W9-AVD-197

THE BADLINGS

To Brian
better read it
till the end
... OR ELSE

XoXo

Xenia Reed

ALSO BY KSENIA ANSKE

Irkadura
Rosehead

<u>Siren Suicides</u>
I Chose to Die
My Sisters in Death
The Afterlife

Blue Sparrow 2:
Tweets on Reading, Writing, and Other
Creative Nonsense

Blue Sparrow:
Tweets on Reading, Writing, and Other
Creative Nonsense

THE BADLINGS

KSENIA ANSKE

Copyright © 2015 by Ksenia Anske
http://www.kseniaanske.com/

All rights reserved.

This work is made available under the terms of the
Creative Commons
Attribution-NonCommercial-ShareAlike 3.0 license,
http://creativecommons.org/licenses/by-nc-sa/3.0/.

You are free to share (to copy, distribute and transmit the work)
and to remix (to adapt the work) under the following conditions:
you must attribute the work in the manner specified by the author
or licensor (but not in any way that suggests that they endorse you
or your use of the work); you may not use this work for
commercial purposes; if you alter, transform, or build upon this
work, you may distribute the resulting work only under the same
or similar license to this one. Any of the above conditions can be
waived if you get permission from the copyright holder. For any
reuse or distribution, you must make clear to others the license
terms of this work.

ISBN-13: 978-1514397510
ISBN-10: 151439751X

To Peter for not being a badling (don't you ever)

CONTENTS

Chapter One

The Duck Pond

What if you found a book stuck in dirt? Would you take a peek inside, or would you chuck it at innocent ducks that happened to waddle nearby? Poor ducks. You wouldn't hurt them, would you? Because who throws books instead of reading them?

Meet Belladonna Monterey, or Bells, as she'd like you to call her—she has decided that Belladonna was too pompous a name for a scientist. See her dark flashing eyes? Her ponytail all askew? Don't try talking to her, lest you want to be throttled.

On this sunny September morning Bells was mad. Mad at her mother, the famous opera singer Catarina Monterey, for calling her a "poor scientist." The argument started with Bells refusing to go to her Saturday choir practice and escalated further into a shouting match when Bells declared that under *no* circumstances would she *ever* become a singer.

"So you want to be a poor scientist?" said Catarina, hands on her hips. It was her usual intimidating pose mimicked by Bells' little sister Sofia from behind her mother's back.

"What does it matter if I'm poor?" asked Bells, stung to the core.

Sofia stuck out her tongue.

Bells ignored it, refusing to descend to the level of an eight-year-old.

"Oh, it matters a great deal," replied Catarina. "How do you propose to make a living? You have seven years left until you're on your own, Belladonna, and every year is precious."

"I told you I don't like that name. Call me Bells."

Her mother's lips pressed together. "As I was saying, *Belladonna*, every year is precious. I've picked out an excellent stage name for you, and I expect you to thank me." Her demeanor softened. "You are destined to become a star, with my talent running in your blood. If you stop practicing now, you might never develop your voice."

"I don't want to develop a voice," grumbled Bells.

"You're a *girl!*" cried Catarina. "What future do you think you have in science?"

"Why does it matter that I'm a girl? I certainly have no inclination toward prancing around in some stupid medieval dresses and hollering my lungs out like you do." As soon as she said it, she regretted it.

Her mother looked hurt. "Is that what you think I do? Holler my lungs out?"

"I hate dresses," said Bells stubbornly. "I hate singing. I hate it that I'm a girl. I want to do science. Stop sticking your tongue out!" That last bit was directed toward Sofia.

"Mom, Belladonna is being mean," she whined.

"Shut up," said Bells.

"You shut up."

"Don't pester your sister," snapped Catarina. "Look at her. She's younger than you, but she has the presence of mind to follow my advice."

Sofia flashed a triumphant smile and twirled, showing off her gaudy pink dress, the type their mother liked to buy for both of them. Bells made a gagging noise. She hated pink or anything decidedly girly. She made sure to never wear dresses, and if she absolutely had to, she smeared them with mud so thoroughly, her mother would pronounce them ruined.

"Well," relented Catarina, "if being a scientist is what you want to do, that is your choice. Go ahead. But don't come crawling back to me asking for money."

"Mom, I'm only eleven!"

"At your age I was already working, modeling and making a considerable sum from every photo shoot."

"I don't want my face plastered on a can of macaroni, thank you very much," said Bells.

"*I* want to be a model," said Sofia.

Bells made a strangling motion that sent Sofia behind her mother's skirt.

"What do you want, then?" asked Catarina. "All I see you do is run around with those abominable boys, doing who knows what and coming home as dirty as a dog."

Bells' face flushed. "I'm not going to change just because you can't stand dirty clothes."

"Then get out of here. Out of my house!" Catarina waved her hand, her eyes throwing daggers. "Go live with your father, and don't you dare come back here unless you're clean and you've changed your mind."

"Fine," said Bells quietly. An iron determination rooted her to the spot. She flung her head high and professed in an injured tone, "I will make it on my own. You'll see."

Catarina took a step forward. "Belladonna Monterey—"

"I'm not Belladonna, I'm Bells."

"Your name is Belladonna."

"No, it's not!" Bells shook so hard, her voice quavered. "I'm Bells, I'm Bells, *I'm Bells!*" She turned on her heel and stormed to the garage.

"Come back this instant!" Catarina shouted, but it was too late.

What do *you* do when you're mad? I'll tell you what Bells did. She grabbed her bike and took off.

"I will run away, that's what I'll do," she said through clenched teeth. "I'll find a way to make it. I don't need her. *That* will teach her to call me a poor scientist."

She pedaled so fast her ponytail whipped in the wind and her eyes spilled over with tears. It took her no more than ten minutes to reach the duck pond where Peacock, Grand, and Rusty were already waiting. Without a glance at them, she dropped the bike and stomped to the stagnant water in search of something to hurl as far and as hard as possible. Her eyes fell on a dark corner sticking out of the mud. She kneeled, clasped it, and pulled. Out came a thick leather-bound tome. It was as large and as heavy as her choir teacher's notebook. Without a second thought Bells chucked it right at the ducks, sending them flying with cries of displeasure.

"There," she said. "Now I feel better."

I imagine you want to know what happened next. Well, it was as expected.

The book landed by the growth of sedge. With an ominous creak, it flung open and lay still, as if waiting to be examined.

Bells frowned.

"Did it just...open on its own?" She walked up to it and bent over. An otherwise ordinary book with ordinarily printed words, it was huge and thick and bloated, containing way too many pages for its binding, all of them yellowing and uneven, as if they were borrowed from various mismatched manuscripts.

A page turned, and Bells thought she saw something move on top of the paper. It was the most peculiar sight. The pages held a miniature landscape. A frozen lake and a dark forest around it, covered with snow that sparkled in the light of a tiny sun. It hung in midair, so close, Bells was tempted to touch it.

She blinked, and it was gone. All of it, the sun and the lake. An old tattered book, albeit enormous, lay sprawled at her feet. She felt her head. It was warm, the normal temperature.

"That's it. I'm seeing things," she muttered.

"Hey, Bells!" called Peacock.

"Hey!" echoed Rusty. "Man, we were waiting for you for like an hour already, right? I mean, come on, you said nine in the morning."

They were ambling over.

Grand made it first. "Um, Bells? Are you all right?" He puffed out his cheeks, taking a laborious breath.

"Huh?" She looked at him and through him.

"Your eyes..." he started, uncertain.

"What's wrong with my eyes?"

"Nothing."

Grand's round face shone with perspiration. He wiped his hands, sticky from a doughnut, and patiently waited for an answer.

Bells called him Grand for his formidable girth and considerable presence. To the rest of the world he was known as George Palmeater. His mother, Daniela Palmeater, worked as a cosmetologist in a funeral home, and his father, Stanley Palmeater, died from heart failure a few years ago—"from being too fat," as his mother explained. He had two little bothers, Max and Theo. They liked to climb him like a little mountain, twist his ears, pull his nose, and poke his sides. This instilled in Grand an admirable patience, as well as a caution in choices and a morbid obsession with death that could be only curbed by eating doughnuts.

"It's not what you think, okay?" Bells sniffled inconspicuously. "I'm not crying."

Grand frowned. "But your eyes..."

"You're seeing things." She glanced down again. "And I'm seeing things. I think. Anyway, it's nothing. I'm just having a bad day."

"A bad day? What happened?"

"Mom again," said Bells in a tone that didn't invite further conversation. "Listen, do you think children can hallucinate? I mean, like, in the middle of the day for no reason?"

"Um. I don't know. I think, yes. But that would mean they have a psychological disorder, and if untreated it could lead to a condition known as schizophrenia, and then they would start hearing voices and seeing things and then they'd become paranoid and start—"

"Okay, I get the point," said Bells weakly. She burned with desire to look down, and made a concentrated effort not to. What if the frozen lake was there again? What if it wasn't? Did that mean she was going crazy?

"Is that a book?" asked Grand.

"Wait." She touched his arm. "Let me—"

"What's up, Bells?" interrupted Peacock.

The gangliest and the tallest of the boys, he slapped her shoulder in a way of a greeting and raked a hand through his blue hair, a fauxhawk, the pride and glory of his appearance. His name was Peter Sutton, but Bells called him Peacock for his cockiness. Changing hair color was his way of getting noticed among the many people present in his house. His father, a real estate agent, had gone off his marbles, in Peacock's opinion, and married a loud artist woman who recently moved into their tiny apartment together with four children from her two previous marriages.

"Okay, I have a favor to ask," Bells pointed down. "Do you guys see what I see, or am I going crazy?"

"See what?" Peacock raised a brow.

The lake was back on the page, more pronounced this time. The snow spread over it in a silvery layer. Wind howled and raged over the miniscule forest.

"Holy buckets...there are trees and a lake and everything." Peacock's voice shook from excitement.

"Wow!" exclaimed Rusty. "Is this for real? That's like, nuts!" He sniggered.

Bells called him Rusty for his rusty voice. His given name was Russell Jagoda. He sniggered a lot. He also talked a lot, which, coupled with his small size and knobbly joints that never seemed to stop twitching, gave him an appearance of a monkey. His parents were killed in a car crash when he was six and most of his childhood was spent in the company of his Polish grandmother Agnieszka who walked dogs for a living and instilled in him the love of animals—and of petting them, regardless of how dangerous they looked.

He stretched out his hand.

"Don't touch it!" snapped Bells.

"Why not?"

"We don't know what it is." She twisted her ponytail. "I do know one thing, though. I'm not going crazy, since you guys can see it too. And that is a good thing, I suppose."

They crowded around the book.

"Where did you find it?" asked Peacock.

"Right over there." Bells pointed to the spot where the ducks sat huddling, their beady eyes shining in condemnation of her outrageous behavior. "I thought someone had thrown it away or something. I didn't know it would have *this* inside."

"You found it?" asked Grand. "On the ground?"

"Yeah, right where the ducks are. See? It was stuck in the dirt, so I dug it out and..." She didn't finish, blushing. "I didn't mean to throw it. I was mad, okay?"

"But how is this possible?" asked Rusty.

"It's not," stated Bells. "Scientifically speaking, it's not possible for anything like this to exist."

"So, what you're saying is," offered Peacock, "this doesn't exist?" He nudged the book with his sneaker, and the wind in it wailed with such ferocity, they all recoiled.

"I suppose it is real," admitted Bells. "Only I don't understand how it works. I guess I could test it and tell you?"

"And how do you propose to do that?" asked Peacock.

"Like any respectable scientist would do, you dolt.

Watch me." Bells hovered her hand over the page.

"Hey, you told me not to touch it," objected Rusty.

"Exactly. Because you wouldn't know *how*." The air froze her palm, and she moved it away. "It's cold. I can feel it on my skin. Because I trust my senses, I conclude this is real." Then, spurred by a rush of curiosity, she touched it.

"What are you doing? Are you off your marbles?!" cried Peacock.

"Are you scared?" Bells challenged him, forcing herself not to wince. The frost bit her fingers, and they got stuck to the ice. She tried pulling away and couldn't.

The lake held her fast.

"Um, maybe this is not such a good idea, testing it," ventured Grand. "The first time I went into the mortuary freezer at my mom's work, I touched one of the walls, and it was very cold and it looked like it was crusted with sugar, so I licked it and my tongue got stuck to it and—"

"Okay, we heard this story a thousand times," said Bells nervously.

"But this is a different one..." Grand sounded crestfallen. He was fond of sharing morbid accounts of stumbling into rooms full of corpses, or eating lunch with his mother right next to a dead body freshly made up, or other unmentionable adventures that nobody except his friends could stomach.

"Well, I think this is very real, actually," said Bells, the first twinge of panic twisting her stomach. She couldn't feel her fingers, and some mysterious force was pulling her arm down, so that she had to plop on the ground, pretending like this was precisely what she was planning to do all along.

Rusty edged closer. "How does it feel, Bells? Can I

touch it now?"

"No!" she cried, a bit too suddenly. "I mean, yes, you can, after I'm done, okay?"

"You're shaking," observed Grand. "Don't you think you've tested it enough?"

Just then something dreadful happened.

Clearly fed up with waiting, the book proceeded to act. It pulled Bells down like a magnet might pull a piece of metal. Her face touched the snow. She decided it was time to panic in earnest.

"It won't let me go!" she cried.

"What won't?" asked Peacock dumbly.

"The book, you blockhead! Don't you see?"

Another tug. Bells cried out, clawing at the dirt to stay put. And then she began to shrink. She looked up at the boys, too stunned to utter any sound or make any movement. Her eyes shone out like two frightened saucers.

For a silent moment, the boys remained dumbfounded at her diminishing shape, until she found her voice and shouted, "Help me!" She was half her size now, a third, a quarter. She took a deep breath and added an insult, in the hopes of persuading them to move. "Get me out, you idiots!"

They rushed to her aid.

Grand grabbed her ankle, Rusty seized her leg, and Peacock clasped her waist. Not that it helped. With a shriek of terror Bells dwindled into a dot and was gone.

A thick silence fell over the pond.

This is what the scene looked like:

A nice and sunny September morning. A rarely visited corner of a park overgrown with yellowing maples. An old pond covered with duckweed so thickly, it was green. A dozen shameless ducks pecking dirt in search of doughnut crumbs that smelled enticingly sweet (Grand always fed them when he came here). Four bikes heaped one over another. A mound of dirt, a giant open book, and three eleven-year-old boys kneeling next to it, their faces lit with a mixture of amazement, bafflement, and fear.

Suddenly—horrible things always happen *suddenly* in books—a fierce wind rose out of nowhere. It rushed across the treetops, tearing off leaves and loose twigs. The sky scudded with clouds. The sun disappeared. Quacking, the ducks fled to the far end of the pond and huddled in a trembling mass of feathers. The book made a slurping noise as if satisfied after a meal. The wind died, and the noise stopped.

"She's gone," said Peacock incredulously. "It took her."

"She shrunk! Did you see that? What do we do now?" Rusty scratched his head.

"I'm going in," said Grand.

"Going where, exactly?" Peacock's eyes widened. "In there? Are you crazy!?"

"Hey, that would be cool, wouldn't it?" said Rusty. "I'd be scared to shrink like that, though."

"You guys do what you want. It got Bells, so I'm going after her." Grand closed his eyes and placed a hand on the lake. In another moment he vanished.

Peacock and Rusty stared at the spot where Grand was a second ago, then at each other.

"Do you want to try it?" asked Rusty. Without waiting for a response, he gingerly extended a finger and touched the page. "Hey, that hurts! Stop!"

But the book didn't intend to stop. Rusty rapidly

diminished in size and disappeared. The book creaked, as if mocking Peacock with its open pages, waiting.

"Rusty!" he cried. "This is not happening. It's *not* happening. It can't be." He took a deep breath. "Okay, okay. I'm coming in, you guys. I'm coming." He felt for the paper. The second his hand made contact with the lake he whittled down to a speck.

The front cover slammed shut.

Happy reading, badlings, rustled the book as it slowly sank back into the dirt.

Chapter Two

The Talking Book

When you open a new book, you hardly know where it will take you. That's the fun of reading. It might plunge you into dark foreboding places, full of terrible monsters, or it could take you into places frighteningly white and empty, like this one.

Bells rubbed her arms. Freezing wind cut through her clothes. She took a step, slipped on the ice, and promptly fell down. The ground met her with a bone-chilling hospitality. She looked around, but there was nothing to see except drifting, twirling snow.

"Hello?" Her voice sunk into silence.

"Anyone here?" She glanced up, fully expecting to see the gigantic faces of her friends. But there was only sky, swept over with depressing whiteness.

"What is this place?" She pinched herself. The scenery didn't change one bit. In fact, it appeared stubbornly snowier.

Bells sighed. "Okay, let's analyze this. Scientifically speaking, and based on the facts of what has just happened, I must be inside the book I found by the duck pond. Right? Right. I *am* inside it. I grew smaller and it pulled me in, and it looks like a frozen lake with a forest around it. What does this mean? This means that maybe it's a part of the story written on these pages, and that means that *I* am now inside this story. That makes sense, doesn't it? What else could it be?" She didn't know to whom she was talking, but the sound of her voice gave her courage. "I'm not scared. I'm not scared at all. I will figure this out." She fell silent. The first twinge of fear poked her like a shard of ice.

Bells rubbed her hands. "Okay, okay. I'm okay." She tried to remember how long Grand said it takes for someone to freeze to death. "I will be fine." Her head began to pound with the injustice of it all. "Why is it always me who has to test everything out? Why couldn't it be Peacock for a change?"

Bells kicked at the snow. "Great. Now I'm inside some stupid book that somehow opened up into this stupid place, and I have no *stupid* clue how to get out of here." As she was talking, she noticed that the wind quieted down and every snowflake appeared to have grown ears, carefully listening to her every word.

A suspicion formed in her head.

"Hello?" she called.

There was no answer, but she thought she heard a rustle that could be the clearing of a throat or the creaking of pages. The sound dissolved into nothing somewhere above her head, and all was still again, as if something was watching her.

"Hello?" she repeated.

No answer.

"Naturally, as my luck would have it, it appears that I'm alone here. But," she raised a finger, "if my hypothesis is correct and this is a story, there must be characters here— it must be a story about *someone*. I don't see anyone, and that is very strange. What kind of a story is this, if it only has a lake and a forest in it? A stupid story, that's what. I get it. This book is dumb, that's what I think." She spoke louder. "It must have been such a boring and dull book, that someone finally got fed up with it and has thrown it away. In fact, I think this book is the most lame and uninteresting book of them *all*!"

The snow stopped. The wind died with a disgruntled sigh.

"Lame?" rustled a papery voice. "Did you call me *lame*?"

Bells' heart plummeted, then sprung into her ears and hammered so hard, she thought she would faint.

"Do I need to repeat myself?" demanded the voice. "Or are you not only rude, but deaf also?"

Bells swallowed. "Who is it?" she asked timidly. "Is anyone here?" She looked about her, but there was nothing to see except snow.

"You're blind, too? Oh, this is getting better by the minute."

Bells rubbed her eyes. "I don't see anyone. Where are you?"

"You saw me well enough to dig me out, did you not?" inquired the voice. It spoke all around her, and Bells trembled from fright.

"I'm sorry, but do you mind—"

"Yes, I do mind. I mind very much."

"You're...the book I found?" Bells faltered. "You can *talk*?"

"So full of insults, boorish and uncultured. All of you are like that. How little respect and gratitude I see from you, for everything I do." A crack ripped through the air, and the ice on the lake shifted.

Bells cowered, expecting the worst, but nothing else

happened. She cautiously looked up. "Er...Book?"

No reply.

"I'm sorry. I really didn't mean to throw you." She paused. "I was mad at my mom, and, well...I tend to throw things when I'm mad. It makes me feel better."

The voice huffed.

"I really *am* sorry. I promise."

Without the slightest warning the ground lifted and threw Bells off her feet. She sat back hard and cried out in pain.

"No, you're not. You're not sorry at all. You all say that, and none of you mean it," hissed the voice.

The snow rolled around Bells in great dunes.

"You're scared, that's what you are. You're trying to placate me. Well, it won't work. You will pay for your offense, you and your pitiful friends."

Bells swallowed. "My friends? Are they *here*?"

"Maybe." The voice crackled in what sounded like papery laughter.

"Where are they? What did you do to them? Please, let us out of here, or we'll freeze to death!"

"Suits me," said the voice with an audible shrug.

"Who *are* you?" demanded Bells.

"I see you don't have much of a brain. But then again, girls usually don't."

Bells choked on her breath. "Excuse me?"

"Excuse you?" boomed the voice. "Excuse *you*! You, the most disrespectful annoying badling who dared to throw me—throw *me*!—like a piece of garbage, like an insignificant trifle, like a...like a..." it burbled with rage.

"Badling?" repeated Bells. "What's a badling?"

The snowy dunes drew closer. "Do you have to

16

know the meaning of everything?" asked the voice cunningly.

"Yes," answered Bells, her teeth on edge. "I need to know the meaning of things so I can understand them."

"How boring your life must be," mused the voice. "Where is your sense of wonder?"

"Facts are the only things that matter for a scientist," said Bells proudly.

"I see now why you would abandon books," concluded the voice.

"What books?"

"You don't even remember."

"I'm really cold. Please. How do I get out of here?"

The voice tittered. "What makes you think you can?"

Bells didn't know. "Can I?"

"Maybe. If you finish reading the pages you have so heartlessly forsaken."

"What pages?"

"The ones you're standing on!"

"But there are no words." Bells looked down. She saw dark lines and cracks and bubbles encased in ice, but nothing else.

"Of course there aren't." The voice cackled.

The sound chilled Bells' blood. "So how do I read it?"

"Enough! You have tired me out. I will go nap now." And with that the voice whooshed away in a shower of sparkling crystals.

"Book?" called Bells. "Hello?"

Hard sun indifferently shone down.

"Grand? Guys? Anyone?"

Bells took a deep breath and marched forward, although it may as well have been backward. The lake around her spread equally in every direction. "So this crazy book is pissed off at me because I threw it at ducks. It got me in here for punishment and wants me to read the pages I left unread. Okay. How do I do that?"

There wasn't anyone to answer, and after a while Bells reached the edge of the woods, where tall pines and firs burdened with snow hunched over like sullen giants. She tucked her hands in her armpits.

"Okay, let's think. What book did I read that had a frozen lake in it?" Her memory refused to cooperate. "I can't think of anything. I must keep walking, otherwise I *will* freeze to death." She waded into the forest.

"Peacock? Grand? Rusty?"

Behind a particularly thick fir something lay sprawled across the ground. Whatever it was, it was warm and breathing and alive. Bells choked back a scream, thinking that it might be a polar bear or some other big predatory animal. White fur covered it from head to toe. Only, it wasn't fur; it was snow, and it fell off in clumps as the figure sat up and dazedly looked around.

"Grand!" Bells rushed to him.

"Bells?"

"You're here! Where are Peacock and Rusty?"

"Back at the pond, I think."

"They are?" Bells sagged a little.

"I didn't see them come after me." Grand stood up, brushing the snow off his shirt.

"Listen! This book we're in, I talked to it. It can *talk*, Grand. It's angry at me for throwing it and for not finishing reading books, or something like that. It called me a

18

badling. I suppose that means I'm bad. So, right now we're standing on a page of a book that I haven't finished reading, and I have to finish it."

"The page of what?" Grand's face puckered in concentration.

"This *book* we're in, the book I found at the duck pond, I talked to it. Can you believe it?"

"Sort of..." said Grand slowly.

"Anyway, it said that Peacock and Rusty are here too. Maybe."

"They are?" asked Grand. Contrary to Bells whose face had attained a shade of blue, he didn't appear to be suffering from cold. His round cheeks blazed crimson. "I'm glad I found you. Did the book tell you how to get out of here?"

"Nope," she admitted. "It got tired of my questions and went for a nap."

"A nap?" Grand smiled. "A book went for a nap?"

"That's what it said."

"That's not good. If we stay here much longer, we will grow so cold, we'll be tempted to lie down and our blood will chill and our hearts will beat slower and slower until—"

"Okay, okay, I get it. Thank you."

"You're welcome," said Grand, nonplussed. "I'm scared of what will happen, that's all."

"Boys aren't supposed to be scared."

"That's not true." Grand looked her straight in the eye. "Everyone gets scared. It's okay to be scared. Girls always—"

"Don't talk to me about what girls do and don't. I'm a girl and I know better." Bells' face flushed and she felt a little warmer. "Let's go find Rusty and Peacock."

This new purpose filled her with energy. She grabbed Grand's hand, marveling at how it could possibly stay so warm in this temperature, and together they trudged to the lake.

An echo trailed on the wind.

Bells stopped. "Did you hear that?" She took a deep breath and yelled, "Peacock? Rusty?"

"Bells?" came an answer from behind a snowdrift.

She looked at Grand. He nodded, and they ran around it, quite suddenly colliding into their friends. There were cries of pain, then cries of joy, and, once they had confirmed that all four of them were whole and uninjured, cries of agitated bewilderment over what Bells told them.

"That is insane," said Peacock, jumping for warmth.

"We're in a book! How cool is that?" Rusty blew on his hands and rubbed them.

"Not cool at all. It would've been cool if it was warmer." Peacock said with feeling. "Are you interested in turning into an icicle? I'm not."

Bells crossed her arms. "Well, nobody asked you to follow me."

"Oh, thanks." Peacock snorted. "We couldn't just leave you, could we?"

Bells squinted. "I bet you were the last one to get in."

"Yeah, he got in after me!" Rusty sniggered.

Peacock gave him a murderous look.

"Guys, please." Grand put up his hands for peace, the gesture he used on his two little brothers. "We need to find a way to get out of here."

"Do we, really?" Peacock smirked. "Why hurry? I

like it here. It's nice and warm and sunny."

Bells pursed her lips. "Stop it."

"Look, someone is coming!" Rusty pointed at a drifting cloud of flurries. It glided. It clopped. And then it snorted in high animal voices.

Chapter Three

The Ice Woman

Fear has big eyes. It makes it easy for authors to fool you. Never trust appearances on first sight, especially those in books. You see one thing, and just when you think you know what it is, it turns out to be something completely different.

Rusty thought he saw a crowd of running monkeys. Grand perceived a rider on a horse, a rider without a head. Peacock feared it could be vampires in white dresses. And only Bells saw it for what it was.

Pulled by three ivory horses, a sleigh carved from ice swished along the lake, spraying snowdust from under its runners. A tall regal figure held the reins, wrapped in a fur coat and muff and wearing an icy crown. It was a woman of frightening beauty, the beauty that stabs you with cold and holds you hostage to its perfection, symmetrical, flawless, and dead.

The horses reared. The woman shouted something and, noticing the children, steered the sleigh in their direction. The horseshoes clacked against the ice, sending an echo that broke off at the trees.

"Guys?" said Bells. "I think I know who it is."

"Yeah?" asked Peacock. "Who?"

"I read this book to Sofia. I never finished it because it became ridiculous, scientifically speaking. I got disgusted and told her to read it herself."

"What book was it?"

"*The Snow Queen.*" Bells took a cautious step back, watching the horses close in on them. "It's a fairy tale about this ice woman. She wants to freeze the whole world, you know, power and domination and all that stuff. She is charming, really, except if she kisses you, your heart will turn into ice or some other nonsense like that."

Peacock had gone white. "She is going to kiss us? Is that part of *reading* this page?"

"I'd like to see her try!" shrieked Rusty. With a cry of war he brandished a stick over his head.

"Where did you find that?" demanded Bells.

"In the snow, that's where. We will just chase her off. That's what you do with naughty dogs, you poke them with a stick!" He stabbed the air a bit too vigorously and knocked himself off his feet.

"She is not a dog, Rusty," objected Grand. "Besides, if you fight her, you might make her want to kiss you, like Bells is saying, and then you will turn black from cold, and after a while—Um, Bells? Does your heart turn to ice right away, or does it take some time?"

"I haven't read that part," said Bells crossly. "And I don't think I want to know."

Rusty pointed an enthusiastic finger. "Whoa! Look at those horses!"

"Rusty, no!" cried Bells, but he had already walked up to the quivering beasts that ogled him like some insane apparition. Their hides were powdered with hoarfrost, and tiny icicles hung from their manes.

"Nice horses, nice little horses..." whispered Rusty, stretching out his hand. The steed in the middle snorted right in his face, and Rusty staggered back, puzzled. "You don't like to be petted?"

The steed gave him a stink eye that clearly signified its protest to such an unbidden proposition.

Rusty scuttled back to his friends.

"Do you *have* to pet every animal you see?" Bells scolded him.

"But...horses..." Rusty fell silent.

The Snow Queen stepped off the sleigh, her face an inflexible mask. Her eyes fell on Bells, and something glistened in them, a deeply hidden hunger.

"Sweet children," she said melodically, "are you cold? Come, I will warm you up."

"No, thanks," said Peacock quickly. "We're not *that* cold."

"She's so pretty!" exclaimed Rusty, utterly mesmerized.

Peacock seized his arm. "Don't listen to her, it's a trick. They're always kissing you in fairy tales, and then you end up dead."

"How would you know? Have you read it?" Rusty wrestled out of his hold. "Hey, Snow Queen! Is that true that if you kiss people, their hearts turn to ice?"

The queen regarded him, amused. "Would you like to find out?" she said sweetly. "Come, boy, let me wrap you in my cloak. You look like you're freezing."

Rusty grinned, the tips of his ears glowing.

It was obvious to Bells that the queen planned something unpleasant. She gathered a handful of snow. It melted in her hands to a perfectly round shape, and she hurled it with commendable precision. It hit the queen in the eye.

Another snowball, thrown by Peacock, obliterated her other eye. The queen staggered back to the sleigh. "Stop!" she commanded. "I'm not going to hurt you. I want to help you!"

Bells scooped more snow. "Help us? I don't believe that for a second." She straightened and froze.

For a moment the queen's face was livid, then she was smiling, not in a cold sinister way, but in a warm friendly way. "I'm so good at this," she said with pride, cleaning the snow off her face.

Bells blinked. "What?"

"I scared you, didn't I?"

"Scared me?" asked Bells. "Pfft. Not one bit." She dangerously weighed the snowball in her hand, as if about to chuck it.

"Oh yes, I did," said the queen. She tossed back her head, and the jewels in her crown sparkled. "It's rather magnificent to be the Snow Queen. I can do things to those who don't obey me. If I breathe on you, you will freeze, turn blue and die." She approached Bells, who hastily retreated. "And if I kiss you, as you already know, your heart will become a lump of ice."

Bells recoiled. The queen's face was so close to hers, she could see her marble-smooth skin and her dazzlingly white teeth. "Would you like to have a power like mine?"

"What for?" asked Bells, looking at the boys for support. They weren't much help. Mouths open, they gaped at the queen, charmed by her voice into a momentary daze.

"She's so pretty," blurted Rusty.

"I know..." echoed Peacock.

Grand didn't say anything, but his cheeks turned the

color of ruddy sunset.

The queen seemed to enjoy the attention. She sent them air kisses, picked up the stick Rusty dropped, and breathed on it. It immediately iced over with glittering frosted patterns.

Suddenly a cough shook the sky and a voice rustled over their heads, "Ahem. What exactly are you doing?"

The Snow Queen paled, if that was possible with her already pallid complexion. "Mad Tome."

"Who?" asked Bells.

"Act scared," she hissed at the children. "Go on. Now!"

It took them a moment.

"Oh no!" cried Bells in mock distress. "She's going to get us!"

"We better run!" picked up Peacock.

"I'm so scared!" Rusty waited for Grand to add something.

"Um," said Grand confusedly.

"Run, run," urged the queen, and together, slipping and sliding, they took off into the woods. The queen ushered them on. They wove between pines and firs and at last stopped out of breath in a murky shadow of a cedar. A cutting wind blew wisps of flurries.

"Snow Queen, where are you?" bellowed the voice.

The queen grimaced painfully. "Unfortunately, I need to be going."

"Wait!" cried Bells. "Who is Mad Tome?"

"Shhh!" The queen pressed a finger to her lips.

"I heard that," boomed the voice.

"Is that...the book talking?" asked Peacock.

The Snow Queen spoke quickly, "You're done with

this page, so you can go to the next one. Go, before it gets really mad!"

"I'm *beyond* mad now," wailed the voice, and large heaps of snow plopped on top of the children's heads, shaken from the boughs overhead. They didn't have time to scream. The ground bulged and careened, then rose as if it were a gigantic turning page, hurtling them to the base of a dirt wall.

They rolled to a stop.

Bells sat up, reeling. "Guys? Are you okay?"

"Sort of," said Peacock, shaking off the snow.

Rusty peered up. "Whoa! What is *that*?"

It was a wall of soil, rock-hard and littered with ends of roots that stuck out like crooked fingers. It stretched from left to right in an endless line, as if the forest had been cut off by an earth divider.

Bells cautiously touched it. "I think I know what it is. We're underground, and this is dirt. The dirt by the duck pond," she turned to the boys. "That means we can dig ourselves out!"

"Oh no, you can't," said the rustling voice. "You're staying until I decide to let you go. Or not," it cackled.

"Mad Tome?" asked Bells. "Is that your name?"

"Mad Tome? Is there no end to your insults, you despicable badling?!" shouted Mad Tome. "Who told you this? The Snow Queen? Blast her. Blast you all. Sometimes I think retirement might be not such a bad idea. I can nap all I want and not have to deal with any of you anymore." It uttered an outraged growl. "I see freezing hasn't cured you of your insolence. How about you bake in the sun and suffer from thirst? Or, better," it dropped its voice, "get impaled on a lance, the old-fashioned way."

The children exchanged terrified glances. Their faces turned grey, and for a good reason. The forest floor slipped from underneath them, and they tumbled headlong onto the next page that felt as hot as a fired up furnace.

Chapter Four

The Petulant Donkey

A good book waits for you to feel comfortable with the story to surprise you with an unforeseen twist. Not Mad Tome. Being a *bad* book, it liked to rudely catapult its readers from page to page without so much as a pause to catch their breath or to take a bite of a doughnut (not that it offered any).

And so it was that instead of munching on something sweet, Grand found himself chewing sand. He energetically spit it out. Close by, Peacock and Rusty did the same. There was no sign of Bells, but plenty of windswept barren land. Bleached knolls rippled into infinity, bright sky held a blinding sun, and the air was so hot and dry, it made them cough.

"What *is* this place?" said Peacock, wiping his mouth. His hands tingled, and his nose burned from the heat.

"Where is Bells?" said Grand with alarm.

"Bells?" picked up Rusty.

"Bells!" they called in a chorus.

"Here!" came a feeble voice.

A moment later Bells slid down the slope of a hill. She descended in a cloud of dust and, caught by inertia, failed to veer aside and rammed straight into the boys. They yelped. Bells squealed. It took them a while to unscramble.

Finally they lay sprawled on their backs, breathless, gradually sinking into the warmth.

"Ahhh," said Bells.

"Ahhh," echoed Peacock.

"Ahhh," breathed Grand and Rusty.

They looked at each other and giggled.

The buzzing sensation of heat was so enjoyable that for a while none of them spoke. All they did was feel their skin hum and their minds melt and their bodies relax.

Bells started sweating. She sat up and redid her ponytail.

Peacock yawned.

"Stop it," she said crossly, suppressing her own yawn.

"I can't," he protested. "I can't control nature. I feel sleepy and I yawn and that's that."

"Well, you should control it. Otherwise we're never getting out of here."

"Do we need to?" said Peacock sarcastically. "I feel comfortable. Don't you?"

Bells pressed her lips into a line.

"I don't feel comfortable at all." Grand mopped his face. "It's too hot."

"Is this a desert? Are we in a desert?" Rusty's eyes shone with the fervor of exploration.

"It's not a desert," Bells corrected him. "A desert is made of sand, endless sand dunes, and this is dry land. See? There are clumps of grass growing. I know they look dead and brown, but they *are* growing, that means there is water here, so, scientifically speaking, it's more of a steppe or a prairie."

Rusty knotted his brows. "What's a *steppe*?"

"An arid grassland devoid of any trees," said Bells slowly. "Do I have to explain everything to you?"

"Either way, it's bad," said Grand with a dejected sigh. "There must be scorpions here, or snakes. They will bite us, and the poison will spread and make the bite marks look like red blisters oozing pus, and in our deathly convulsions we wouldn't even—"

"If you don't stop, I will bite you instead of a snake," said Bells with feeling. "My venom is worse than that of a cobra, did you know that?"

Peacock snorted. "I have no doubt."

"Snakes? Where?" Rusty scrambled up the hill, sending down clouds of dust.

Bells clasped her forehead. "He'll get us in trouble, I have a feeling he will."

"Don't let the scorpions eat you!" called Peacock after him.

"I'll only take a look, I'll be right back!"

They watched him climb to the top and crawl around, peering at the ground and poking it.

"This is not logical," said Bells.

"What's not logical?" asked Peacock.

"It's not making any sense," she reflected. "So, we're in this book, and it's called Mad Tome. That's not its proper title. Remember how upset it got? It must be a nickname."

The boys nodded.

"Okay," continued Bells, encouraged. "Let's apply logic to this. If Mad Tome is a book about the Snow Queen, the next page should've been covered with snow, right? It should've been winter, not summer."

"What are you saying?" asked Peacock, interested.

"I'm saying that this is not an ordinary book. Well, naturally it isn't, because somehow it managed to shrink us and get us in, but also because it's not a coherent story. I think this page is from some other book."

"Um," began Grand timidly, "that would explain why it's called Mad Tome."

Bells raised her brows. "How so?"

"Maybe it's made of pages from different stories." He shrugged. "It can't be called any one story in particular, so it has its own name."

"That's exactly what I thought," said Bells breathlessly. "I thought it's made up of pages from different stories." She looked at Grand with new appreciation. He turned bright magenta.

"You guys so sure it's a book?" blurted Peacock. "Maybe it's not a book at all. Maybe it's come crazy guy called Mad Tom."

"It's not Tom," snapped Bells. "It's *tome*. A tome is a thick book. And it's mad because, well, I suppose it's gone mad, and that's why it's called Mad Tome."

The ground underneath them trembled.

Peacock paled. "Did you feel that? What do we need to do to get out of here, again?"

"Read the pages, as far as I understand," said Bells. "Only I don't know how we can do it, maybe we should dig and there will be words underneath?"

"But the Snow Queen said we were done with her page," remembered Grand.

Bells' mouth opened. "Grand, you're a genius. That's it."

"What's *it*?" Peacock's question went unanswered. "I hate it when you do this. Can you tell us already?"

"We don't need to read it," croaked Bells, her voice breaking, "all we have to do is live through the page. I mean, we're *inside* it. So all we have to do is..." She looked across the steppe, noticing the silence. Apart from their own voices and an occasional breeze, no other noises reached them, and Bells' stomach jolted unpleasantly. They were in the middle of nowhere, with no water or food. She suddenly felt very thirsty.

"I think," she began, "because I didn't finish reading some books, Mad Tome is punishing me by making me live through them. But then why are *you* guys here? I mean, I don't remember reading this book, so it must be...wait, do any of you know what story we're in right now? Did any of *you* abandon it?"

Grand and Peacock shook their heads no.

"Are you sure?" Bells narrowed her eyes.

"What's that look for?" asked Peacock.

"Nothing. Just wondering."

"If we stay here much longer," observed Grand, "we will fry alive. In my mom's funeral home they have this incinerator, and when the relatives want their dead to be cremated, they—"

Bells interrupted him. "Can we not talk about dead people, please?"

"Guys!" On top of the hill Rusty was waving both arms. "Look who's here!"

Bells sighed. "What now?"

Next to Rusty stood a plump dappled donkey, happily chewing a wad of grass. It brayed and galloped down until it stopped right by the children. Rusty caught up to it, beaming, as if it was the most exciting thing in the world to bring a donkey to his friends stranded in the wasteland of an unpredictable book that was obviously mad.

"Hello, badlings," said the donkey. "Feeling warm yet?"

Bells gaped. "A talking donkey? Why am I not surprised."

"Um," said Grand, feeling his forehead. "I think we all had a heat stroke and are delirious. Soon we will lose consciousness and—" Bells nudged him.

The donkey bared its yellow teeth. "Who of you would like to be a donkey?" it asked.

"Why would any of us want to be a donkey?" said Peacock.

The donkey pouted, sticking out its moist lower lip. "I was going to risk my precious position to help you. Maybe I shouldn't have bothered. And you said your friends are nice," it looked up at Rusty accusingly.

"They *are* nice," he grinned. "This is Bells, Peacock, and Grand. Guys, this is Dapple."

Dapple hiccuped. "Peacock? That's a funny name."

"What's so funny about it?" Peacock smoothed his hair, giving Bells an accusatory look.

She pretended not to notice and said slowly, "Can...everything talk in here?"

Dapple balked. "What do you mean, everything? I'm not a thing, I'm a person."

"Oh, I'm sorry, I was assuming..." Bells hesitated. "A person?"

"This is so irritating." Dapple flicked his ears. "I must confess, I'm getting tired of this camouflage." He plodded closer to them, speaking quietly and throwing cautious glances around. "I'm not really a donkey. I want to help you."

"Help us with what?" asked Bells.

"Would you like to get out of here?" offered Dapple.

"Yes," answered Bells at once.

"Here is the deal. Mad Tome is getting madder and madder. There is no telling what it might do next. Do you want to get home?"

They nodded.

"Well, I'd like to get home too. And—"

"Home where?" interrupted Peacock.

There was a flicker of sorrow in Dapple's eyes. "Promise me you won't breathe a word about this to Mad Tome."

"Promise," said Peacock in a single breath.

"We promise," picked up Bells and Grand and Rusty.

Dapple waited for a beat and said quietly, "*Destroy it.*" When none of the children comprehended what he meant, he added, "*Mad Tome.*"

"What?" said Bells incredulously. "How?"

"Why?" said Peacock.

"Right now?" said Rusty.

"Will we die in the process?" said Grand.

There was a sound like the crackling of bones in a huge mouth yawning somewhere in the sky. Dapple's eyes widened. He raised his head and brayed. "There you are! I found you! My master will call his master, and he'll skewer you on his lance!"

"Skewer us?" repeated Bells, startled by this sudden change.

"It's terrible that I can't help you!" continued Dapple. "There is absolutely nothing I can do! Prepare for your torturous and imminent death!" He winked and cantered off.

The ground rumbled alarmingly. A harsh wind beat on the children, throwing sand in their faces, and a rustling voice announced overhead, "That's enough, Dapple! Next thing you know, you'll tell them who you really are. Can't rely on any of you these days, how very annoying."

"Guys?" Rusty pointed to the knolls. They formed a mouth that sneered in the most unpleasant manner.

"Hey, Mad Tome!" he called. "How was the nap?"

"Do you happen to have anything against naps, you brazen badling?" asked the mouth.

"No," Rusty backtracked. "I love naps, actually. I always take naps on weekends with my grandma."

"Perhaps I should separate you four, to make things a bit more fun. What do you say?"

Before Rusty could answer, Mad Tome's mouth disappeared. In its place the knoll swelled into an enormous hand that seized him by the scruff of his shirt and tossed him across the wasteland to the dirt wall, where the page peeled off, curled, and swiped him out of sight.

"Rusty!" cried Bells and, together with Peacock and Grand, rushed after him. By the time they made it to the spot where he vanished, the page was back in its place.

"Where did he go?" asked Bells.

"Um, to another page?" wondered Grand.

"Let's go after him."

"And how do you suggest we do that?" said Peacock in a tone too high-pitched for comfort.

"Dig, stupid." She studied the ground.

Peacock's brows lifted. "Dig? What for?"

"Don't you get it?" Bells placed her hands on her

hips. "We're on a page, so underneath all this soil there must be paper. That means, if we dig it up, we could turn it and get to the next page." She scraped at the ground with her nails, which proved to be useless, as it was baked into an impenetrable crust.

"I don't think it will work," said Grand with a tinge of panic.

"That's right, at least one of you is wise," rustled Mad Tome. "How about some bloodletting, since freezing and frying you doesn't make you more agreeable?"

Bells looked up, fuming. "Are you going to keep throwing us from page to page?" she shouted.

"Oh, feisty, are we?" Mad Tome cackled. "I must say, despite your naïve impertinence, immaturity, and foolishness, you are dispelling my boredom. If you keep going like this, I might skip my naps to watch you even *closer.*"

The page heaved.

Bells pitched forward, toppled over the boys, and they all rolled into the widening gap by the wall. It opened with grim familiarity, welcoming three screaming children into its depth. The last thing they saw before hurtling out of sight was a sneering face made of dust shimmering in the hot steppe sun.

Chapter Five

The Enormous Puppy

It's unadvisable to delegate your tasks to those who abhor you. They will most likely make you fail. Mad Tome wrongly concluded that those living on its pages would obey it. On the contrary, bereft of their homes, they conspired against it from day one.

Take this enormous puppy, for example. Tail high and ears alert, it pranced around the patch of thistle and chewed on one of the purple flowers, blatantly neglecting Mad Tome's instructions and spying on the boy instead.

Rusty lay sprawled on the turf. It smelled fresh and spicy. With a groan he propped himself up on his elbows, reeling. It took him a moment to remember who he was.

"Rusty," he said, testing his voice. "That sounds familiar. It's my name, right? I think it is. No, wait...my name is Russell. Russell Jagoda. Rusty is my nickname. I must have hit my head pretty hard." He absentmindedly touched the grass and gazed up at the giant flowers. "Is this a prehistoric wood or something?" Blades as tall as trees hung with globules of dew. At the nudge of his foot one of them quivered, slid, and burst over his head, drenching him in the process.

"Cool!" He licked off the water. "I was thirsty anyway."

He pulled himself up. Above him fragrant flowers

formed a canopy of colors. Shafts of sunlight pierced through the greenish haze, and the air smelled so enticing, Rusty's thoughts muddled and his nose took over.

"It smells like Grandma's jam..." he said to himself. "I wonder what I'm doing here. We were at the duck pond waiting for Bells, right? But what happened after?" Nobody answered, but somebody looked at him. Rusty sensed eyes on his back and twisted around.

By a thistle of epic proportions sat a puppy of equally epic proportions. Soft curly fur covered it from a sniffing nose to a wagging tail. Its large round eyes blinked in friendly curiosity.

They stared at each other for a second, then the puppy pounced on a stick and pushed it with a paw toward Rusty, its tongue lolling.

"Wow, you're big!" said Rusty. "Want to play? Is that what you want?"

The puppy yelped delightedly and said, "Please pardon me if this looks silly, but I absolutely have to have at least one good catching game before I do anything serious. If you don't mind. It's been too long, and I'm itching for a bit of exercise." It crouched, waiting.

Rusty grinned. "You *talk*? Wait. The donkey talked too. The donkey I found...Dapple." His stomach turned. "I remember! We got into this book, this, what's its name..." He snapped his fingers. "Mad Tome! That's it. Bells? Guys? Where is everyone? How did I get here?"

His words drifted off.

The puppy watched him, one ear twitching.

Rusty clenched and unclenched his hands. "We were in this desert with the donkey, and then Mad Tome threw us here, right? But where is everyone? Come on, guys, it's not funny anymore." He ambled around, calling his friends' names. But the more he did it, the more he was certain that he was alone.

He plopped down by the puppy and scratched its huge paw. "I guess it's only me. Hey, do you have any idea why I'm here?"

"I'm pretty sure I do," obliged the puppy. "You must have angered Mad Tome and it sent you here for punishment." It stuck its nose so close to Rusty's face, he thought he'd suffocate in puppy breath. "I've been instructed to make you suffer. Well," it explained, prompted by Rusty's horrified expression, "I'm not going to do that. I promised someone else to keep you untouched. Although, I must confess, I'm tempted to bite you myself."

"Bite me?" croaked Rusty. "Why would you want to bite me?"

As adorable as the puppy was, its two gigantic rows of teeth at close distance looked like they could snap him in two.

Rusty drew back and bumped into a stalk of grass. It shook with indignation. He spun around. "What was that?"

"Oh, that's just grass," yapped the puppy. "It's upset at you."

"Upset at me? Why?"

"*Why?*" The puppy sized Rusty up and down. "You pushed it!"

"Oh." Rusty scratched his head, confounded. "That was an accident. I didn't mean to. I mean, there is grass everywhere!"

"Doesn't matter," said the puppy. "You need to apologize to it."

"Apologize?" Rusty stared. "To grass?"

"Silly badling," swished the grass.

At this the puppy barked at the grass, and the grass slapped it on the head. The thistle clapped its spiky leaves, urging on the spectacle.

"Look at this," said one flower to another. "They're fighting again."

"How childish." The other flower shook its head and doused Rusty with dewdrops.

"Right," said Rusty. "They're all nuts here. I need to go find Bells and the guys." He resolutely stalked around the thistle, only to be picked up by the puppy and placed back to where he began.

"You're not going anywhere," said the puppy, and this time its large eyes didn't have any friendliness in them. "You're staying here."

"Hey!" cried Rusty, brandishing his fists. "Let me go!"

"I thought you liked animals," said the puppy.

Rusty knotted his brows. "How do you know?"

"Dapple told me. Would you like to become a puppy?"

"Why would I want to be a puppy?"

"Why not?" The puppy bristled, and for a second it changed into a cunning beast. "Look at me. I'm cute and soft and fluffy, am I not?"

Rusty swallowed, backing off. "Sure thing. Nice puppy, nice little puppy..."

"Well, if you like me so much, what's wrong with being a puppy?" It advanced, sniffing the air with a dangerous determination.

"Nothing, nothing at all," stammered Rusty, feeling

behind him for the treacherous grass stalks that shifted and squirmed. "I didn't say there was anything wrong with being a puppy. I love puppies. My grandma delivers puppies. She walks dogs, too, all kinds of dogs, and I help her. I wash them and feed them and clean their paws with a wet towel and..." He gulped.

"Do you?" asked the puppy dreamily.

"Totally," said Rusty, starting to grin. "I cut up raw pieces of meat, so tender and juicy, and I feed them right off my hand."

The puppy rolled up its eyes. "Tell me more."

"Right." Rusty tromped into the thistle and stifled a cry from brushing against its thorns. "I scratch behind their ears and part their fur and pick their fleas and...and..."

The puppy growled. "Fleas? I don't have any fleas."

"Sorry, sorry. I said the wrong thing. Good puppy, nice puppy..."

"Go on, badling," said the puppy demandingly.

Rusty frowned. "Wait. Dapple called me a badling too, and the grass. What does it—"

A shrill whistle cut him off.

The puppy flattened its ears and tucked its tail.

"What was that?" asked Rusty.

"Quiet," and the puppy was upon him, snarling in his face, "or I will bite you, and you *will* replace me, want it or not."

"What's that supposed to mean?" Rusty tried wiggling out, but the puppy overwhelmed him with its weight.

The whistle trilled impatiently over the flowers.

"You better go to her," said the thistle, speaking up for the first time.

"I could do it right here, right now," said the puppy, "and be free. Free of you and of all these flippant flowers that talk gibberish from morning till night. I'm sick of you, if you must know."

"Oh, are you?" The cluster of flowers, so peaceful and aromatic, suddenly started beating on the puppy with all the ferocity of carnivorous plants deprived of dinner.

Rusty wisely used the ensuing commotion to his advantage and tore off into the greenery without looking back.

"I'll never pet another puppy again," he promised himself, climbing over monstrous roots. "Forget it. That thing was scary. I wonder what book this is. I'm sure it's one nutty story."

A series of whistles erupted behind him, and Rusty sprinted, running blindly, until he slammed into something spongy. Panicking, he tumbled to the ground, hands over his face in the desperate attempt to hide from this new menace.

When nothing sniffed him or licked him or talked to him, he opened one eye.

"It's a mushroom!" he said.

And it was, a fleshy leg crowned with a big brown cap. Elegant gills fanned out from its center like spokes of a bike wheel. It smelled pungent and earthy, and Rusty patiently waited for it to speak, searching for eyes or for a mouth.

When it did talk, it talked from above, first coughing and then saying nasally, "Who are you?"

Rusty drew himself up and craned his neck, but the mushroom's cap came to his nose and even when he stood on tiptoe, he couldn't see where the voice came from.

"If only I was a little bit taller," he sighed.

Whatever it was that was talking to him uttered a little cough. "What do you mean? It is wrong," it announced.

"What is wrong?" asked Rusty.

"You said the wrong line. That's not what you ought to say. You ought to say, 'I hardly know.'"

Rusty scratched his head. "I'm not sure I understand?"

"Wrong again!" said whatever sat on the mushroom.

There was a shuffling noise, and suddenly Rusty was staring into a pair of blue eyes on a face so velvety smooth and violet-blue and inhuman, he knew immediately who it was, and it gave him comfort.

But we shall leave Rusty to his conversation and get back to Bells and Peacock and Grand who have been deposited into a tale so desolate and wretched, it didn't promise anything good apart from what Mad Tome already predicted—plenty of unsightly and messy bloodletting.

Chapter Six

The Red Menace

Books die every day, just like people do, together with the characters that live inside them. It can be a slow demise, with page after page falling out in sorrow of not being read anymore. Or it can be a brutal execution via ripping.

Terrible, wouldn't you say? I agree. Let us shelve this depressing subject for a while and focus on three dots rushing through the air. As you know, these would be Bells, Peacock, and Grand. Hollering in fright, they landed at a somber wall that girded an abbey of many turrets and towers gripped by dead vines. A couple of naked trees flanked an iron gate beyond which a path led to a pillared porch. The last ray of sun colored everything ruddy, and the narrow windows seemed to scrutinize the intruders with many dead eyes.

Bells shivered and glanced at the boys. Her dread reflected in their faces. Not only had they lost Rusty, they appeared to have landed in an obviously spooky story. On top of it, they were hungry, thirsty, and sore.

"Where did it send us now?" asked Peacock, picking bits of gravel out of his scraped hands.

Grand sighed. The impact didn't have as devastating an effect on him as it did on his friend. "Um," he said, rubbing his forehead, "I don't know, but it doesn't look friendly."

Peacock kicked a stone. "This is dumb. I don't like it. What did that donkey mean by not being a donkey? And how are we supposed to destroy this thing? Mad Tome or whatever?"

Grand shrugged.

"I might have an idea," voiced Bells brightly, dusting herself off and redoing her ponytail.

Peacock cocked a brow. "Care to share?"

"I'll have to think about it first," she stated, "see if it makes sense."

"Well, hurry up then," he snapped.

Bells propped her hands on her hips and said heatedly, "Look, Peacock. Forgive me for being blunt, but can you be any more selfish? First we need to find out where Mad Tome has sent Rusty and get him back. Don't you think?"

Peacock glared at her. "Leave it to a girl to slobber guilt all over you to make you feel even worse."

"Oh, we're talking about *girls* all of a sudden, are we?" hissed Bells. "Okay, let me tell you something." She advanced at him. "For a *boy* you're sometimes too much of a blubbering sissy. I thought boys were supposed to be braver than girls, you know, valiant knights that brandish swords around and protect us, feeble maidens, with fierce cries of war."

Peacock stared. "What?"

Sensing her victory, Bells continued. "I'm not saying you will stay a coward your whole life. There is hope for you yet. I'm just worried about Rusty, okay? It's not like he will drop on our heads. We need to actively look for him. What if he is being devoured alive by some monster right now? Did you think about that?"

A faint smile played on Grand's lips. "I thought I was the only one thinking about morbid things."

Bells hastily cleared her throat, "I do too, *sometimes*. For the purpose of examining facts."

"Don't tell me you're not scared," said Peacock, motioning to the abbey. "This place gives me the creeps. Look at it!"

"Scared?" asked Bells with forced bravado. "Pfft. Not at all."

"You're not scared of dying?" said Peacock, amazed.

"Nope," Bells lied. "When Death shows up, I will punch him in the face and tell him he can beat it."

Peacock snorted. "Spoken by a true scientist."

Bells opened her mouth to retort and closed it. "It is beneath me to descend to your level of petty bickering." She turned on her heel and decidedly stalked to the gate. Unlocked, it swung open on the first try with a grating noise that sent goose bumps along her arms. She raised her head and stalked inside, turning and looking at the boys.

"Coming?"

"Are you crazy?" cried Peacock. "Where are you going?"

"Inside, where else?"

"Don't you think it's a better idea to find the edge of the page and dig?"

"I thought you didn't like that idea."

"Bells is right," reflected Grand. "There might be tools there. And food."

"Food?" exploded Peacock. "How can you think about *food*?"

A crow landed on one of the towers and croaked.

The children jumped.

"Shoo! Go away!" Peacock grabbed a stone and flung it at the bird. It took off, but not before swooping right over his head. He barely dodged it.

Grand cleared his throat. "Um," he began cautiously. "We need to get going. My mom says it's no good talking about doing things. She says people who *do* things have no time to talk. That's why she loves her job. She doesn't talk to dead people, and they don't talk to her. They accept her, and she makes them look nice. She really does," he said, answering their astounded stares, "I saw it. It's the last thing she can do for them, to make them lie all pretty in a coffin and—" He checked himself. "Sorry. Got carried away."

"No," said Bells, "it's okay."

"Yeah," added Peacock in a rather high-pitched tone, "we don't mind *at all*."

"You don't?" Grand smiled sheepishly.

"Guys, look." Bells nodded at the abbey.

A couple windows lit up with sickly reddish glare.

"There is definitely someone inside," she whispered.

"Still want to go in?" inquired Peacock.

Bells didn't answer. The boys followed her gaze and saw an appearance that almost made them soil their pants.

Between the silhouettes of the trees hovered a figure in a red cloak. A draping hood hung so low, they couldn't see the face underneath. But the worst part was not the way it looked, it was the way it moved. It didn't walk, it *glided* over the ground as if weightless.

The children froze, mortified.

The figure drew closer.

They could hear its shallow breath and the swish of the cloak. They could see icky splodges of blood it left glistening on the ground. It passed them within inches, cracked open one of the double doors, and slunk inside.

Bells shook all over. "Who was *that?*"

"Does it matter?" Peacock took a step back. "Let's get out of here."

"But we must go in," she insisted.

"How is that going to help us?"

"We'll live though the page and go to the next one. At least we'll keep moving and looking. Who knows, maybe Rusty is there."

"Oh yeah? And what if some medieval maniac will make us into mincemeat? Didn't Mad Tome say something about bloodletting?"

"There won't be any bloodletting," said Grand.

They gawked at him.

"I read this book. I know what will happen," he said quietly, "it will be worse than bloodletting."

Bells and Peacock stole a glance at each other.

"How much worse?" breathed Bells.

"Well, it's one of Poe's stories, about Red Death," explained Grand. "I can't recall the title, but it's about this disease. It's like a plague. If you're infected, you get sores all over your body. They grow and burst and leak pus and blood and then—"

The doors flung open.

There stood a regal man dressed in velvet. His face was concealed behind a domino mask. "Welcome, new badlings!" he intoned. "Please, do come in. It's getting rather chilly. You don't want to catch a cold, do you?" He patiently waited for response. Behind him milled people in extravagant outfits and masks, accompanied by noises of merriment.

"There it is again, *badlings*," muttered Bells.

She exchanged a look with the boys.

The man didn't appear to be insane or murderous, quite the opposite. He instilled a sense of wealth and prosperity. He beckoned them with his gloved hand into the warmth and the light and the smells of food, and that won their internal argument. They climbed the steps and walked into the strangest assortment of individuals they had ever witnessed in their lives.

Chapter Seven

The Creepy Masquerade

Life goes out of a book that has lost all of its pages, unless you collect them and rebind them in a new cover. But if you tear or crumple or bend even one page, its characters will suffer mutilation and thirst for revenge. Imagine them lurking on paper, looking for you. It's an unsettling thought.

This is what flitted through Peacock's mind for reasons I'm not going to disclose. Not *yet*.

He quailed, reluctant to go further. Endless pairs of eyes fastened on him. Eyes of pomaded partygoers dressed in wigs, ladies in gowns, jugglers in leotards, musicians, magicians, dancers, performers, stoutly matrons sipping drinks and gossiping in sibilant whispers. Everyone present wore a mask, which made the entire congregation seem eccentric and eerie.

Spooked, Peacock hurried behind the man in velvet, gawking at the costumes and the getups and the lavish disguises the kind you see in illustrated history books.

"Prince Prospero," spoke the voices around—"Who do you bring in our midst, Prince Prospero?—Why are they unmasked?—Where is their respect for our etiquette?—How dare they—"

"Who speaks?" commanded Prince Prospero. "Be grateful. I'm bringing you new badlings. Soon we shall divide them among ourselves and you will thank me for my generosity. Now hush!"

The voices dropped and the crowd parted for them like a silky feathery river.

"*Divide* us?" whispered Peacock.

"I don't like it either," admitted Grand.

Peacock felt unnerved. "What is this, murders' ball? Are they going to kill us, is that why they're wearing masks?"

"No, they're not going to kill us," explained Grand patiently. "They're wearing masks because it's a masquerade."

Peacock shook his head, not convinced. His eyes fell on a man in a black cape that folded down like leathery wings, each wrinkle a rigid bone. His face was hidden behind an animal mask frozen in a snarl. "Is that a *bat*?"

"No, it's a nice cuddly puppy," scoffed Bells.

"That's not funny."

"Okay, chill, it was a joke. Obviously, it's a man in a costume of a bat with a bat mask. What else could it be? See the wings on the back?"

"Why is he following us?"

"He's not following us. Why would he be following us? You're being paranoid."

"Yes, he is," insisted Peacock, anxiously watching the man's cape flicker behind them. The man, sensing the stare, hissed, and Peacock flinched, his heart pounding.

The prince led them on through a vista of rooms, each a new dazzling color: blue, purple, green, orange, white, violet. At last they entered a spacious suite decorated in black. Everything was black here, everything *except* the windows, their tinted panes glowing disturbingly red.

"This is hideous," said Bells in a loud whisper.

"What is this place?" asked Peacock.

Before Grand could answer, a heavy chime of a clock shook the walls. It rung out one creepy ding and stilled. Thick silence enveloped the abbey.

Prince Prospero spoke. "Go on. Get on with it already. We do not have the luxury to dally."

Peacock couldn't see whom he talked to. Masked guests blocked his view. They pressed through the doorway, steadily edging closer.

The clock struck twice.

Peacock winced. "Why is it so loud?"

A couple more chimes shook the air. The clock appeared to be mocking him, waiting for him to be terrified out of his mind.

"Is everyone present?" asked the prince.

The guests answered with obedient cries. "We are, Prince—We are ready—Bestow on us your generosity—We cannot wait any longer, have pity—Must we suffer so?—Do not prolong our torment, we beg you, it is but unbearable!"

The clock appeared to have lost its patience and struck several deafening ding-dongs in a row.

Not paying it any heed, the mob jabbered and jostled and drew closer to get a better look at the children and to touch them with a quivering finger or even lick them with a grating tongue, which Peacock, to his horror, saw flick out of a mouth of a monkey. Several of them knuckled to and fro between skirts and suits, crude masks stretched over their furry faces.

"Holy buckets." Peacock gripped Bells' arm. "Did you see that?"

"See what?"

"Monkeys!"

His exclamation drowned in the next angry chime.

"I do believe the time has come!" began the prince, as soon as the echoes died. "Hereby I shall decree—"

The clock, apparently very upset at hardly anyone paying attention to its horrifying performance, sounded out the rest of the twelve hours.

"We hear you, loud and clear," called Prince Prospero.

The clock added another chime. Spitefully.

"That is thirteen, which is a trifle too much," observed the prince calmly. "Wouldn't you agree?"

The clock plinked once and stopped, satisfied. All noise faded. The music quieted. The voices fizzled out. A somber silence hung in the room, and through it strode the figure in red. Its face was finally visible: it wore a mask of death.

Prince Prospero bowed in welcome and said, "At last! I was beginning to think you had insulted me by rescinding your duties. Badlings, I'd like for you to meet Red Death. Red Death, these are—"

"Do pardon me for interrupting," said the Red Death in a spine-chillingly tone. "I bring you urgent tidings."

"Tidings of what nature?" inquired the prince. "Is it still napping? How long do we have?"

"Half an hour at the most," was the Red Death's answer.

The guests murmured uneasily. "This is a tiresome affair—Why do we have to wait?—Let's grab them for ourselves—What right do *they* have to decide—Do our desires count for nothing?—I daresay—"

"Silence!" rung out a woman's voice, followed by a stomp of a foot that brought a sudden calm to the fidgeting assembly.

"The Snow Queen!" cried Bells, forgetting herself.

The Snow Queen didn't grant a single glance in her direction. Drawn up to her full height, she strode into the circle and addressed Prince Prospero sternly, "Enough of this amusement. I want my share and I want it *now*." She threw a chilling glance at Bells, her ice-blue eyes hard as stones.

"I was the first to come here. It's my right to claim the one I want. I claim the girl." She seized Bells by the wrist.

"Ow!" cried Bells. "Let me go!"

"I beg to differ," said the man in the bat mask, noiselessly appearing next to the queen. "If anyone in here has any claim on them, it's me."

"Them?" the queen repeated, her lips curling. "You cannot claim all of them. Take the one who caused you damage and be off with you, you bloodthirsty vagrant!"

"Is this a new diversion to your boredom," said the man softly, "calling me names?" His long-fingered hand emerged from under his cloak and crept toward Bells, his eyes holding the queen's attention hostage.

"Do not attempt to draw me into one of your witty games," said the Snow Queen, "I know exactly what you're scheming. Today we will vote on the division of the loot. Then and only then will you get your share, *if* you get it at all. Do you understand me, or would you like me to repeat this one more time, Dracula dear?"

Whatever Dracula answered, Peacock didn't hear.

His ears felt stuffed with cotton, and his stomach flopped and dropped to his feet, bursting to pieces. "Dracula?" he said to no one in particular. "It's...Dracula?"

"Excuse me," said Bells through clenched teeth, "please let me go. You're breaking my wrist." She wriggled her arm.

"Oh, I'm so sorry," said the queen, her expression promptly changing from indifferent to the one wrecked with worry. "Come. Let me warm you up."

"Time," pronounced the Red Death. "Time is scarce."

"Indeed it is," agreed the prince. "I decree we rejoice in our fortune. For years we have suffered, but enough of our lament. Welcome freedom!" He pushed the children forward.

There were cries of excitement, mixed with the sounds of clapping hands and snapping teeth.

"Four lucky badlings get to shed the chains of their unjustified confinement and return to their homes while the rest of us wait to be avenged!" The prince foamed at the mouth.

"Avenged?" mumbled Peacock. "What for?"

"For the crimes we did not commit," helpfully supplied Dracula. His putrid breath gave Peacock deathly chills. "You, on the other hand, very well know what you're guilty of, *badling*."

Peacock gulped. "I don't know what you're talking about."

"Would you like me to remind you?" asked Dracula, and Peacock thought that in the next second he would faint.

Sudden wind slammed into windows. The trees

outside groaned alarmingly.

Dracula's mouth folded into a line. "We shall see each other again soon. Farewell." And he withdrew, vanishing from sight.

"Was that really Dracula?" asked Bells breathlessly.

Peacock nodded.

"What was he talking to you about?"

He shook his head, unable to speak. They were surrounded from all sides with greedy gleaming eyes.

"Enough with this nonsense." A stocky man in a worn travel coat pushed through. He looked quite ordinary, if not for his imposing size and his beard. Blue beard. It fell to his waist, a curly bushy treasure.

Peacock reached for his fauxhawk. Yes, it was blue, but not as blue as *this*.

"Upon my beard," boomed the man, his eyes popping out of their sockets, "this one is perfect for me." And he unceremoniously seized Peacock by the scruff of his shirt, lifting him clear off the ground.

Peacock gasped for air, his throat locked in panic.

"Put him down, Bluebeard!" shouted the Snow Queen.

"Who are you to tell me what to do? Go freeze at your lake, icicle witch."

The queen hissed at him, frosting his beard.

Frightened cries erupted.

Bluebeard chuckled. "You think you can scare me with a little bit of cold? I don't give a rat's skin over what you lot decided. I came here to take what is rightfully mine, and that's that. What are you going to do, tear me to pieces? I'd like to see you try." He gave Peacock a jubilant shake, tucked him under his arm, and marched off, his heavy boots punctuating every step with a bang.

"Peacock!" Bells rushed after him, but the queen stopped her.

"Hang on, Peacock." Grand made two steps and tripped over Dapple the donkey.

The floor trembled. The earth under the abbey hummed.

"It's awake," said the Red Death.

"Quick!" cried Prince Prospero. He took out a dagger and thrust it forth with the words, "Unmask yourself!"

The Red Death touched him, and the prince dropped to the floor.

Peacock heard the thump of a body followed by a volley of shrieks. His face was firmly pressed to Bluebeard's grimy coat. He closed his eyes and opened them only when the noises subsided and the sweet smelling air hit his nose. The gentle slope of a hill, no more than a line against the dark sky, bobbed up and down.

Bluebeard stopped and tossed him on the grass. "Don't you even think about running away. I'll break your spine like that." He snapped his fingers.

Peacock nodded, horror flooding his stomach.

Bluebeard tucked his precious beard under his belt and bent over, groping for something at the foot of the dirt wall. Misty tendrils rose from the ground, when a cry made him look up.

"Upon my beard...looks like we got company."

A swarm of figures ran down the hill. Two of them broke off, jogging at a frightening pace.

Peacock recognized them. "Grand? Bells?"

Grand pumped his legs with an iron determination,

one arm outstretched, another tugging Bells. At least a dozen guests pursued them, with the Snow Queen in the lead.

Bluebeard grasped at something and pulled. He was lifting the page from under his feet. Clumps of turf peeled off and fell, and solid darkness leaked from the gap.

"Don't just sit there. Get in!" He reached for Peacock just as Grand and Bells ran into them. They knocked Peacock back, and all three of them somersaulted into the yawning void.

Seeing that he had no time to follow, Bluebeard let go of the page. "I'm afraid you're a bit too late," he said as he stepped aside.

Carried forward by inertia, the Snow Queen dove after the children but instead slammed her face into dirt.

Chapter Eight

The Forbidden Dungeon

Don't think that the longer the book, the more gripping its story. Some very short tales have penetrated the minds of generations and remained there, unwilling to leave. People like to call them "classics," although there is nothing *classic* in them, but plenty of blood, murders, and treachery.

The children were presently rushing toward one such tale. Murky fog whooshed past them, or they whooshed past murky fog—it was hard to tell. The lower they hurtled, the chillier it got. Even Grand's typically warm hands lost all feeling. A fine layer of dew formed on his hair. At one point he thought they would fall like this forever, sinking further and further into a uniform greyness that clung to them like spider webs.

It *was* spider webs.

They shot through a tangle of them and landed on stone with a muffled thwack. Shaken and disoriented, none of them moved.

A minute passed.

Grand patted the uneven floor, groaned, and rolled to his side. He was sitting in a dark room. Weak light trickled in from a barred window high up by the ceiling. The air was dank and drafty, and it smelled foul. He stood up, took a step and froze. His worst nightmares had materialized right by his feet, splayed along the wall in a neat, gruesome row.

Grand stopped breathing. A single drop of cold sweat rolled down his nose and hung at the very tip. He willed himself to wipe if off and couldn't.

"Grand?" called Bells from the darkness.

"Um." The sound of his own voice startled him so much, he nearly jumped.

"Oh, good, you're here. Peacock?"

Peacock coughed. "I'm okay."

"Just making sure," said Bells. "It's so dark in here, I can't see a thing. Where are we, do you know?"

Grand swayed.

"Are you okay?" she asked, groping for him. "Your hands are cold!"

Grand opened and closed his mouth. No sound came out.

"I don't remember your hands *ever* being cold. What's wrong?" Bells glanced around until her eyes fell down and she stifled a shriek.

"What is it?" Peacock wiggled in between them. "Why are you guys shaking..."

Grand had forgotten about his friends. Nothing existed for him except the horrible dreams he had every time after visiting his mother at the funeral home. They were always the same: he entered the mortuary fridge, and someone turned off the lights and slammed the door shut, locking him in. For the rest of the dream, he blundered around the room, walking into dead people's clammy arms until he panicked and woke up drenched in sweat, his heart pounding like a hammer.

"Grand." Bells tugged on him. "Grand!"

He remained motionless, rooted to the spot.

Bells dug her nails into his palm.

He didn't flinch.

"Peacock," she squeaked, "help me!"

Peacock stumbled backward, retching.

"Come on, guys, don't fall apart on me now. We need to...we need..." She held it, held it, and lost it, hanging onto Grand so as not to faint.

Right by their feet, on the cobblestone floor blackened by wear and grime, stood a wooden block with an ax wedged into it. Next to it, carefully arranged along the wall, lay bodies of five dead women, their unseeing eyes open, their hair caked with blood, their stiff feet peeking out from under the hems of white nightgowns.

Grand made a concentrated effort and moved his foot. It touched a puddle of something sticky. His body turned wooden and his leg refused to make another step. Bells clung to his shoulder, and Peacock pressed into a wall, barely breathing.

Hurried footsteps broke them out of paralysis. Someone skipped down the stairs, skittered the length of the hallway, and halted by the other side of the door.

A key turned in the lock. The door swung open and there stood a young woman with a candle in her hand. The flame threw dancing shadows over her organza-veiled face. She entered the room, her dress trailing over the cobbles, saw the children, dropped the key and the candle, and screamed.

This must have had an inspirational effect on Bells, because she let go of Grand's shoulder and joined the screaming.

Their voices bounced off the walls in dull echoes. After a good few seconds of this they stopped and proceeded gawking at each other in pitch-black darkness.

The woman picked up the candle, struck the flint and lit it again. The scent of melting wax blotted out the stink. She studied the children with a disgusted expression, as if it were they who smelled bad, not the bodies.

"Well?" she inquired. "What book are you from and what are you doing on my page? I don't remember inviting anyone."

"Er," Bells said hesitantly. "We're not from...*any* book?"

The woman tensed. "Don't lie to me."

Bells flushed at this injustice. "I'm not lying. Grand, tell her."

Grand stared down at the dead women. "It's only a story," he muttered to himself. "A story of Bluebeard. We're in the dungeon where he killed his wives, and these are their bodies. They're not real, so there is nothing to be afraid of." It seemed to him that one of them winked, but when he squinted to see better, she appeared to be as dead as before.

"Only a story," he mumbled.

"Is that what Bluebeard did? Killed his wives?" Bells rolled her eyes. "What kind of a book is this?"

"It's actually a fairy tale," explained Grand.

"This? A *fairy* tale?" Incredibly, Bells chuckled.

"Well?" prompted the woman. "Explain yourselves. You." She pointed to Peacock. "Why are you not saying anything?"

He coughed into his fist. "Sorry, lady, I'm feeling sick. I think I'm going to puke."

One of the dead wives tucked in her legs, perhaps in an attempt to avoid being puked on, or for some other reason.

Peacock gulped. "Did she just...*move?*"

"Are you going to answer me or not?" said the woman impatiently. "I don't have all day, you know."

"Look, we have no idea why we're here, okay?" began Peacock. "Ask that Bluebeard guy. He said I was perfect for him or something. He must have liked my blue hair." Peacock nervously ran a hand through it.

"He said that, did he?" the woman smirked. "Without consulting me, of course. I understand now. You must be the new badlings." She looked at them appraisingly.

Someone sniggered on the floor.

"What are you laughing at?" demanded the woman.

"You, Boulotte. I'm laughing at you. You take your role so seriously," said a voice that sent chills along the children's backs.

"Is that...*them* talking?" asked Peacock, his eyes huge. "They're not really dead, are they?" He began edging toward the door.

"I don't think so," said Grand, following him. "I think they are acting like they're dead. It's good that they aren't. For a moment I thought I was in the morgue at my mom's work—it's where they store the corpses so they won't decompose before the funeral and—"

Bells put a hand on his shoulder. "Do you mind? I'd rather not think about anything decaying just now." She forced a smile. "And sorry for screaming. I hope I wasn't too loud."

"Funny to hear you apologize," Peacock tried to sound sarcastic. "Isn't that what girls do when they're scared?"

Bells stared at him, burning with desire to throttle him right there and then.

While Boulotte was absorbed in a muffled conversation with Bluebeard's dead wives, the children tiptoed through the door into a narrow hallway lit by torches.

"Where do you think you're going?" called Boulotte. She waved the candle, and in its flickering light they saw the wives struggle up.

"Um," ventured Grand. "You know how you're supposed to escape mortal danger in books?"

"Yeah?" said Bells and Peacock as one.

"I think now would be a good time."

None of them moved. All three of them wanted to leave this dreadful place, but a strange curiosity held them hostage, and instead of running they stayed put, staring at the doorway with a mix of horror and amazement.

First a pale foot emerged from the darkness, then the nightgown, and finally a grey face of one of the wives. She held her head together with both hands, since it was cleaved in two by an ax, making her look rather asymmetrical.

Bells made a mewling noise. Grand slammed into a wall. And Peacock flung a hand over his mouth, retching.

The second dead wife stepped out of the dungeon and patted the arm of the first one. "Stop it, Eleonore," she said, brushing hair out of her blood-streaked face. "You're scaring the children."

"They're not children," snorted Eleonore, "they're *badlings*. I'm claiming that one." She pointed a decomposing finger at Grand.

Boulotte's eyes narrowed, and she hefted the candle higher as if ready to throw it. "I'm claiming the girl. How dare Bluebeard not tell me?"

"He told *me*," said Eleonore proudly.

Boulotte gasped. "He told *you*, but not me?"

"Of course he did," teased Eleonore, "I was his *favorite*."

"Liar," hissed another wife. "It was *I* who was his favorite. I was the first one."

"Little do you know, Rosalinde," smirked the fourth wife. "When we married, he told me how lazy you were. He said you never cooked for him and never ironed his shirts. He even said you never—"

"Shut up, Blanche!"

Their quarrel escalated into shouting, and soon they were grabbing each other's hair and pulling and tearing and snarling.

Bells watched them with a grimace of distaste. "That is precisely why I want to be a scientist and not some wife cooking dinners and mending shirts," she stated.

The wives heard her and stopped fighting.

"What did you say about wives, badling?" asked Boulotte.

"Er, nothing." Bells quickly smiled, and glanced at the boys. "Guys? I think we have a bad reputation here."

"I think," said Grand, "it's time to flee."

"Agreed," said Peacock.

"Get them!" shouted Boulotte.

Pursued by five dead wives and one living one, the children bolted into darkness.

Chapter Nine

Bluebeard's Revenge

There must be an ancient hostility between a book and its characters for them to turn against it. It rarely happens to good books, but it's what happened to Mad Tome, the *bad* book that didn't care for its inhabitants. Not one bit. Yawning, it sensed unrest on one of its pages but didn't bother investigating, too lazy to rouse from a nap.

The unrest quickly escalated to a deadly chase. Six women hunted for three badlings through the halls of Bluebeard's chateau.

Bells rounded a turn and bumped into a winding staircase.

"Where are you going?" called Peacock.

"Up," she answered, leaping two steps at a time.

"You don't even know where it leads!"

"Who cares? It goes up, and that's good enough for me. Are you guys coming or what? Or would you rather be smothered by a bunch of crazy cadavers?" Her ponytail flipped and winked out of sight.

"I guess," Peacock reluctantly followed. "Grand?"

"Coming!" Grand reached the staircase last, huffing and sweating. His stomach grumbled, and he made himself think of doughnuts to move faster.

They reached the top, crashed through a door, and found themselves in a large hall bedecked with medieval décor: suits of armor, lances, shields, tall candelabra with hundreds of candles. The shifting light they cast on the walls made the shadows look alive and creepy.

Bells waited for Grand to labor out, slammed the door shut and leaned on it. "I need to catch my breath. Help me hold it."

"Can't we lock it?" asked Peacock.

"I don't see a lock. Do you?"

He shook his head.

"Then quit whining and help!" She glared at him.

Peacock pushed at the door with both hands, but it was Grand's weight that saved them. He slumped into it, shuddering under sudden blows from the other side. Muffled screams trickled through. The door trembled but held. It was thick and heavy, made of solid oak, and after a few more tries to force it open the commotion behind it faded. The pounding stopped too, and they heard retreating steps.

"I'm sure this is not over yet," said Bells with conviction. "This place looks like a castle, and as far as I know, castles have lots of hidden passages. I bet they just decided to take another way. Let's get out of here before it's too late."

"I hate castles," moaned Peacock.

"Maybe there's some food here," blurted Grand. "Maybe we could go look—"

"Are you insane?" Peacock shook his head. "How can you talk about food when we just saw butchered bodies? How can you even...doesn't it make you queasy?"

Grand shrugged. "I have lunch with my mom all the time."

"Yeah, I've heard that before. I'll believe it when I

see it."

"Guys?" said Bells with alarm.

High under the vaulted ceiling a harsh cry rebounded, followed by the sound of bare feet slapping on the stones. The wives gathered on the balcony overlooking the hall.

"There they are!" Boulotte pointed down. "Get them!"

The children dashed across the room to a pair of doors so big, a giant could pass through them.

Bells struck them with wide-apart palms and pushed. The doors slowly swung out. Moist air washed over her face. It was dark, and it was raining. A horse whinnied, and moments later a carriage manned by a humpbacked driver sped into the court. It stopped abruptly by the porch. The door flipped open, and, just their luck, out stepped Bluebeard.

"Upon my beard, how did you make it out of the dungeon? Did you happen to meet my wife Boulotte?" His eyes sparkled with menace.

The horse whinnied. The driver spurred it on, and the carriage rolled off.

Bells followed it with her eyes into shadows. "Look, Bluebeard," she stammered. "What do you want from us?"

"Like he will tell you." Peacock snatched her hand and rushed down the steps. It was futile. Bluebeard swept them into his powerful arms and stood them back on the porch as if they didn't weigh an ounce.

"What's your problem?" said Peacock hoarsely. "What did we do to you?"

"You found Mad Tome." Bluebeard smiled. Rows of crooked teeth shone from his beard. "We have been waiting for you for *years*. Just one, we hoped for, at least one. And look, we got four. *Four* new badlings, and three of you are in my hands." His tone dropped to a dangerous low. "What did it feel like to be alone and scared? To be in a dungeon with maimed bodies?"

He thought a moment.

"Forget the ritual. I cannot wait any longer. I shall do it right here, on these very steps that have suffered my wary feet for I have forgotten how long." He reached under his coat and took out an ax, spitting on it and sliding his thumb along the blade. "Should be sharp enough."

"Um," said Grand, his mouth hanging open, "are you going to split our heads with that?"

"Oh, there is no need to be *that* dramatic," said Bluebeard amiably, "unless you want me to?" His smile suddenly folded into a pout of dismay.

Disheveled and red in the face from running around, Boulotte stepped out on the porch. "There they are! Wretched scoundrels." Then she saw her husband. "Bluebeard! How on earth will you explain this, I'd like to know?"

Bluebeard shrunk under her fiery stare. "Boulotte, my dearest, I missed you so. Here, this is for you." He produced a crumpled bouquet of bluebells from one of his pockets, still holding the ax in his other hand. "Look, I brought us new badlings. One for you, one for me, one for Eleonore. Aren't you happy, my honey bee? We've been waiting for so long, my dulcet darling, and our salvation is finally here." He talked in a simpering voice that dripped with artificial sweetness.

Grand rubbed his nose, then said, "I don't think you're the real Bluebeard. Real Bluebeard wouldn't talk like that. Real Bluebeard wouldn't be scared of his wife, he'd kill her. And, to be honest, I don't think you're his wife either," he looked at Boulotte, whose cheeks sprouted pinkish blotches.

"Do it, before he talks any more," she snapped. "I should've grabbed my scissors, I knew I should've." She patted her corset and her skirt.

"Are you trying to be smart with me?" bristled Bluebeard at Grand. "You haven't even finished my story!"

"I have. I read it to the end," said Grand. "My mom read fairy tales to me when I was little, but when she got to Bluebeard she said it was too scary and wouldn't read it. So I snuck out of bed at night and read it myself."

Bluebeard's eyes widened. "Then why are you here?"

"Because of me," volunteered Bells. "I haven't finished reading The Snow Queen. I did finish reading the page I stopped on, though. I mean, I *lived* through it. We all did. And I think we just lived through your page too. See? There is no reason for you to be mad." She lowered her voice. "When we were in the steppe, I mean, on a different page, we met a donkey. Dapple. He said we could go home if we destroyed Mad Tome. Is that true?"

Bluebeard's face sagged, but Bells failed to see it, because just then—bad things always happen in stories when you think all is well—the ground jolted and tilted to the side, throwing everyone off balance. Bells dropped into a puddle, Peacock spread-eagled next to her, and Grand sat down on the steps.

A rustling voice spoke from above. "Can't nap in peace without one of you betraying me. I know what you're after, Bluebeard, you spoiled nasty badling."

"Mad Tome," said Bells in horror.

Grand followed her gaze. It was so dark, and the rain lashed so hard, he had to squint to detect a shadowy mouth hanging above them.

"Do you?" yelled Bluebeard into the sky, his knuckles white, his ax trembling. "A fat lot of nonsense you know, you brainless piece of carton. I should've done this a long time ago." He heaved the ax and with a grunt brought it down between his feet. It sunk into mud with a squelching plop. Mad Tome's shriek filled the clouds with whistling echoes and shook every windowpane in the chateau.

"How do you like *that*, Mad Tome? Would you like some more?" Bluebeard wrenched the ax out and brought it down, again and again and again.

Boulotte screamed and dashed down the steps, throwing herself on Bluebeard. He shook her off like a fly and delivered another blow.

Mad Tome squirmed and bellowed, sending shivers through the page that felt like an earthquake. The walls crumbled, the roof shingles shifted and fell, sinking into puddles like darts, and where Bluebeard had struck the ground it cracked, the resulting fracture widening with an alarming speed.

Grand seized Bells by one hand, Peacock by another, and dragged them away from the porch. They ran blindly. The night flashed an ominous yellow. An ear-splitting boom of thunder crashed on their heads. Fierce wind picked up wet leaves and flung them in their faces.

Bells shielded her eyes. "What is he doing?"

"He's breaking...the page," wheezed Grand. "We must get...to the wall."

"What wall?" cried Peacock.

"The dirt wall...to hold on..." Grand drew short breaths, "when the page turns."

"That's brilliant!" exclaimed Bells.

"Look out!" screamed Peacock.

There was a terrible noise, as if the page was tearing in half. A dark jagged line ran down the path and it split, leaving Peacock and Bells on one side, and Grand on the other.

"Grand!" Bells reached for him and grabbed only air.

"Hang on, we'll jump over!" Peacock crouched, but Bells stopped him. The gap was too wide. With a final resounding groan, the page tore in two.

For a moment Grand remained still, as if carved from wood. Then the page side he stood on sagged, and he toppled into the void.

"No!" screamed Bells. She crawled to the edge and looked down, expecting to see layers of soil. Instead she saw pages stacked like floors of a building. Each presented a different landscape: snowy mountains, a forest, a city, a silver river cutting through a dale. Some pages were farther away, others close enough to see characters milling about.

The nearest one was twenty, maybe twenty-five yards down—an ancient city that had been reduced to ruins. Dark bodies crawled over its sun-bleached stones, and on a central plaza stood something grey and bulky. An enormous bird swooped down and snatched it.

"Was that an *elephant?*" asked Peacock.

The bird lifted its head, one mean orange eye looking directly at him, the elephant wiggling and trumpeting in the hold of its powerful talons.

"Why did you have to say that, you idiot?" grumbled Bells. "It heard you. Look. It's coming right at us!"

The bird opened its giant beak and screeched.

Bells covered her ears, losing her hold in the process. The last thing she glimpsed was Peacock lunging for her, and then they were airborne, falling into the path of the feathery flying monstrosity.

Chapter Ten

The Missing Head

Ever find yourself rereading the same page over and over again? Over and over and over and over...how boring and repetitive. Envision the toil the characters have to go through to tirelessly act it out. They'd rather you turn the page, unless you're a badling, in which case you're prey for Mad Tome.

Grand loved morbid stories, the gorier the better, but there was one he couldn't bring himself to read. Each time he started, he shuddered in horror and set the book aside. How fortunate for him to drop exactly into it.

The moon shone on a prairie like an eye of a cyclops. The grasses chirruped and swished. The nocturnal rodents scurried on their nightly business. A stag grazed nearby, flicking its ears to and fro. All seemed peaceful, yet a sense of dread encircled Grand's throat with cold slimy fingers.

"Bells?" he said probingly.

No answer.

He cleared his throat and tried again. "Peacock?"

Unsettling silence.

Grand's stomach lurched and beads of sweat stood out on his nose. He sat still for some time, taking in his surroundings, then quietly said to himself, "I'm alone, I guess, but there is nothing to worry about. This is just a book. It's not real; it's the product of a writer's imagination."

The night around him appeared to have an opposite opinion.

The peaceful chirring was disturbed by a new noise: a clop of hooves against a rocky knoll. A horse with a rider approached at a steady gait.

Grand looked up and froze. His legs went soft, his lungs collapsed, and he promptly fell back into grass. The rider was a man wrapped in a long travel cloak. There was nothing wrong with him except for one small detail.

He had no head.

He *did* have it, but not on his shoulders, where one would expect it. He held it in his hands, and Grand thought that it was just his luck to come here on an empty stomach, because it shrunk to the size of a nut, and if there were anything in it, it would've surely escaped him.

The stag that grazed nearby flinched and dashed away, plunging though a shallow river. The rodents promptly hid in their holes. Whatever breeze there was, it hiccupped and died.

The horse snorted, trotting straight at Grand.

I won't look, I won't look, he thought, but as it clattered by, despite his best self-restraining effort, Grand glanced at the head, saw it wink, and fainted.

Time passed.

Some more time passed.

Then some more time passed.

The nightlife, spooked by the presence of an unusual guest, quietly resumed. Shrews dug holes. Mice escaped owls. A prairie dog cautiously sniffed at the warm, breathing shape unceremoniously splayed right over its burrow. The shape smelled like doughnuts, and the prairie dog followed its nose to Grand's pocket. It was about to steal the leftover crumbs, when Grand groaned and sat up, clasping his head.

The prairie dog peeped its complaint and scuttled off.

Grand, oblivious to this minor disturbance, scrambled to standing. The night stretched around him, unperturbed. He was about to take a step when clopping ascended the same rocky hill, and Grand witnessed with horror the same horse and the same headless rider bypassing him in exactly the same fashion. This time he didn't faint, but merely stood nailed to the ground, watching them cross the river and gallop away, a stark silhouette against the flat moonlit prairie.

He blinked at me, thought Grand.

A wolf's howl raised the hairs on the nape of his neck. He crawled into a cluster of grass and sat still, listening.

The howling stopped. A cicada chirred in his ear. Startled, he snatched at it. It hopped out of reach.

Grand held his head. He wanted a doughnut, he *needed* a doughnut. If there was ever a time in his life when eating a doughnut needed justification, this was it.

He sighed. *Why did I get stuck here? Why not in some story with food?* He sighed some more. It didn't help. He knew perfectly well why he was on this page, and he didn't like thinking about it.

I'll think about what happened. I'll think like Bells, I'll use her scientific method of analysis. That cheered him up, and he smiled. *I guess Bluebeard was upset at Mad Tome, to hack at it like that. And Mad Tome called him a badling. I wonder what that means? I wonder if book characters read books. I guess they do. I guess characters in books can read books, and inside those books characters can read books, and inside those books...*

His stomach rumbled, diverting his attention.

If I sit here much longer, I will expire from hunger. I'll get thinner and thinner. I'll eat insects and get so bony that even the wolf won't bother with me, and then—

Clopping yet again reached his ears, and he shrunk deeper into his shelter, watching the horse's legs flash past. He waited until the splashing of the water fainted, drew a breath and whispered, "I think this page is repeating itself."

A burning desire to share this new insight with his friends trampled his fears. He stood up, energized. Unfortunately, at the same moment the silhouette of the headless rider crested the hill, and Grand flopped down like a sack of potatoes.

This is ridiculous, he thought.

The rider seemed to be mocking him, daring him, waiting for his patience to run out. It wasn't lack of patience that won in the end, it was Grand's overwhelming wish to find Bells, Peacock, and Rusty.

Poor Rusty, thought Grand, *I hope he's okay.*

"A badling! What a surprise," twanged a voice.

Grand spun around.

The horse stood behind him, and the rider's cut off head was grinning.

An indistinct moan struggled up and out of Grand's throat.

"Do I look *that* ugly?" asked the horseman, a trifle offended. "I was handsome in my time, every woman told me so."

"Um," managed Grand. His armpits grew wet.

"But I digress, as usual. My memory is not the same nowadays. I wonder if it has to do with the fact that my head is no longer on my shoulders." He laughed as his own joke.

Sweat rolled down Grand's face, but he didn't dare wipe it. It was one thing watching the headless horseman from a distance, and quite another seeing his severed head close-up, animated and talking.

"Are you a badling too?" hazarded Grand.

The horseman hesitated. "Why do you ask?"

Grand shrugged. "I guess I'm curious."

"Who told you about the badlings?"

"Nobody," answered Grand. "Mad Tome called Bluebeard a badling, and I thought...I thought maybe you're one too."

"Mad Tome?" the horseman snorted. "That dumb bundle of paper is mad indeed." He regarded Grand through narrowed eyes.

Grand stood still, willing his luck to continue.

"We're all badlings," said the horseman at last. "I see no reason to hide it from you, as you'll be one of us soon. In fact, I think I'll claim you this very moment." He stretched out his arms, and Grand felt his legs turn to jelly.

"Ah, curse me!" exclaimed the horseman vexedly. "My hands are tied. I tell you what, badling, drop to your knees and crawl to my boots. Right by the spurs, over there, if you would be so kind."

"What..." Grand stammered, "What do you mean, you'll *claim* me? I don't want to be claimed. I'm fine on my own."

"Did no one explain to you what your role is?"

Grand shook his head.

"Of course they didn't. They were scared you'd flee. Well, there is nowhere for you to go here, badling, just as there was nowhere for me to go when I got here."

Grand rubbed his nose. "If you got here like us, that means you're not the *real* Headless Horseman."

"I beg your pardon! Don't I look scary enough?"

"You look plenty scary to me," said Grand, trying to reassure him.

"Good," said the horseman gravely. "I was beginning to worry." And then he added in a whisper, "Since you're so clever, I will tell you. It's my first time claiming a badling. Don't tell anyone, okay?"

"I won't," agreed Grand, not quite understanding what he agreed to.

The horseman sneered, pleased. "You never finished reading the book, did you?"

Grand sighed. "I couldn't. I honestly tried, but I got too scared."

"How scared did you get?" asked the horseman.

"Um, that picture on the cover, it made me shudder when I looked at it, and when I read the first page about the stag in the prairie and the wrongness of it all, I got so terrified, my hands started shaking and I closed the book and tried not to think about it."

"Go on," said the horseman. "What else?"

"I don't know. I ate a doughnut to feel better."

The horseman looked disappointed. "That's all?"

"I had bad dreams," admitted Grand.

"Nightmares, I hope?"

"Awful ones."

"Well, that's good enough for me." The horseman proclaimed cheerily. "You belong here, badling. You belong in this book."

The horse whinnied impatiently, tramping the

ground.

"If you'll pardon me but for a moment, I have to enact the page again," said the horseman eagerly, as if he was lonely and wanted more conversation. "Wait for me and don't go anywhere."

Grand watched him gallop away, thinking.

If they're all badlings, that means that...that maybe they're kids like us who got here because they didn't finish reading books. But they don't look like kids. Did they turn into characters somehow?

Grand's face lit up with an incredible idea.

That is why they want to claim us, to replace them, so they could get home. The Snow Queen wanted Bells, and then Prince Prospero said four lucky badlings get to toss their chains or something, and Bluebeard said they were waiting for years—

The wolf howled, interrupting Grand's thoughts. Once more the horseman rode down the hill and stopped in front of him.

"May I ask a question?" said Grand shyly. "Before you...make me replace you?"

"Shoot." The horseman seemed to be in high spirits.

Grand smiled, secretly elated that he took his bait. "If we destroy Mad Tome, do we all return home?"

The horseman's jolly demeanor slid off his face. "We hope so. We don't really know."

Grand felt a pang of fear. "Is there anyone who knows?"

"Mad Tome did, before it got mad."

They shared a moment of silence.

"How old are you?" asked Grand.

"Twelve," said the horseman. "Although I don't

remember what it's like to be twelve. I don't remember what it's like to be me. It's been too long since I talked to anyone," he added quietly.

Grand thought about Bluebeard. "May I ask what happens if your page gets ripped?"

The horseman's face hardened. "You die."

"But...my friends are still there."

"The other new badlings? Don't worry about them. Before they become one of *us*, they're safe. You're safe. For now."

Grand let out air. "Then Bluebeard must be dead," he said sadly. "I wonder if his dead wives are double-dead. Is that even possible?"

"Bluebeard is dead?" cried the horseman.

Grand sensed an idea form in his mind. "He ripped his own page. I mean, he split it with an ax."

"He *what*?" the horseman gasped. "But that's suicide! Why didn't you tell me right away? That is grave news!"

Grand shrugged. "Sorry."

The horseman fumed. "That changes things. We cannot tarry. On your knees, badling!"

"But if I have my head cut off and my hands tied like yours, how will I help my friends destroy Mad Tome?" said Grand smartly.

The horseman sneered. "By then I'll be out of here and it won't be my problem. On your knees!"

Grand couldn't come up with another objection. He thought of every story he has ever read, anything that had monsters in it and how to fight them, and it came to him. He needed to climb on the horse. If he did that, he'd be like one of those heroes riding the beast and making it impossible for the beast to snatch him.

With an unexpected adroitness he lunged for the saddle. Alas, his body betrayed him, and what he imagined as a magnificent leap ended up as a clumsy shove.

The animal reared, neighing its offense.

"This is how you repay me for my kindness!?" screamed the horseman and charged.

Grand ran for his life. He had never run so fast before. He positively flew, smashing through grassland like a rolling boulder.

"Stop!" cried the horseman. "You can't run away from me!"

The prairie suddenly moved; the ground shifted. The horse neighed and shot like a bullet in the opposite direction.

"Get back here!" shouted the horseman.

Grand turned to look and lost his balance. His foot sunk into a hole—one of the prairie dog's burrows—and he hydroplaned, sliding uncontrollably and coming to a stop by the dirt wall. His palms scraped bloody. His lungs were on fire, and sweat stung his eyes. He noticed none of it, staring.

An enormous hand emerged from the gap. It was the same size as Grand, each finger as thick as his leg. It felt about until it found him, scooped him up and whisked him into another story.

Chapter Eleven

Giant Birds and Giant Diamonds

Every book has characters—as without them there would be no books—but not all characters like to stay put. It gets lonesome and boring, particularly if the book hasn't been read for a while. Tired of waiting, those best equipped for travel give in to wanderlust and visit other pages.

One such restless individual was returning from precisely such an excursion. Bells clung to its feathery back, half-dead from fright. She hadn't dared open her eyes since slamming into its moving body.

I'm not dead, she thought. *I'm okay. I might catch a cold, but I'm alive.* She sneezed. Her thoughts switched to her friends, and her stomach twisted from worry. *I wonder what happened to Grand. I hope he didn't just fall to his death. And what about Peacock? And Rusty? How will I find them?*

She gripped the feathers harder. *I hope this monster bird doesn't eat me once it discovers me. That would be a great end to* my *story.*

The steady whistle of the wind acquired a new sound. Bells' heart sped up. She heard a thin whining noise. It came from behind her. It sounded like Peacock screaming.

It *was* Peacock screaming.

"Peacock!" Bells opened her eyes. Rushing air hit them, producing tears. She blinked, astounded. She was clinging to the back of a giant bird, its plumage brown and glossy, its wingspan as wide as their backyard where Sofia liked to prance around in her gaudy dresses. Everywhere she looked there was clear blue sky.

Another noise broke through the drone—a desperate pitiful trumpet, followed by a shrill screech.

That was an elephant, thought Bells. *Poor thing. I'm sure this stupid bird is planning to eat it.* She considered kicking it, but thought it unwise in her position. Behind her erupted a volley of upset exclamations.

"And that is *definitely* Peacock," she said, smiling.

Two quivering hands clasped her back.

Bells flinched at the touch of damp clothes on her skin. Still, she grinned. It was the most welcome change of events.

Peacock pulled closer. "We're going to fall!" he screamed "We're going to fall and die!"

Strangely, his panicky outburst gave Bells a surge of confidence. Somehow things would turn out all right. She rolled her eyes, which made her feel even better, wiped her dripping nose on her shoulder, and twisted back as far as she could.

"Can you stop freaking out?" she shouted. "I'm glad you're with me, but please don't spoil it!"

"What did you say?" yelled Peacock.

"Stop screaming, the bird will hear you!"

"What?"

"Shut up, you ninny!"

It finally produced the desired effect, and Bells exhaled in relief. "Boys," she said to herself, putting all kinds of meanings into a single word.

Peacock promptly pinched her.

"Oww!" she yelped. "What was that for? I thought you said you couldn't hear me!"

"Stop calling me names! Or I'll pinch you again!"

"Since when is that an issue?" shouted Bells with indignation. "I've always called you names, and you never had a problem with that! If you don't like *ninny*, how about *sissy*?"

Peacock pinched her again, but Bells was ready. Holding onto feathers with one hand, she seized Peacock's arm with another and dug in her nails.

Among other battles between Bells and her mother, the nail-cutting battles were the worst. Catarina insisted that her daughters take care of their nails, which meant trimming them regularly, filing them to a fine oval shape, and scrubbing away the dirt with a special brush. Bells considered it a pointless waste of time. As a result her nails were long and jagged, with a layer of grime underneath. And now they came in handy.

"Ouch!" cried Peacock.

Bells waited.

No pinches or acerbic commentary followed. *That is how you deal with obstinate boys,* she thought with pride.

The bird suddenly tipped and swooped down. Bells gazed at the view in a stunned agitation.

A blue-green ocean lapped at a rocky island, a squat solitary mountain its only attraction. On one of its snowy peaks sat a giant nest from which a trio of enormous chicks cried for food. They looked pitiful from this height, but there was no doubt in Bells' mind as to what they were capable of. She supplied the missing details with her imagination.

Apparently Peacock thought the same thing. He

gripped Bells so hard she thought her ribs would break.

"Stop!" she yelled. "You're hurting me!"

"Sorry!" His hold slackened. "Where are we?"

Bells took a deep breath. "Like I know?"

"You're the one who reads most books!"

"And you're the one who likes others to think for you!"

Peacock fell quiet.

They dove into warmer air. The sky blinded them with azure intensity. The bird descended in tightening circles, making Bells dizzy.

"Look, a giant nest!" shouted Peacock.

"With three giant hungry chicks! In case you failed to notice!" Whether Peacock heard her or not, she couldn't tell. He didn't comment.

They were now low enough to make out a craggy valley that surrounded the mountain. It appeared desolate, with no sign of trees or vegetation of any kind. But there were things crawling along its gulches. At first Bells thought they were mice pursued by snakes. They moved comically slow. Then she saw them for what they were: dozens of elephants escaping monstrous serpents that coiled and uncoiled, clearly on a hunt.

Bells shivered. *What a bizarre assortment of animal life,* she thought. *I wish I could stay here and study it, as revolting as it is.*

"It's about to drop us!" cried Peacock.

The bird screeched, rocking over the nest. In the midst of broken shells and animal bones squatted three chicks the size of little dragons. They squeaked in a deafening chorus.

The bird let go of the elephant. It uttered its last

helpless cry and crashed down. The chicks pounced and began to devour it. Bells heard terrible noises of rending, snapping, and slurping, and they made her sick. *Okay, this has got to stop,* she thought. *I'm a scientist, and scientists are not supposed to faint when witnessing the lawful course of nature.*

Having delivered the meal to her offspring, the bird alighted on the rim of the nest and folded its wings.

With a shriek, Bells and Peacock tumbled down.

If not for the ledge of tangled branches over the precipice below, they would've plummeted to their unquestionable deaths. Instead they rebounded into the nest, rolling to a stop on a surprisingly soft surface of moss, down, and animal skins decorated with bird droppings and, strangely, diamonds. In the middle of this horrendous interior, three hungry nestlings were picking away at the elephant's remains. The thing was gone in minutes, its carcass stripped to bones.

Bells crept behind the pile of animal skulls. Peacock hesitantly followed.

The mother bird screeched and took off to procure another juicy creature. Its colossal wingspan covered the sky like a dark cloud. As it cleared, the diamonds sparkled in the sun, and suddenly Bells knew where they were.

"The Seven Voyages of Sindbad the Sailor," she said, picking up one of the gems. "Peacock, we're in the valley of diamonds!"

"Where?" he squinted at her.

"The valley of diamonds, it's in one of the Sindbad the Sailor stories. Haven't you read them?"

He shook his head.

Bells was too excited to notice his anguish. "Oh, you

should read them. They're great. Sindbad is this guy who sails the sea and gets into all kinds of trouble. So one time he lands on this island that's full of diamonds and serpents, and he meets these merchants. They throw huge chunks of meat into the valley. The diamonds stick to them, and Roc birds pick them up and carry them to their nests. The merchants wait for the birds to fly off, then show up and collect them. That's it, Peacock. We must be in one of those nests! That was a Roc bird, and these are Roc chicks. They eat elephants and snakes." She paused and added under her breath, "I'm not sure if they eat people. I can't remember reading about that." She pocketed the gem and picked up a couple more, all of them the size of quail eggs.

Peacock stared at her, his pupils huge. "Snakes? Did you say, snakes?" He frantically looked around.

"They're giant snakes, Peacock," clarified Bells. "You'd see them if they were here."

He didn't answer, pointing instead.

The three chicks turned their attention to the newcomers, appraising them for edibility.

"Don't move," whispered Bells. Peacock gripped her hand.

One of the chicks tilted its head in that jerky avian fashion. At any moment it could strike. The tension seemed unbearable.

"Why are they called rock birds? They don't look to me like they're made of rock," whispered Peacock nervously.

Bells frowned at him. "What?"

"You said they're rock birds?"

"Oh. No, not that rock. *Roc.* R-O-C."

"What kind of a name is that?"

The chick gave them a scrutinizing eye, as if it heard them and wasn't happy about what they discussed. Bells and Peacock crouched lower, flattening themselves to the floor.

"They've seen us," whispered Peacock. "They'll eat us."

"No they won't," hissed Bells. "Stop freaking out. Let's focus on getting out of here."

"Oh yeah? And where will we go? Jump off the mountain and smash our skulls?"

"Will you stop fretting?" said Bells with feeling. "They haven't eaten us yet, have they? They don't even think we're food. But if you keep squirming like a worm, I'm sure they will."

The chicks appeared to be listening.

"What happens next?" asked Peacock.

Bells gaped at him. "What do you mean?"

"You read the book, didn't you?"

"Some of it," she admitted, blushing. "I flipped through it at the library, mostly for pictures."

"So?" demanded Peacock, fidgeting. "You must have *some* idea."

"Why are you so upset?"

"Are you kidding? I'm about to be eaten alive!"

Bells' face grew hot and for a moment she forgot about the danger they were in. "Oh, I see. It's all about you. It's always about you. But what about Grand? And Rusty? Don't you ever worry about them?"

Peacock blinked. "Why would I?"

For a second Bells couldn't say a word. "Because...because...how can you *not*?"

"You girls worry too much," declared Peacock.

"Oh, we do, do we?" She propped her hands on her hips. "Well, that is very *manly* of you to say, the boy who's about to pee his pants, scared out of his mind because some birdies might peck him death!"

She suddenly noticed a curious silence and looked up.

The Roc chicks towered over them.

"Go on, continue," screeched one.

"Yeah, like, it's very entertaining," screeched another.

The children froze, stunned.

"Dude, you scared them," screeched the third with conviction. "What if they die of fright?"

"No, I didn't," rebuked the first. "You did."

"Anyway," said the second. "What are you doing here?"

"I think they're new badlings," ventured the third. "Aren't you?"

Bells eyed with horror the scaly legs the size of tree trunks, the sharp claws, the powerful beaks, and the orange unblinking eyes.

"We are," she said finally.

"Dude, that's awesome. Mother must've gotten you for us. But why aren't there three of you? How are we supposed to share you?"

"Why do we need to share them?" asked the first chick. "I'll get this one, and you guys can have the other one."

"That's not how it works!" protested the second chick.

"You're not getting anything, Haroun," said the first.

Haroun sulked, his orange eyes full of grudge. "Why not?"

The first chick ignored him. "Anyway, as I was saying—"

"We should wait for Mother, Hinbad, that's the rules," said the third.

"Don't interrupt me, Hossain," Hinbad snapped his beak warningly. "As I was saying—"

"Dude, take it easy." Hossain spread his wings and set his legs apart in an aggressive stance.

"Here comes Mother," announced Haroun. "We missed our chance, you idiots."

A large shadow covered them.

"That's not Mother, that's Alice!" screeched Hinbad.

A queer thing occurred.

The nest tilted. The chicks fluttered their wings and fell into a panicked confusion. The children smashed into the pile of skulls, too startled to scream. The same hand that stole Grand from the headless horseman snatched Peacock and Bells and lifted them high in the air. In another moment it placed them in a lush meadow overgrown with thistle, burdock, and mushrooms. Huge floppy mushrooms, the cap of one of them prominently occupied by a caterpillar as blue as the sea.

Chapter Twelve

The Badlings in Wonderland

Look closely at your bookshelf. Are you sure every book is where you left it? Doesn't one seem to stick out from the rest? I thought so. It wants to be noticed. The more you read it, the thicker it will get, bursting with pride. And the books you haven't touched in years will get thinner and thinner until they perish.

Lucky for Alice, her story has never been abandoned, and she certainly didn't plan to abandon it herself. She loomed over the children like an oversized doll, her wavy hair combed back, her face alert and curious.

"Who is *that?*" said Peacock, backing off.

"I think that's Alice," said Bells. "Alice from Wonderland."

And Alice it was.

"You poor things," she said kindly, "those dreadful birds must've scared you silly. Why, I'm sure by now you don't know *what* to think about us anymore. It must be so confusing." She pouted. "You sad creatures. Well, *I* don't approve of what they want to do. *I* certainly don't want to leave my story. *I'm* perfectly fine here, and here is where I'll stay, so, you see, you don't need to fear me." She waited for them to answer.

"Are you Alice?" asked Bells. "Alice from—"

"Wonderland? Why, yes, I *am*," answered Alice and

frowned as if she thought of something unpleasant. "At least that was my name this morning. You see, I've changed since then so many times, I'm not quite sure who I am anymore."

"Holy buckets," said Peacock, "you talk just like her."

"I *am* her," said Alice petulantly.

"You never know," confessed Peacock, recalling what Grand said to Bluebeard. "What if you're fake?"

"Do I look fake to you?" asked Alice. Her eyes glinted with a carefully concealed fury.

Peacock noticed it. "No, not you. You look very Alicey. I mean, Alice-like. I mean, like a proper Alice."

Alice smiled triumphantly. "Thank you, Peacock. And you must be Bells?"

"I am," said Bells, impressed. "How do you know?"

"Your friends Grand and Rusty told me."

"Grand and Rusty?" Bells brightened. "Where are they?"

"Here, as a matter of fact." A smug tone crept into Alice's voice. "I have rescued them all by myself. It's so much nicer to be in *my* story than in any of the others, particularly the one where dead women chase you all over the page."

Bells opened her mouth. "You *know*?"

"Everyone knows. News spreads fast here in Mad Tome. Besides, Bluebeard told me himself. He floated by on his way out." Alice sighed theatrically. "Poor chap."

"What happened?" asked Bells.

"You saw what happened," interrupted Peacock. "He axed it."

"No, I mean to Bluebeard."

"Why do you care? He's a freak!"

"Peacock!"

"What? Let's figure out a way to destroy this *Mad Tome* or whatever and get out of here instead of talking all day. How do you *girls* get anything done is beyond me."

Alice regarded him sternly. "How rude."

"Ah, don't mind him." Bells waved a dismissive hand. "He's a *boy*."

"And that makes you better than me how?" bristled Peacock.

Bells propped a hand on her hip. "I didn't say I'm better than you."

"Maybe you didn't say it, but you thought it," he scoffed.

"Nonsense," snapped Bells.

"Grand told me you two like to fight," observed Alice with mild curiosity.

Bells glared at Peacock. "He is the one who always starts it."

"I just don't understand what we're doing here, okay?" he said in his defense. "I want to get home. Don't you want to get home?"

"Home?" repeated Alice wonderingly. "This is your home. You don't need any other home. What's wrong with a meadow full of flowers and mushrooms?"

The children exchanged a look.

"Nothing, nothing is wrong with it, Alice," said Bells soothingly. "We love your story, and this page; it's so summery and nice and warm, we would *love* to stay here with you." She hesitated, then added in a lower voice. "Forever."

"You would?" asked Alice. Her eyes grew round, all

trace of malice gone from them, replaced by hope.

"Of course!" lied Bells. "Could there be anything better than Wonderland?

"I'm glad you think so," said Alice happily. "Isn't it absolutely wonderful? I love it here. You see, it's much better than home. I don't *ever* want to go back. I'm perfectly fine being Alice, if not for one little thing." She paused, waiting to be prompted.

Bells took the cue. "What little thing?"

"Well, it does get a bit boring sometimes, but that is why I want you to stay with me. All four of you. That way I won't need to hurt you, and we can be friends. Do you agree?"

"Yes," nodded Bells and stepped on Peacock's foot.

"Yes!" he piped up.

"Splendid!" Alice clapped her hands. "Would you like me to give you a tour?"

"Actually, would it be possible for all four of us to go on the tour?" Bells willed her face to look innocent. "We'd love to go together with Grand and Rusty, if you don't mind, to share this unique experience."

A strangled noise came from the thistle. Alice flicked her eyes to it then peered at the mushroom with suspicion.

Bells followed her gaze but all she saw was the underside of a fleshy cap spiked with gills like a wheel of a bicycle.

"I gave them permission to explore it on their own," Alice told Bells without looking at her, "I should think they'll be back very soon, so there is no reason for me to worry. Is there?" This last question was clearly addressed to the caterpillar who sat on top of the mushroom.

The caterpillar coughed politely and said in a creaky

voice, "I'm afraid, dear Alice, we have a visitor."

A gust of wind hit the meadow, ruffling leaves and tearing petals from the flowers.

Bells' eyes widened. "Mad Tome."

Peacock paled.

"Oh dear," piped Alice in a small voice. "I must hide you at once. Puppy?" She stuck two fingers in her mouth and expertly whistled. "Come here, puppy!"

A big fluffy thing gamboled out from behind the thistle and roved its eyes over the children. It would've been a cute gesture if not for the broken capillaries in the whites of its eyes and their bulging appearance. The puppy looked quite mad, and when it growled, revealing two rows of sharp teeth, there was no doubt as to what it would do if they attempted to flee.

"Watch over the new badlings for me," commanded Alice.

"That's one huge puppy," said Peacock, amazed.

The puppy gave him the look of death.

"If you'll excuse me," said Alice to the children, "I must go talk to Mad Tome. Or it might think I'm planning something. I sure *do* hope it doesn't." She made to stand up.

"Wait!" called Bells. "What about our friends?"

"You'll see them soon enough," said Alice mysteriously, rising to her full, gigantic height and strolling across the meadow to the dirt wall, where she stopped and looked up.

"Hello, Mad Tome," she said nicely to the sky. "How are you this morning?"

"Oh, don't ask," Mad Tome rustled. "Terrible, simply terrible." Its face was an accumulation of cloudy wrinkles that hung so low they almost touched Alice's head.

"I thought you looked rather sad," she echoed and threw a quick glance over her shoulder.

The children, no taller than the mushroom, were hidden from view by a large burdock leaf. It threw greenish shadows on their startled faces.

"Is *that* thing Mad Tome?" asked Peacock.

Bells gripped his arm. "What else would it be, you noodle? I think it takes shape from whatever things are around it. When we were on that frozen lake, the snow moved like giant lips. And then in the steppe, remember? It made a hand—"

The puppy growled, and they fell quiet.

"The badlings have been misbehaving lately," whined Mad Tome. "I fear mutiny, or worse, they might go to war. Bluebeard injured me. Can you believe it? He stabbed me with an ax, the hotheaded duffer! I'm hurting, Alice, hurting so badly! And the pages, all these pages make me feel bloated, I can hardly hold them all inside my covers." Whatever it said next faded to garbled whispers.

Peacock turned to Bells. "Why is she talking to it? Isn't she supposed to hate it like the rest of them?"

Bells rolled her eyes. "She said she likes it here. Don't you remember?"

A stifled groan came from the thistle.

"Did you hear that?" whispered Peacock.

"Yes," said Bells breathlessly, peering into the shadows between stems as thick as trees adorned with prickles the size of her hand.

"Pardon me, but I must warn you," spoke up the puppy. "If you won't keep quiet, I'll bite you, and then you'll understand what it's like to beg for scraps and chase a stupid stick, pretending like it's the height of doggy entertainment." It sneered not unkindly.

Peacock raked his hair. "It talks."

"Obviously," added Bells.

"I asked you to be quiet," yapped the puppy, peeling back its lips and showing sharp teeth.

Bells and Peacock hastily nodded their agreement.

A change overcame the puppy. Its eyes darkened. It quickly looked around as if to make sure they were alone, flattened its ears, and snapped its jaws so close to Bells she jumped.

A creaky voice coughed and said, "I saw that."

"Caterpillar?" asked Bells.

"Where?" Peacock craned up his neck.

The puppy's ears drooped, and it sat on its tail. "I can bite you in half in no time," it threatened, "slimy worm."

"Do so," said the caterpillar. "I would be glad to grow four legs instead of these six pitiful stumps and ten useless prolegs that are more a decoration than a locomotion."

"I can't believe it," smirked Peacock, "it's smoking a pipe, just like in the book."

"I beg to differ," said the caterpillar, crawling to the edge of the mushroom. "It's a hookah." It inhaled and blew smoke right into Peacock's face.

Peacock coughed, waving it off.

The thistle growth shook. Someone moaned.

The children looked at each other and without a word dashed inside, shielding their faces from the sharp prickles. On the ground, cocooned in silk and gagged, lay two boys.

"Grand!" cried Bells. "Rusty!" She fell to her knees, clawing at the hardened skins. "What happened to you? Are you okay? Peacock, help me!"

But Peacock was afraid to move: the puppy's head loomed right over him.

"So that's what you've been doing, you nasty grub," barked the puppy. "You stole them for yourself. Wait until Alice finds out. Alice!" It backed out of the thistle. "Alice!"

Grand and Rusty wiggled, impatient to get out of their predicament.

"Teeth!" cried Peacock. "Do it with your teeth!"

"Great idea!" Bells bit a hole in Grand's cocoon, gripped the edges and pulled. After a couple tugs the silk gave with a soft ripping sound. She frantically tore the rest of it off and loosened the rope around his head.

Grand spit out the gag, coughing.

"Are you all right?" asked Bells.

"Um," he rubbed his mouth. "The headless horseman almost cut off my head, and then the caterpillar almost turned me into a pupa, but I'm still me and still alive. So I guess I'm okay." His cheeks reddened.

Bells sighed. "I was so worried about you!"

"That she was," confirmed Peacock, freeing Rusty from his gag. "Rattled my head off about how insensitive I was not to worry as much as her. *Girls.*" He gave Bells a sly look.

"Shut up," she scolded him, hiding a smile. "That's not what I said at all. I said—"

"Thanks, man," interrupted Rusty, moving his jaw to make sure it worked. "I'm so happy to see you, guys! I thought I'd never see you again. That puppy is nuts. It wanted to bite me—"

"Okay, Rusty, you can tell us later," said Bells nervously. "We need to get out here before Alice gets back. Obviously we can't trust anyone here. They're all after us."

"But where have you been?" gushed Rusty. "Did you get to see other stories? I've been stuck here since that hand threw me in from the desert. And guess what. Grand met a headless guy—he's dead and he's riding a horse. His head is cut off, right? And he's holding it! So he wanted to cut off Grand's head too. The nerve the guy has, I tell you."

Bells looked at Grand with a new appreciation. "For real?"

"For real," he confirmed proudly, sweating a little. He wasn't sure if that was what the horseman intended to do, but it sounded impressive.

"So how did you end up in cocoons?" asked Peacock.

"Shhh," Bells shushed him. "I hear voices." She stealthily poked out her head. "Alice is small again. Look!"

Alice, the same size as Bells, was standing on tiptoe next to the mushroom, talking to the caterpillar.

"It's because the page is repeating itself," said Grand.

"What do you mean?"

"It happened in *The Headless Horseman*. He kept riding by me, again and again and again. There is only so much story on one page, so I guess it kept replaying itself." He shrugged.

"That must've been scary," said Bells compassionately.

"Hey, where did the caterpillar go?" asked Rusty.

Indeed, it was nowhere to be seen. Alice was alone, breaking off a piece of the mushroom.

"She's about to eat it," commented Grand. "When

she does, she'll grow big and catch us like flies."

Peacock gulped. "Then what are we waiting for?"

"Not what. *Who*," said the caterpillar from behind.

The children spun around.

"What do you mean?" asked Bells.

The caterpillar puffed out a ring of smoke and said, "I don't *mean*, I *say*, and I'm not *mean*, but what I do *mean* is what I *say*, and I say you are waiting for me."

Bells looked at the boys, utterly confused, then back at the caterpillar, greenish-blue in the shadow of the thistle.

"What are you trying to tell us?" she asked.

"I'm not trying, I'm saying," stressed the caterpillar, "that I'm too slow to weave you four into cocoons before Alice gets her hands on you, and I most certainly don't wish for her to have you if I can't. Therefore, I will show you my hole."

"What hole?" asked Rusty.

"The hollow hole," said the caterpillar. "I bore it when I was bored, to wade through the pages."

"You mean to say..." began Bells.

"I don't mean, I say!" The caterpillar shrunk back, offended. "It's over there. Suit yourselves," it turned and crawled under a leaf.

"What was that about?" asked Peacock.

"Look! There it is!" cried Rusty, diving into shadows.

"Wait!" Bells rushed after him, Peacock and Grand on her heels.

"I told you to watch the new badlings for me!" said Alice's voice from above.

"I beg your pardon, I did," yapped the puppy.

"Then how do you explain this?" Two gigantic

hands parted the thistle.

Bells shrieked, squirming under a pile of rotting leaves and sliding into the hole that ran down at a sharp incline. Peacock followed her. Grand made it last and just in time.

The nose of the puppy plugged in the entrance. It snapped and growled and barked hysterically, sending showers of dirt on top of the children's heads. Slipping and sliding, they rapidly descended down the passage that bore through this page to the next one like a wormhole in an apple, all twisted and pitted and dark.

Chapter Thirteen

Down the Caterpillar Hole

How fascinating would it be to visit all the books you have ever read? You know perfectly well who lives *on* their pages, but what about *between* them? What about characters that get lost, disfigured, or worse, depart from life? Where do they go?

Our friends were about to find out.

They crept on their hands and knees through tunnel after tunnel after tunnel. Scattered light that seeped out of nowhere illuminated the fibrous walls, made of grey paper pulp. The air smelled like wet cardboard, and it got colder the deeper they went. It wouldn't have been half bad, if not for a new unexpected problem.

First one, then a couple more, then a whole cluster of ghostly shapes appeared, casually floating in the air. They quivered and curled and fizzed. And then they started talking.

"Badlings," they whispered, "look, here come new badlings...where are you off to...stay with us...we are in no hurry...we have no homes...why won't you talk to us...we are so lonely..."

"What are these things?" whispered Peacock.

"They're like jellyfish!" Rusty stretched out a hand.

"Um," said Grand. "I don't think it's a good idea to touch them."

"Why not, man? They're so cool and slimy. Look, I think they like it." The shape he stroked undulated, its empty mouth stretching into something that could be called a creepy smile.

"You and your petting, Rusty. Leave them alone. Let's keep moving," said Bells crossly and suddenly stopped.

Peacock bumped into her. "What's the holdup?"

She stared at a yawning face next to her.

"Badling..." sighed the face, "lovely badling...stay with us...there is no hurry..."

"Er," said Bells, "I'm really sorry, whoever you are, but we need to get out of here to get to the next page. If you don't mind?"

But the apparition did mind. It was joined by scores of others who blocked the tunnel with a multitude of their foggy bodies, reducing the visibility to that of milk.

"Fantastic," commented Peacock. "What are we going to do now?"

"Move forward, you dupe," snapped Bells. "What else?"

"Hey, I thought we agreed on not calling me names."

Bells regarded him with a stink eye. "We didn't agree on anything, and I will keep calling you names until you stop asking stupid questions and acting like a coward."

Peacock was about to parry, but a particularly large phantom sallied up to within an inch of his nose and hung there, whispering garbled nonsense. "Shoo. Shoo!" He waved it away. His fingers passed through its gelatinous surface and he uttered a horrified whimper.

"There is my proof," said Bells and rolled her eyes to

solidify the sweet feeling of superiority.

"Rusty, you sure it's not going to bite off your hand?" asked Grand worriedly.

Rusty, unperturbed, an exuberant grin shining on his face, was petting something teethy and horrendous. It didn't exactly have a body or any kind of a presence, except an ethereal head that seemed to enjoy the attention. It tilted back so Rusty could scratch whatever was left of its neck.

"Over here...yes, right here...a bit to the left..." It directed him in a nasal voice. "Ohhh...this feels so good...I haven't been properly scratched in a millennia..."

"You're not alone...move over...it's our turn now..." murmured the voices belonging to a line of spooks that were eager for some tenderness.

Grand pulled Rusty by the hand, breaking this lovely exchange of pleasantries to a pouty dismay of the apparitions that immediately glided after Rusty, nuzzling to him to solicit another dose of affection.

Bells stopped again.

To the left and to the right branched out more burrows and hollows and passages than she could count.

"You know what?" she said, thinking out loud. "Maybe it's a good thing that we're here. At least we can rest for a bit and think, without every character trying to catch us or Mad Tome throwing us from page to page."

"Do you have any idea why they're trying to do that?" asked Peacock in an attempt to forge peace. He even made a conciliatory face.

Bells regarded him suspiciously. "Are you trying to make fun of me?"

"No, I'm not. Honest."

"Cut it out, Peacock. I know as much as you do."

"No, seriously," he said without a trace of sarcasm.

Bells sighed. "I can only guess."

"Um," began Grand, but Peacock overrode him. "And? What did you guess so far?"

"You don't like to tax your brain with thinking, do you?" She sensed a change in the air.

The diaphanous glops around them huddled and tensed.

"Well, here is one thing I guessed," said Bells a little louder, "I'm not sure why the characters are trying to catch us, but I'm sure what these things are," she waved vaguely, "they're *ghosts*."

There was a general susurration of agreement.

"I see that much," said Peacock disappointedly. "But whose ghosts are they?"

Bells was gripped by an idea. She willed herself not to smile, although the corners of her lips turned upward. "Ghosts of *ducks*."

"Ducks?" repeated Peacock.

"Ducks?" asked Grand and Rusty.

"Ducks?" scattered through the hazy crowd.

"You know, ducks die too," continued Bells in a very serious tone. "So why can't they have ghosts like people?"

"I thought, as a *scientist*, you don't believe in ghosts," delivered Peacock smugly.

"I was just getting to that," said Bells, keeping her cool. "You're absolutely correct. Scientifically speaking, ghosts can't exist. But, as a scientist, I must trust my senses. If I can touch it, that means it's there," she demonstrated on the nearest ghost, unceremoniously plunging in her hand. In the next moment she yanked it out.

"Yuck! It's cold and slimy!"

"I will see...what you will become...when you are dead...badling," moaned the ghost unpleasantly. "I don't like you...I like that other badling...better." It floated up to Rusty.

"Fine. Suit yourself," said Bells, trying to sound brave.

The rest of the ghosts pushed closer to her in an angry, muttering wave. "We are not ghosts of ducks...what nonsense is that...we are ghosts...of characters...and of badlings..."

Bells' throat constricted. She was right. They fell for it like flies for honey. Only instead of triumph she was flooded with horror. "Are you really ghosts of badlings?" she asked.

"Good work, Bells," said Grand.

Peacock gaped at him. "What's that supposed to mean?"

"I get it!" exclaimed Rusty. "So Grand told me how Bluebeard axed his page, right? Maybe when the page is gone, the characters are gone too? Like, if they don't go to some other page, they become ghosts?"

"Smart badling..." clamored the ghosts.

"But why are they after us? The characters? What do they want?" asked Bells. She wanted to ask more questions, other questions, and had to force herself to stop, afraid to break the delicate trust they had established.

"Um," began Grand again, and again was interrupted by Peacock.

"Hey, ghosts. What's a badling anyway?" he said. "Come on, tell us. Don't just hang there like some sorry clumps of fog."

"Peacock!" cried Bells, horrified.

"What?"

"You're hurting their feelings."

"I thought you were the expert of that," he said acidly.

Bells ignored him. "I'm sorry, ghosts, he didn't mean to offend you..." She trailed off.

There was no one to talk to. The spell was broken. The ghosts whirled up in a tide of vapor and dispersed along the length of the tunnel.

"Why are you looking at me like that?" demanded Peacock, pressing into the wall under the glares of his friends.

"Did something happen to him?" asked Grand quietly, speaking into Bells' ear.

She shrugged. "Nothing I can think of. He's been like that since that Red Death place. No matter what I say, he gets all upset and irritated."

They exchanged a glance.

Bells crawled up to Peacock. "Hey, what's wrong?"

He crossed his arms. "Why do you care? Leave me alone."

"What is it?" pressed Bells.

Peacock looked away and mumbled something.

"Listen. If you tell us, you'll feel better. I promise."

"Nice try, Bells," he scoffed, but without acidity.

"Come on, Peacock," called Rusty. "What's up, man?"

"Shut up." Despite his best efforts, Peacock sounded miserable.

"All right, you know what? Stop being a baby and man up!" commanded Bells. "Either tell us what's going on, or sit there all upset and alone, because we're moving forward." She expected a snide remark, but Peacock only looked at her, small and frightened, his blue hair hanging in snaggles.

"It looked like..," he whispered, trembling.

"What?" Bells leaned closer.

"It looked like a *vampire*."

Her eyes widened. "What looked like a vampire?"

"That ghost, the one that got in my face."

"So what? It was probably a ghost of a vampire. What difference does it make?"

"Aren't you scared of them?"

"Who? Vampires?" Bells sat back. "Not any more than I'm scared of any other freaks. Why?"

Peacock wrapped his knees and stared at the ground.

They patiently waited for him to crack.

"It's the book," he said finally, "the book I didn't finish reading. It's *Dracula*."

Faint voices around them picked up the name. "*Dracula*...he said *Dracula*...did you hear...he didn't finish reading *Dracula*...he will be mighty mad..."

The ghosts were back.

Peacock jerked his head, mortified.

"Hey, I know that book," exclaimed Rusty. "It's about vampires, right? Man, vampires are cool! I mean, they're scary, but—"

"Can you let him finish?" hissed Bells.

Rusty sniggered embarrassingly.

"It's a bad idea...to mention books...you haven't finished reading...badlings," said a ghost with a beard.

"I don't think...they will listen to you...Bluebeard," observed a ghost in a nightgown.

"Bluebeard?" Bells squinted.

Peacock looked in horror at a misty arm that playfully tickled Rusty. It belonged to Eleonore, one of Bluebeard's dead wives, looking uglier as a ghost than when she was simply dead. She giggled, her hands creeping up his neck.

"Bells?" called Peacock.

She turned to look.

Eleonore squeezed her fingers, and Rusty gasped for air. "Nice ghost. That's enough playing," he said. And then, in a sudden panic, "You're choking me! Get off me!"

They rushed to his help, but when they tried prying Eleonore's fingers, their hands came away with strands of goo.

"Let go of him, you dead pudding!" shouted Bells.

"Dead...*pudding?*" The shock of the insult made Eleonore slacken her hold. Rusty took a shuddering breath, color returning to his cheeks.

"Run!" screamed Bells.

Unfortunately, running in a tunnel wasn't possible. Instead, shrieking their heads off, the children scurried off without any sense of direction, only wanting to get away from the ghosts and the murk and the chill.

Bells turned into the first passage on the right and stopped, her ears assaulted by a cacophony of explosions.

"Get back!" she cried, trying to push past Rusty.

Rusty was enthralled and wouldn't move. "Whoa!" The end of the burrow seemed to open into the sky. He crawled to the edge and looked out.

About thirty feet below lay a field. A garrison of horsemen in navy coats and beaver hats, sabers aloft, galloped through fire and smoke toward an army of men in kaftans most of whom walked, yet some rode elephants decked out in brocades with colorful tassels.

"I know this book. It's Baron Munchausen! There he is!" shouted Rusty.

"Are you out of your mind?" Bells tugged on his arm. "Get back before you get shot!"

"You can't go out there, Rusty," said Grand wisely. "They will kill you."

"But it's Baron Munchausen!" Rusty pointed at a man in a red topcoat and a triangular hat, his face one curly mustache. "Right there, see? That's him. Watch what he's going to do. He's going to attack the sultan!" The Baron charged at the most decorated man who rode the biggest elephant, knocked him down, dismounted and rained lashes left and right.

Rusty's enthusiasm infected Bells and Grand, and even Peacock sidled up to them, looking over their shoulders. They watched the sultan fire at the Baron from a pistol, to which the Baron responded by slicing off the sultan's head.

Bells gasped.

Peacock and Grand gaped.

And Rusty said in awe, "Did you see that? He just lopped it off, just like that!"

The Baron cleaned his saber, stashed it away, caught a shooting cannonball with bare hands, mounted it, and flew off.

"Holy buckets. That's impossible!" said Peacock.

"I know, right?" rattled Rusty excitedly. "It's crazy! But listen to this. He also pulled himself out of a swamp by his own hair, *and* he shot a deer with cherry pits so a cherry tree grew from its head the next morning, *and*—" Rusty gasped for air, "—he shot ducks in the air so when they fell down they were already roasted! *And* he turned a wolf inside out!"

"I don't know why you'd turn a wolf inside out," said Grand, shuddering at the memory of the wolf howling in *The Headless Horseman*, "but roasted ducks sound good. Come to think of it, I wouldn't mind a roasted wolf either," he patted his stomach sadly.

"Come on, guys," said Bells. "Let's find a quieter story. Looks like all these tunnels open into different pages. Maybe we'll find one where there's some food."

This was met with a unanimous agreement.

And so they crept through the maze of holes for another hour, halting to rest, when at one of the stops they glimpsed a turnout into what looked like a bedroom with a bed, a desk, and a window looking over a peaceful night. Uplifted by this discovery, they scrambled toward it, oblivious to a small dark shape spying on them from the shadows.

Chapter Fourteen

The Underground Throne Room

Book characters must lead remarkably easy lives. Rarely do you read about them wasting time on such trifles as eating, sleeping, or making trips to the bathroom. This presents a curious problem for new badlings: food and drink are hard to find, as are places to take a shower or lie down for a nap.

Filthy, tired, and hungry, the children climbed out of the opening in the wall, dusted themselves off, and looked around.

They were standing in a dark room. A tall wardrobe flanked a simple wooden bed on which a child slept under the covers, blond locks spilled on the pillow. By the bed stood a chair and a desk with carefully arranged papers, an inkbottle, and several quills. A clock tick-tocked in the corner. Apart from that no other noises disturbed the night.

"What story is this?" whispered Peacock.

Bells shook her head. "No idea."

"I wish it was *Hansel and Gretel*," muttered Grand.

Rusty's eyes rounded. "Is that where a witch catches two children and eats them?"

"Um," began Grand calmly, "not exactly. It's about a cannibalistic woman who forced Gretel into slavery and locked Hansel in an animal cage. Then she fed him to fatten him up so she could fry him in an old-fashioned stove. It operates similarly to a funeral incinerator, except that it burns at lower temperatures and more unevenly, so his dying throes would be longer and more painful, and nobody would hear his screams. Once she decided that he was sufficiently crisp, she would take him out and start carving him and—" He stopped under his friends' mortified stares. "I'm just exploring what could happen. She doesn't eat him in the end. They escape."

"Thank you for clarification," said Peacock nervously. "Why would you want to go into a horrible story like that?"

"Her house is made of cakes and candy," said Grand dreamily. "Which is almost as good as *doughnuts*."

His last word rang out a bit too loudly.

The sleeping child mumbled something and turned to the side. The bed springs groaned, the blanket billowed, then sagged, and all was still again.

"Shhh!" hissed Bells. "You'll wake her up."

"How do you know it's a girl?" asked Peacock. "Maybe it's a boy."

Bells goggled at him. "Are you blind? Look at her hair." She continued before he could answer. "I hope this is *The Secret Garden*. I would like for it to be *The Secret Garden*, because there's food there."

"Is that about an orphan girl who lives with her uncle?" whispered Rusty.

"Yes, it is," said Bells, impressed. "Her parents die of some disease and she comes to live in this mansion with her sick brother, and all they do is play in the garden and eat muffins and cakes and currant buns."

"For the whole book?" asked Rusty.

"For the whole book," confirmed Bells.

"Cool. I'm in!"

Peacock smirked. "Sounds like a nice life."

An irregular clop of hooves echoed from the street. Bells frowned and stole to the window, drawing back the curtain. Two stories below a horse pulled a carriage across a bridge that was dusted with snow, yellow in the light of the lanterns.

"It's a city," whispered Bells. "It shouldn't be a city, it should be a garden."

"Do you recognize it?" asked Grand.

"No. And it's winter. Are we in *The Snow Queen* again?" She glanced back at the child. "Maybe it's Gerda."

"Would be cool if we were in *Dwarf Nose*," said Rusty. "Grandma read it to me when I was a kid. It's about this boy who lives in a witch's house with guinea pigs and squirrels. They wear nut shells on their feet and skate on this glass floor, and he learns how to cook all these dishes." He poked Grand. "Hey, if we asked him to make doughnuts, I bet he would."

"Warm, fresh doughnuts." Grand's eyelids fluttered and closed. "With sugar glaze..."

"...and chocolate syrup..." breathed Peacock.

"...and when you bite into it..." added Bells.

"...it melts in your mouth!" finished Rusty excitedly.

That did it.

The child yawned and sat up. It was a boy of about ten with long blond hair, dressed in a long nightgown. He saw the children and beckoned to them without a word.

Peacock flashed an I-told-you-so look at Bells. She pretended not to notice.

The covers on the bed bulged, and out snuck a little black hen. Its eyes shone like two candles. It clucked, fluttered to the floor, and scuttled out of the room. The boy padded after it. When he reached the door, he turned back, put a finger to his lips, and beckoned them once more.

Bewildered, the children exchanged a glance and tiptoed out in a single file.

The boy led them along a dark corridor that ended in a large bedroom lit by moonlight. In it slept two old ladies in two white beds. On one of the nightstands sat a cage with a parrot, and next to it reclined a big grey cat. Both of them were sleeping. The boy leaned to the cat as if to pet it, and it suddenly sprung up, its fur standing on end. The parrot spread its wings and started squawking shrilly, "Fool! Fool!"

Startled, the boy and the hen rushed across the room to another door and vanished through it. The old ladies opened their eyes. The cat hissed. The parrot screeched.

Unnerved by this spectacle, the children darted after the boy to the door that stood slightly ajar as if left open on purpose. Behind it a narrow staircase led down to another floor. They skipped two steps at a time, descending deeper and deeper until they emerged in a long gloomy hall. Ahead of them two figures receded into shadows, their words bouncing off the walls in a muffled echo.

"You woke them up, Alyosha!" the hen berated the boy.

"I'm very sorry, Blackey, I will be more careful next time," said Alyosha anxiously.

"Did you hear that? It can *talk*!" said Rusty in a loud whisper that carried rather well. "The chicken can talk! Man, I tell you, everything talks here. I wonder if the walls talk too. Hey, wall, how you doing?" He patted it.

"Rusty, we're not deaf," snapped Bells. "So can you

please keep your exuberance to yourself?"

Blackey stopped and peered back. Alyosha followed suit. He shook his head and put a finger to his lips, indicating silence.

"Sorry," said Bells, her face glowing like a furnace, "we'll be quiet." She gave Rusty a murderous look. He slapped both hands on his mouth to hold back a snigger.

Blackey nodded.

They continued walking. The further they went, the more it smelled like molten wax and smoke. Faint yellow glow flickered ahead, showing them the way. At last they came upon it.

The hall ended in a spacious chamber. A candle chandelier hung off a low ceiling; its golden light threw dancing shadows on the walls. Two armored knights guarded a pair of heavy doors. Without a warning they sprung up and charged at the hen. It flapped its wings, rapidly growing in size, clucking and pecking at them until they fell apart. Their armor scattered on the floor with loud clatter. There was no one inside. They were empty suits animated by some mysterious force.

The fight was over in seconds.

Alyosha threw up his hands, swayed and fainted, crumbling down like a wilted flower.

Blackey turned to the children. They slowly retreated, staring up in horror at the bird that could no doubt kill every one of them with a single jab in the head. "Don't be afraid," it said, "I'm not going to hurt you. I want you to listen to me. Listen carefully. You must go through these doors and wait for me there. Don't go *anywhere* until I come back." Then it picked up Alyosha and they melted from sight.

For a moment no one moved, stunned.

"Okay," said Bells weakly, "that was entertaining. I like it how everyone wants to help us, and then it ends up being a big fat lie. What do you guys think? You think it's a trap?"

Without waiting for an answer she marched to the doors.

"Stop!" cried Peacock. "You don't know what's there."

"Relax," said Bells, "I was only going to take a peek. There is a—" she broke off abruptly.

Something clicked in the doors, and they slowly swung inward. Beyond them lay a hall with a low ceiling. It was no bigger than the room where the old ladies slept with their pets, but it seemed enormous because everything inside it was miniature, made for people no higher than a couple of feet. Golden candelabra threw a warm glow on the marble floor. Chairs draped in velvet lined the walls that were hung with tapestries. And on a raised platform at the far end stood a gilded ornamented throne.

"Whoa," said Rusty, stepping in. "This is cool." He ran his hand over the backs of the chairs as if they were furry animals. "Looks like little people live here, with a little king and a little queen." He sat on his hunches by the throne, studying it.

"Doesn't seem like they're here at the moment," said Bells and plopped to the floor. "Finally it's nice and quiet. I hope nothing happens for a long time."

"There is nothing to eat," observed Grand disappointedly.

Peacock raised a brow. "Is food the only thing you think about?"

"You know what, Peacock? You're starting to sound like Sofia," said Bells with feeling.

"Oh, am I?" Peacock smirked. "Care to elaborate?"

"Sure," said Bells sweetly and proceeded to fix her ponytail with deliberately slow movements, holding Peacock's glare. "She's always nagging me, 'Belladonna, can you draw me a princess?' 'Belladonna, what do you think about this dress?' 'Belladonna, how do I look?' 'Belladonna, do you think mom will like it?' She can't shut up and won't stop calling me Belladonna, when I told her a thousand times that my name is Bells. All she cares about is her dresses and books of fairy tales. Bleh." Bells made a gagging noise.

"I fail to see the similarity," said Peacock airily. "Should I start calling you Belladonna?"

Bells squinted at him. "Don't you *ever.*"

Before Peacock could retort, Grand came to the rescue. "Fairy tales like *The Snow Queen?*" he asked.

Bells gave him a grateful look. "Yeah, that's one of them. Now I wish I read it to her till the end, maybe then we wouldn't have gotten here. I thought it was silly girl stuff, I didn't know it was a pretty scary story."

Her words sunk into a frightened pause.

"I think we need to rip it," she said quietly.

Peacock looked up. "Rip what?"

"Mad Tome." She passed her eyes over the boys one by one. "I think the only way to destroy it is to rip it to pieces. Remember how Bluebeard—"

"No!" cried Peacock, starling everyone.

Bells was dumbfounded. "Why not? I thought you wanted to get home."

"What if..." Peacock fidgeted with his hair, "what if

something bad will happen?"

"Of course something bad will happen," said Bells. "It will die. But then something good will happen too— we'll be back by the duck pond."

Peacock was not convinced. "How do you know?"

"I don't," said Bells honestly. "But that's what usually happens in books when the villain dies, doesn't it? Everything returns back to how it was before."

"Totally!" cried Rusty. "That's brilliant, Bells!"

Peacock stubbornly shook his head, getting more and more agitated. "And what if it will go after us?"

"It'll be dead, Peacock," said Bells with a sigh.

"And what if its ghost will go after us?"

"Listen, what's wrong with you? Why do you keep—"

"Wrong?" Peacock straightened his back. "*Wrong?* We got sucked into some crazy book and now we're supposed to rip it to pieces, or we'll end up dead. That's what's wrong!"

"We don't know that for sure," objected Grand, "if we'll end up dead or not. And, um, there's something I wanted to—"

"We know *nothing* for sure!" Peacock's voice skipped a register. "How can you all just sit around and not even care?" He gazed at them with hard eyes. "We need to figure out a way to get out of here."

Bells felt stung to the core. "You know what? You're a hypocrite." She placed both hands on her hips to stop them from shaking. "I just offered a solution on getting us out of here, and you rejected it. And now you turn around and tell me I don't care?"

Peacock was taken aback. He had nothing to say.

Something flashed through his face. Guilt? Remorse? Whatever it was, it quickly receded, hidden underneath irritation. "It's your fault we're here," his tone was low and bitter. "You're the one who found Mad Tome, you're the one who picked it up and threw it at the ducks. We can all die because of *you*, and you're not even bothered."

"Oh, I'm not bothered. I see." Bells' nostrils flared at this unjust accusation. "And you're apparently being a great help, whimpering like a little boy. Of course you would. It's the easiest thing to do, to feel sorry for yourself and blame everyone else. Great strategy, Peacock, I'm impressed. Next time you pee your pants, make sure you blame us too."

Peacock gaped at her, splotches of red creeping up his neck. "Are you accusing me of peeing my pants?"

Grand glanced at Rusty, who put a hand over his mouth to suppress a snigger.

This is going to be a while, Rusty seemed to be saying.

Might as well take a nap, Grand seemed to respond. He leaned on the wall and closed his eyes.

The throne room rang with insults. They bounced off the ceiling and faded, to be quickly replaced with new ones. Bells twisted her ponytail; Peacock gripped his fauxhawk. They looked like fighting roosters, their faces so close, it was a wonder they didn't touch. This heated exchange went on for another few minutes then abruptly stopped. The opponents were out of breath.

When no more shouts shook the air, Grand opened one eye. "You guys done?"

They turned on him, fuming.

"Man, you were *loud*," commented Rusty. "I thought my eardrums would break. If you were grandma's dogs, I'd smack you to make you stop."

"Hair pulling works too," added Grand with a faint smile.

"Or tail pulling. Very effective," nodded Rusty.

"Shut up," said Peacock.

"No, you shut up!" Rusty balled his little hands into fists. Astounded at his own dare, he looked at Peacock, expecting a comeback, but Peacock only sagged and said nothing. He was looking at Bells.

She stormed to the doors, tried them, and when they didn't open, uttered a cry of dismay and sat down, her back to the boys.

"Hey, Bells?" called Peacock.

She didn't answer.

"Look, I'm sorry. I didn't mean what I said..."

Her shoulders began to shake.

The boys exchanged a horrified look that meant something along the lines of, *But...Bells never cries. She didn't even cry when she fell off her bike and scraped her hands bloody. What do we do? If we say something wrong, she'll bite our heads off.* They sighed, thinking one single word that contained an exorbitant amount of meanings, *Girls.*

Grand rubbed his nose and said timidly, "Bells?"

She shook her head.

He took a deep breath and walked up to her. "Um, I just wanted to say...it's okay. We'll be fine. We'll figure out something. We'll rip Mad Tome, like you suggested—"

"It's not that," she muttered into her knees.

"Oh," Grand hesitated, "it's not?"

Bells was silent.

"My mom says it's no good holding things in,"

began Grand thoughtfully. "We always talk about—"

Bells couldn't hold it anymore. She lifted her tear-stained face and sputtered. "She doesn't want me to become a scientist, she thinks it's not a proper job for girls, she wants me to become a stupid opera singer, she always tells me, 'Why aren't you like your sister?' I hate her, I hate her, I..." She paused to catch her breath.

Without a word Grand pulled a crumpled napkin from his pocket. It was smudged with chocolate glaze and faintly smelled of doughnuts. He offered it to Bells. She gratefully accepted it, dabbed her eyes, and blew her nose.

"You don't know what it's like," she hiccuped. A couple of tears fell on her cheeks. "None of you have any idea, so don't tell me that you get it!"

Grand spread his arms, "We're not saying we do."

"Then don't say anything at all!" She dropped her face into her hands and proceeded to cry.

Carefully, as if afraid he might get burned, Grand sat next to her and touched her back. When she didn't push him away or told him to get lost, he began to stroke it, like he would stroke the heads of his two little brothers after a good session of roughhousing.

"I don't *ever* want to go back," whispered Bells.

"What?"

"I don't want to go back."

Grand's mouth fell open. "You don't want to go back home?"

Bells raised her head, looking crushed. "No. I'd rather stay here than see my mom. She...she called me a 'poor scientist' and kicked me out of the house."

More sobbing followed.

Grand shifted uncomfortably. "At least she doesn't

call you *names*. My mom calls me fat, to motivate me to lose weight, only it works backwards. It makes me feel awful." He glanced down at himself and sighed.

"At least you guys have moms," said Rusty absently.

Bells immediately stopped crying and turned around. "I'm sorry, Rusty. I'm sorry I forgot."

He shrugged, avoiding her eyes.

Bells sensed Peacock's stare burn a hole in her head but refused to acknowledge him, passing her gaze through him as if he didn't exist. She used this maneuver on Sofia when she got particularly annoying, successfully driving her to tears.

"Look, Bells," began Peacock. "I didn't mean that...about you throwing the book at the ducks and everything."

Grand stood up so suddenly, he nearly fell over. "Ducks," he said, "ducks!"

"What is it?" asked Bells.

"I think," Grand started, sweat beading on his forehead, "I think I know how to destroy Mad Tome."

"How?"

"Well, if we could somehow find a way to..." He wiped his face, hesitating.

"A way to?" Bells prodded him.

"The thing is, we're too small to do any kind of damage to Mad Tome, unless we find a way to grow bigger. We should've grabbed a piece of that mushroom from Wonderland. It's too bad we didn't, and it's too late now. So I was thinking...I thought if we could somehow make the ducks rip the book, back at the pond..." He frowned. "Never mind, it's a stupid idea."

"It's not stupid, it's genius!" exclaimed Rusty.

"Why would ducks bother about some book?" blurted Peacock. "Ducks are dumb."

"No, they're not," said Rusty, offended. "We just need to find a way to get them interested in it."

"And how would you do that?"

Rusty opened his mouth, but nothing came out.

"We could go back to the caterpillar hole," pondered Grand, "and...I don't know..."

"Exactly," Peacock finished for him.

They contemplated this in silence.

"How about climbing up that dirt wall?" offered Bells. "The one that's at the end of each page?"

"What for?" challenged Peacock. "So we can make it half-way up, see there's nothing there, and get stuck? You know how hard it is to climb down? We might fall and die. We don't even know how far it goes. We don't even know what it *is*!"

Bells avoided his stare. *I can't fight anymore,* she thought, *I'm too tired.*

Grand saved her. "I think that's a great idea, Bells. The wall must be some kind of a border, and every border ends. Only I wouldn't be able to climb with you guys. I'm too heavy." He looked down at his hands.

Desperation settled on them.

After several minutes of thinking over every possible way of destroying Mad Tome and coming up with nothing Bells suddenly yawned. Rusty picked it up, then Peacock.

"I'm tired," said Grand and yawned so wide, his jaws cracked.

"Me too," agreed Rusty.

"We need to sleep," said Bells with finality that didn't invite any objections. "We're all tired and hungry, and unless we rest, we won't come up with *any* ideas, good or bad, so I suggest you make yourselves comfortable."

There were no objections.

Peacock stretched out along the row of chairs, one arm under his head, another over it. Rusty curled up by the throne, using its canopy as a blanket. Grand slumped in a corner not too far from the doors, his legs and arms splayed out, his chin resting on his chest.

Bells pulled the band off her hair and shook it out. "Grand?" she called quietly.

He turned to look.

"I like your idea about the ducks. I don't know why, but I have a feeling that it might work."

His face lit up. "You really think so?"

"I do."

They yawned at the same time and smiled, the tension of the day whooshing out of them. Bells made her way over to the corner and settled next to Grand, lying on her side. His body radiated so much heat that although there was at least a foot between them, she could sense it, and before she knew it, she was sleeping.

Soon the throne room filled with steady breathing.

Every one of them forgot about the little black hen, but it didn't forget about them.

Chapter Fifteen

The Hen Uncovers the Culprit

Where there are *big* bad characters, there are always *little* bad characters helping *big* bad characters do mischief. Sometimes authors themselves don't know what to expect and get so frightened by their characters' behavior that they hide until the trouble is over.

It was precisely trouble that brewed over the children's heads while they were happily snoozing. Rusty snored with amazing regularity. Peacock lay still, an arm over his face. Bells' eyelids twitched—she was watching a dream. Only Grand didn't sleep well. He kept dozing off and snapping awake.

I miss my soft bed, he thought. *It's so comfortable.* He pulled up his legs and accidentally nudged Bells.

"Whuh?" she said, blinking.

"Sorry," he whispered. "I didn't mean to wake you up."

"Grand? Is something wrong?"

He sighed. "Nothing. Just can't sleep."

"Why not?" She sat up, stretching.

He wouldn't meet her eyes.

"What is it?" she insisted.

He shrugged.

"It's probably because you're uncomfortable. The only reason I was able to fall asleep is because of you."

"Me?" he looked puzzled.

"You're so warm that you warmed the floor around you, so thank you for that." She smiled.

"Oh. You're welcome," he said appreciatively, and then added, "at least some use out of a *fat* kid."

Bells sucked in air. "Please don't say that."

"Why not?" He spread his arms with passion. "It's the truth. I *am* fat. Everybody thinks that."

Bells began to object.

"Yes, you do," said Grand stubbornly. "Don't deny it. I was fat my whole life. My dad died from being fat and I will die from being fat, so I might as well get used to the idea." His arms hung limp and he sagged.

"You're not fat," said Bells in a tone she used to contradict her mother.

"Sure I am," he said, "see this?"

He inspected his bulging stomach, his plump fists, his thick calves and big feet. "I hate my body," he concluded. "I wish I could stop it somehow, but I can't. When I feel bad, I have to eat a doughnut, or something sweet, it's the only thing that helps me feel better." He raised his eyes at her. "You honestly don't think I'm fat? You're not just saying it?"

Bells took a deep breath. "You are a bit overweight," she said tenderly. "That doesn't mean you're *fat* fat, you know? There are fatter people out there. It just means that you weigh more than a healthy eleven-year-old should, according to some stupid standards devised by some stupid doctors. What do they know? In my personal opinion, it's a load of nonsense. It's how you feel that's important. If you feel healthy, then you're healthy. And I can't imagine you any other way, I like you the way you are. You're like a...like a...cuddly bear cub." She suddenly threw her arms around him, surprising herself.

Grand's already red face turned bright magenta, and he thought it would melt off any second. "My mom says I'm fat," he mumbled in her ear. "She says if I won't stop eating sweets, I'll die like my dad."

"What an awful thing to say. How can she know?" said Bells fervently. "Moms sometimes say things they regret later. And sometimes they make us do things they think are good for us instead of just letting us be." She gathered her hair into a ponytail with shaking hands, snapped on the band, then pulled it off and started all over again. "It always snags," she complained. "And there is no mirror."

"You don't need a mirror, you look great," said Grand. "It's me who's ugly."

"Stop it," said Bells. "Who says you need to be thin? You look cute like this. I like your cheeks. They're so...*round.*"

"Are they?" Grand stared at her and in the flickering candlelight noticed for the first time that her eyes were the color of thunderous sky right before it erupted. Which was, essentially, Bells in a nutshell—a constant threat of eruption.

He felt his cheeks. "You really think so?"

"I really think so." She nodded. "I want to grab them and squeeze them, like Rusty's grandma does."

"Um. Okay," said Grand, encouraged. "You can, if you want to." He closed his eyes and offered his face.

Bells didn't expect this. After an awkward moment, she quickly touched his cheek and tore her hand away. His skin was smoldering like a hot griddle.

"Um, Bells?" said Grand. "There's something I wanted to tell you, about the badlings. Well, I wanted to tell everyone. When I was with the headless horseman, he said that—"

Someone coughed.

The children started, turning around.

By the doors stood a little man about two feet high. He was dressed all in black. A red wedge cap sat at an angle on his small head, and his neck was draped in a starched white collar. He coughed again. It sounded like a hen's clacking. In fact, he looked like a hen, missing only the wings.

He walked up to Bells in measured dainty steps, doffed his hat, and bowed. "Blackey, the King's Ambassador, at your service." His movements were refined and courteous, and his manner of speaking old-fashioned, like he belonged to a different era.

It took Bells a couple seconds to compose herself. "Er...Belladonna Monterey. Very nice to meet you, Blackey."

Blackey took the very tip of her forefinger and lightly kissed it. "Pleased to meet you, Belladonna. I'm grateful you have waited for me here as I have requested. For that I thank you."

Bells waited for him to say something else, but he only gazed at her serenely with his black shiny eyes as if it was her turn to talk. The pause stretched on uncomfortably. Finally Blackey looked up at Grand, only it seemed as though he was looking down, and Grand felt like shrinking.

Bells flushed. She suddenly understood what she was supposed to do. "Oh, I'm sorry, Blackey. Let me introduce you to my friend. This is Grand."

Blackey didn't speak, waiting.

"My real name is George Palmeater," offered Grand shyly. "Grand is my nickname. You can call me either way, I don't mind."

Blackey bowed. "My pleasure, Grand." He turned to Bells. "May I call you by your nickname as well?"

"Please do. That's what I prefer, actually," said Bells, and then asked suspiciously, "how do you know I have a nickname?"

"Everyone knows your names, badlings. Everyone sends to you their greetings and their welcome."

"Everyone?" asked Bells, confounded.

"Every badling in Mad Tome."

"You mean, every badling that got turned into a character?" hazarded Bells.

Blackey regarded her silently. "I see you have surmised much on your own. I'm impressed. Perhaps you also guessed the title of this story?" He tilted his head.

Bells sensed the tips of her ears beginning to glow. "No, unfortunately I haven't. I've never read anything like it. If I did, I wouldn't have remembered, because it looks fascinating."

Blackey's eyes glinted with pleasure.

"Would it be okay if...I asked you what it is?" She spoke in a reverent manner that Blackey instilled with his poise, hoping she wouldn't offend him with her directness.

To her surprise, he answered. "You are in the story called *The Little Black Hen,* written by Antony Pogorelsky."

"I never heard of it," she said.

Blackey's face darkened. "That's a pity."

Bells glanced at Grand for help.

"Um," he began, "I have a question. Are you a badling or a real character?"

Blackey stiffened. "I humbly ask you to grant me *your* understanding of the matter," he said in a steely tone.

"You mean, you want me to tell you what I think?" asked Grand.

"Very much so."

"Just about you, or about other badlings too?"

"However you prefer," said Blackey curtly.

"Okay," agreed Grand, "well, the first part is easy. The headless horseman said you're all badlings, every one of you. That's what I wanted to tell you, Bells," he answered her questioning stare.

"Oh." She nodded, not sure what to say.

"Sorry it took me so long. I tried a couple times but someone always interrupted. Anyway, he wanted to claim me so I'd replace him. I don't know how this *claiming* works, but I think he wanted to cut off my head. The sad thing is, he's just a kid like us. He said he's twelve. So I figured all badlings must be children who don't finish reading books, and then Mad Tome collects them for punishment. The next part is a bit more complicated. I think Mad Tome is lying. I don't think living through the pages is the real punishment, I think the real punishment is for the badlings to replace the characters and stay here forever," he caught his breath, amazed and horrified by his idea.

"Wow," said Bells quietly. "That makes sense."

Grand stood a little taller, encouraged by her reaction. "That's not all, though. There's more. When I was thinking about it, I thought, wait, if the badlings replace the characters, then where do they go? Then I figured it out. Mad Tome must've killed them. We saw their ghosts. They live between pages." Grand wiped the sweat out of his face.

"The last part is the worst. At some point every single character must've gotten replaced, but new badlings kept coming, so Mad Tome must've started getting rid of the old ones. They didn't want to die, so I think they came up with something clever. They started replacing themselves with new badlings before Mad Tome did. That way they could escape death." He looked at Blackey who seemed to shiver slightly.

"I mean, you could probably replace yourselves forever, as long as there's enough new badlings. But it looks like we're the only ones who came in the last few years, so now you're all after us." He fell silent.

For a tense moment everyone stared at him, including Rusty and Peacock who were awake, their mouths agape.

"Quite astute of you to deduce this much in such a short period of time," said Blackey smoothly. "It'll be a pity to lose you."

"I can't believe this, Grand," whispered Bells. "When did you figure all of this out?"

"Holy buckets," came from Peacock. "Are you sure about this?"

"Is that what Mad Tome will do?" sputtered Rusty. "Kill us?! Hey you, chicken guy, is that true?"

Blackey gave him the stare of death. "My name is Blackey," he said levelly. "And I'm not a chicken, I'm a hen and the Ambassador to our King."

"Sorry, hen. I mean, Blackey. I mean—" Rusty fell quiet, embarrassed.

Blackey looked at Bells expectantly. Shocked by Grand's conclusions, she didn't understand right away what he wanted. "Oh," she said breathlessly. "Yes, I forgot. Blackey, let me introduce you. This is Peter Sutton, or Peacock." Peacock barely nodded, his face white. "And this is Russell Jagoda, or Rusty."

"Nice to meet you!" Rusty stretched out his hand.

Blackey took a frightened step back.

"Sorry! I only wanted to—"

Bells silenced him with her stare. "I apologize, dear Blackey, if we have offended you."

Blackey pursed his lips. "No apology needed. I'm pleased to be at your service, new badlings." He bowed. "I do hope that you are well rested, for as much as I regret this, I must send you on a journey right away. This page is no longer safe for you."

"No longer safe?" repeated Bells.

"I'm afraid so," said Blackey sadly. "I truly wish we could spend more time together to get to know each other. I would've loved to show you our underground zoo—"

"There is a *zoo*?" Rusty's eyes widened. "Can I see it?"

"Another time, perhaps."

"What kinds of animals are there?"

"Rusty," hissed Bells.

Blackey smiled. "It's perfectly all right. It's not every day that a new badling gets interested in our old musty story."

Grand shifted uncomfortably. He could sense resentment lurking under Blackey's polished conduct. *I should ask him if my idea was right. He never really said if it was or wasn't.* "Um," he began.

Blackey spoke over him. "We have rats, moles, and other rodents. We go on rat hunts in the underground tunnels. If you," he faltered for a second, "ever come back, I'll show you our English garden where paths are strewn with diamonds, emeralds, and rubies."

"Real diamonds?" breathed Rusty.

"Yes, indeed," said Blackey.

Bells inconspicuously felt her pockets.

"Right on! But how do I get here?"

Blackey appeared to have mulled over a distant memory. "All you have to do is read this book."

"I will. I totally will!" said Rusty hurriedly.

"Thank you." Blackey bowed. "You give me hope."

"You're real," whispered Grand. "You're not a badling, you're one of the real characters."

Blackey flashed him a painful look and stole a glance behind him. "I hate to bring our conversation to an end, but we don't have much time. We must hurry."

A faint noise of struggle reached them from the chamber. Then something heavy slammed into the doors, and they groaned under its weight. Blackey jumped. "Follow me!" He skittered into shadows behind the throne and tugged on one of the tapestries. It slid off the wall, folding down and sending up a cloud of dust. Behind it was a door about four feet high.

"Blackey, wait!" called Bells, but he was gone.

They scrambled after him, squeezing through the opening and stooping so as not to bang their heads on the ceiling. A narrow corridor ran up at a steep incline. There were no steps, and it was very cold.

"Faster! Faster!" called Blackey.

"We're coming!" Bells pressed her hands into the

walls to give herself more speed. "You guys all right back there?"

"We're fine!" answered Rusty.

"Speak for yourself," said Peacock angrily. "I don't trust this guy. What if it's a trap?"

"Maybe it is," panted Grand, "but maybe it isn't. I don't think turning back is a good idea, though."

The doors of the throne room banged open. There was a terrible roar of triumph, and that put an end to everyone's doubts. Panicking, the children rushed up the passage and suddenly emerged into the light, blinking.

In front of them lay a snowy backyard, empty save for a shabby chicken coop, its wooden boards black with age. Across the snow ran a pair of tracks that ended in a huddling figure of Blackey. Behind him loomed the omnipresent dirt wall, and the ground by his feet was peeled. From the void below swirled up tongues of mist.

"Quickly!" He waved.

Bells took an uncertain step. "Are you sending us to another page? What story is it?"

Blackey's face contorted in annoyance. "You must hurry!"

The wind picked up, pushing the children forward. They glanced at each other. The hatchway on the side of the building from where they emerged coughed up unsettling noises. Something furious was coming up. By an unspoken agreement they crossed the yard and stopped at the void.

"Where are you sending us?" asked Bells.

"Somewhere where you deserve to go," said Blackey darkly.

Through the rift in the mist below they saw a

cobblestone court by an ancient castle shrouded in a pitch-black night.

"That looks creepy," concluded Rusty.

"What do you mean, *deserve*?" demanded Peacock.

"I'd prefer it if you got in of your own volition," intoned Blackey, "unless you want me to push you in."

"Why would you do that?" asked Peacock. "See? I told you it's a trap!"

Blackey pinned him with a piercing stare. "Why? You *dare* to ask me why?"

"Stop staring at me, chicken guy. How about *I* throw you in?" Peacock stomped at Blackey, coming within a couple of feet.

Blackey began to quiver. First one feather, then another, then a handful of them sprouted from the back of his suit. "Would you like me to enlighten your friends as to what has transpired between you and a certain book?" he clucked.

Peacock paled. "What are you talking about?"

"I'm talking about a boy who has gotten terribly upset at a book he was reading two days ago," said Blackey sharply, his civility gone. "This boy committed a monstrous crime. Instead of finishing the book and putting it back on the shelf, he flung it out the window. When that didn't seem enough, he went outside, found it, picked it up," Blackey paused dramatically, "and *ripped* it. He ripped it almost in half and threw it in the trash."

Peacock raked his hair. "So what? What does this have to do with me?"

"Who was it, Blackey?" asked Bells.

"Make a guess!" Blackey began rapidly changing. His arms flattened to wings, his coat changed to a shiny plumage, and the cap on his head molded into a fleshy red comb. Where the ambassador stood a moment ago now sat the little black hen.

"The most feared, the most popular story of all time ended up in Mad Tome as a result of this crime," clucked Blackey. "Not only has this badling brought misfortune to the book he maimed so cruelly, he unleashed Mad Tome's wrath upon all of us, and for that he deserves to suffer."

"But who was it?" repeated Bells softly.

Blackey said nothing. He only gazed at Peacock with his beady glistening eyes.

Peacock got very quiet. He looked over the ambassador and then over his friends one by one.

"Is that true?" breathed Bells. "Did you really rip a book?"

Peacock smirked. "What book? What are you talking about?"

"That's what I'd like to know," said Bells icily. "Did you rip a book like Blackey is saying, or did you not?"

Peacock opened and closed his mouth without a sound.

Bells advanced. "Did you?"

The wind whistled angrily around them. The air, already cold by winter standards, grew freezing, but neither the children nor Blackey noticed it. They waited for Peacock to say something. He's gone grey, and suddenly shrieked, "I didn't mean to, okay? It scared me! It...*they* talked to me! I thought I'd gone off my marbles—"

"What book was it?" Bells interrupted him.

Peacock took a deep breath and bellowed, "*Dracula!*"

The ground rocked and they all swayed.

"Um, Bells?" called Grand.

She didn't hear him. "Why did you have to rip it?"

Peacock had gone from grey to splotchy bluish. "Because they whispered to me."

"Who?"

"The sisters," his lips quivered, "the vampire sisters."

"Guys?" said Grand in alarm.

They turned around.

At the other end of the yard stood a throng of badlings who had quietly assembled while Bells questioned Peacock. They were guests from Prince Prospero's masquerade headed by the prince himself together with the Snow Queen, the Red Death trailing behind them.

"You were going to hand them over to Dracula," said the queen, glaring at Blackey, "you disgusting pitiful *traitor*."

"Prepare to pay the price!" The prince took out his dagger. But whether he wanted to stab Blackey or only to scare him, none of them found out.

A familiar voice rustled over their heads.

"Ahem," said Mad Tome. "What's going on here?"

The entire company looked up. Above them, in the sky laden with clouds, solidified a hideous face, then a neck, then a pair of crooked claws that snapped and clicked like pincers.

"It's quite a gathering you have here," Mad Tome said, astounded. "How did you manage to escape my notice? Clever, clever." It squinted at the little hen. "Blackey, you treacherous buffoon. Why, of all you fools and layabouts it was *you* who had to deceive me. I should've disposed of you a long time ago. Well, no use talking about it, is it?" Its eyes swiveled around, daring anyone to contradict it. It raised its claws and brought them down, snapping them right over their heads.

A collective *ahhh* of horror went up from the crowd. None of them moved, pinned by Mad Tome's glare.

"Shall I do it now?" it asked.

No one responded.

"Answer me!"

The silence was absolute. Someone shifted, and the crunch of snow sounded like a crash of icebergs.

"You're a bunch of spineless nitwits, that's what you are. Can't decide on your own fate, how pathetic is that? What would you do without me? You'd be lost. Lost!" It suddenly yawned. "You see what you do to me? You're tiring me out. I shall punish you, all of you, lest I forget after my nap." And as if it was as casual as crumpling a napkin, Mad Tome scooped a few badlings and squashed them. They seeped through its claws as ghosts and floated away.

This was followed by a second of stunned silence, then pandemonium erupted. The badlings screamed, dashing about in terror. Prince Prospero dropped his dagger and fell to his knees. The Snow Queen elbowed her way to the chicken coop. Only the Red Death remained still, standing amidst the chaos like a red pillar, as it pertains for a proper death to behave.

In the midst of this confusion Blackey inflated to ten times his size and slammed into Peacock with a frantic screech. Peacock tottered over the void and tumbled in. Blackey then picked out the rest of the children one by one and tossed them in after Peacock as if they were unsavory seeds. That done, he turned around to face his demise.

With a demented cackle Mad Tome grabbed him

and squeezed. At once the color went out of Blackey, and he imploded. In his place appeared a ghost of a little man with a wedge cap sitting jauntily on his head. He gazed forlornly at the Snow Queen who swooped down on her sleigh and snatched Prince Prospero by the arm, pulling him in.

"You got what you deserved, you snitch!" raged Mad Tome. "Your turn, badlings...where did you go? Where are my new badlings? Dracula, you bloodthirsty beast! Give up my loot at once!" It shoved a claw down into the gap and screamed.

A crack shot across the backyard.

Mad Tome writhed in agony. "Ahhh! You rascals! You made me rip my own page!"

But the children didn't hear its lamentations. They finished their descent by thumping to the ground and rolling to a stop. The earth beneath them rattled. The stale chilly air condensed and enveloped them, molding into ghosts. Dim voices murmured in a chorus, "Run, badlings! Run!"

They struggled up and bolted, half-conscious from fear. In front of them loomed a castle as tall as a mountain and as cold as a mortuary freezer, its formidable walls scarred with narrow windows, jet-black in the light of the moon.

They passed under a series of elaborate arches, reached the courtyard, and collapsed on the steps by an old massive door. A pack of wolves howled nearby, and the sound of their hunger rapidly drifted closer.

Chapter Sixteen

The Vampire Hospitality

Never damage a book in any way. In fact, never open a book you don't intend to read from cover to cover. Who knows what awaits you if you decide to forfeit it in favor of doing something else? Like riding bicycles or chasing ducks? Don't. You may bitterly regret your nonchalance later.

That is precisely what Peacock did: he bitterly regretted mistreating *Dracula*. His eyes were glued to the inviolable door that didn't bode anything good. He struggled to standing and swayed.

Grand caught him. "You okay?"

Peacock mumbled a string of words.

"What?"

"I don't..." came out of Peacock's mouth. "I don't want to..."

"You don't want to *what?*" inquired Bells, hugging herself. She regarded the windows with suspicion. Someone was watching them, she was sure of it, someone's eyes glittered dully and retreated as soon as they met Bells' prying stare.

"If someone is in there, I hope that *someone* will open the door before we get eaten by wolves," she said and knocked on the door. "Hello? Anyone?"

No answer, only a muffled echo and another volley

of howls, much closer this time.

Peacock suddenly broke into a hysterical gibber. "I don't want to die, I want to live! I'm just a kid! I didn't do anything wrong. Since when is it a crime to rip a book? Why do I have to pay for this with my life? That's a bit harsh, don't you think? What is this Mad Tome anyway? What right does it have to do this to me? *Dracula* is just a book, it's just stupid a book—I hate this place! I want to get out of here!" He pushed Grand aside and belted.

"None of us want to die," said Grand absently, watching Peacock catch his foot on a rock and sprawl.

"What's wrong, man?" asked Rusty.

"You're scaring us, Peacock," said Bells. "We're already scared, and you're scaring us even more."

"I don't care." Peacock glared at her, tears in his eyes.

"Yes, you do," countered Bells.

"No, I don't!"

"Then what *do* you care about?"

"Go away! Leave me alone. Just...leave me alone..." He hid his face.

Grand and Rusty looked at Bells.

She took a deep breath. "I really want to throttle you right now. You disgust me. You're the reason we're here, and now you're abandoning us? Thanks for being a great friend." She glanced up, a tingling sensation telling her that someone was not only watching them but eavesdropping too.

"Man, I never expected this of you," said Rusty and shook his head.

"Shut up," muttered Peacock.

Rusty staggered as if slapped. "Stop shushing me. Why do you always shush me? You're the one who needs to shut up. You blamed Bells when it was *your* fault all along!"

Peacock covered his ears. "Stop talking to me! I don't want to hear it!"

Bells shook from an urge to punch him.

"It's okay, Peacock," said Grand tiredly. "I guess you can apologize to Dracula for hurting his book and maybe he won't bite our necks and drain our blood and—"

Heavy footsteps approached the door.

The children turned to face it.

Rusty nudged Bells lightly. "Hey, we get to see a vampire, a *real* vampire. That's a positive thing, right?"

She couldn't help but to smile. "Yeah, I guess it could be. I didn't think of it this way. Thanks for being so cheery."

"No problem. That's what you have *me* for." Rusty stuck out his chest, glancing at Peacock to see what effect this exchange had produced. Unfortunately, Peacock missed it. He was staring at something under the arch, his mouth open in horror.

"Okay then." Bells scrutinized the boys. "Ready?"

"Um." Grand pointed to what Peacock was staring at, a dozen red dots hanging in the air and slowly advancing from the darkness. "I don't think I've ever been more ready in my life."

With an agonized wail Peacock lunged to his friends. The wolves whined hungrily and drew closer.

"Wolves!" said Rusty. "Can I...never mind." He let his arm fall under the unblinking stare of the nearest beast. "I see you don't want to be petted. I got it, man, I got it."

Bells was frantically looking for a knocker or a knob or a handle of some kind. The door had neither. It was flat, studded with iron nails. Desperate, she lifted her leg and kicked it. There was a clatter of chains and a bang of a heavy bolt drawn back. Muffled reverberations streaked into the depths of the castle and died.

Their hearts thrumming like hammers, the children listened intently. No sounds reached them, except claws scraping on stones and jaws snapping in the anticipation of a nice dinner.

"Let us in, please!" Bells pounded on the door with both hands until it suddenly swung back. They tumbled inside, and it shut behind them. The wolves slammed into it, yowling in dismay.

"That was close," whispered Bells. "Who opened the door?"

There was no one in sight. The entrance vestibule stretched dark and empty. Vague shapes of statues fringed a staircase that led into the gloom of upper floors.

"No idea," said Rusty. "Dracula's butler?"

"He doesn't have a butler," said Peacock. "It's just him and the sisters."

"And wolves," added Grand, giving Peacock a look of reproach. "I'm sure they're sad they have nothing to eat now."

Peacock snorted.

"You feeling better, then?" asked Bells tartly.

He avoided her eyes. "Having the time of my life."

"Can you tell us about the vampire sisters? Do they live here?"

"Can we not talk about this right now?"

"What else would you like to talk about? You didn't have to tear this book, you know," she said crossly.

"You didn't have to throw Mad Tome," taunted

Peacock.

Bells gaped at him in surprise. "I thought you were fainting from fright."

"I am. You're so scary, I peed my pants," said Peacock sarcastically.

Bells smiled. "You *are* feeling better."

"Say you're sorry," butted in Rusty.

"Don't tell me what to say!" Peacock's cry rebounded off the walls.

Startled, the children went quiet, waiting for the echoes to die. In the ensuing silence footsteps came to life as if leading them on.

"Is that Dracula, you think?" asked Bells.

"I think so," answered Grand.

"All right. I guess we have no choice but to follow him."

They climbed up the staircase and walked along a corridor lined with doors and dusty portraits.

"I wonder how old this book is," whispered Bells. The atmosphere didn't invite loud talking.

"A hundred years?" volunteered Rusty.

"Peacock, do you know?" she turned to look.

He shrugged without raising his eyes.

"So is Peacock the only one who read it?" continued Bells. "I mean, part of it. Because I didn't."

"Nope," said Rusty. "I didn't read it."

Grand was about to answer when his stomach rumbled. He threw both hands over it, embarrassed by the noise. "I read other books about vampires but not this one. Too bad vampires don't eat human food," he concluded miserably.

The footsteps slowed as if waiting for them to catch

up.

The children came to the end of the corridor and turned into a great hall. It ended in an archway flanked by stone gargoyles. Their ugly faces grimaced in silent scorn. One of them winked at Peacock, and he stopped dead, the hairs on his neck rising.

"Come on, Peacock," said Bells, "we need to get going."

When he didn't move, she marched up to him and took his arm.

"I wonder," she said, pulling him with her, "how Mad Tome ended up by the duck pond, you know? How did it get there? Who put it there? Did it just...*appear?* And why us? I'm sure there are lots of other children who don't finish reading books or rip them, so why would we be any different?"

Peacock drew a ragged breath. "Why are you asking me?"

"I don't know, I'm just wondering. Something is not right. What did the vampire sisters tell you?"

"I don't want to talk about it," he said stubbornly.

"Maybe Dracula asked Mad Tome to punish Peacock?" said Rusty.

"But why would Mad Tome listen to Dracula if he's a badling?" theorized Bells. "How does it pick new badlings, that's what I'd like to know."

"Um," said Grand.

They all looked at him expectantly.

"Um," he repeated, red in the face. "I think...if all the characters here are badlings, then they're in it together. They were probably looking for a way to escape for a long time."

Bells knotted her brows. "So they *made* it, is that what you're saying? They made it look for new badlings? Bluebeard said they've been waiting for us for years, and he said it finally worked. Does that mean Mad Tome stopped looking for some time?"

Rusty scratched his head. "They call it Mad Tome because it's gone *mad*, right?"

"Maybe they planned it," continued Grand, "maybe they made it so that some kid wouldn't finish reading a book on purpose."

Bells suddenly stopped. "The vampire sisters. What if they planned to scare Peacock so that he wouldn't finish reading *Dracula*?"

This idea made them study their friend with a new understanding. Peacock nervously raked his hair.

"What did they tell you?" pressed Bells.

The footsteps halted, and there was a creak of hinges.

The children rounded the corner to investigate.

The hall abruptly ended in two ornate doors flung open in mute greeting. Beyond them lay a richly decorated room lit up by a fire roaring in a chimney. The windows were draped shut, and in the semi-darkness it was just possible to make out a table set with dishes: a basket of bread, a couple wheels of cheese, a bowl of stew, a carafe with water, and a platter covered with a silver dome lid.

"Food," said Grand in a voice not quite his own.

It acted like a signal.

The children stormed in and began filling the plates, grabbing bits of everything and stuffing their mouths.

"No doughnuts," said Grand, biting into a bun.

Rusty lifted the dome lid. "Chicken!" He tore off a

leg and sunk his teeth into it, chewing so fast, he almost choked.

Peacock quietly sat down without touching anything. "He's coming for us."

"Listen, you have to eat *something*," Bells instructed him between spoonfuls of stew.

"She's right. You need to eat," said Grand.

"If he wants to starve, let him starve." Rusty tore off another chicken leg. "It's his choice, right?"

There were no objections to that. Sounds of chewing and swallowing filled the room. Hands reached for food. Forks scraped plates. Tumblers filled and emptied. At last everything edible was consumed.

Grand leaned back on the chair and belched.

Rusty belched louder.

They proceeded to belch in turns.

"Stop it, you guys," said Bells, but her tone lacked conviction. Her face grew warm, her stomach full, and her thoughts slurry.

Peacock looked slightly better. He was nibbling on a piece of cheese, sniffing it occasionally.

"You should've eaten more than just a piece of cheese, Peacock," said Bells. "That stew was very good. I'm so full now."

He didn't reply.

"You know, to be honest, I don't want to do any more speculating or analyzing or any of that," she sighed. "I wonder how scientists do this every day. It's making my head hurt. I just want to go home."

Peacock looked at her quizzically.

"Yes, imagine that. I want to see my ridiculous mother with her ridiculous demands. And I miss Sofia. Can you *believe* it? I thought I wanted to stay here, but not anymore." She shifted closer. "Do you miss home?"

"Maybe," said Peacock to the cheese. "Why would I? They don't miss *me*."

"I'm sure they do," said Bells passionately.

Peacock narrowed his eyes. "Why are you talking to me all of a sudden? You're not mad at me anymore?"

Bells raised her brows. "Is that what you're worried about? Me being mad at you? I thought you didn't care."

"I was upset," said Peacock quietly. "I *do* care."

"Well, *that's* a relief to hear," scoffed Bells.

"You can be pretty scary, you know that?"

"Who, *me*?" she gaped. "You're kidding."

"No I'm not," protested Peacock. "I'm dead serious."

"Well, don't be scared of *me*, be scared of Dracula. I suppose you plan to apologize to him?"

"How can I apologize to him if he's not here?"

A chair fell with a clatter and startled them.

Rusty was chasing Grand around the table. Grand tripped. Rusty stumbled over him and pounded on his stomach, both of them laughing.

"Stop it, you two," commanded Bells.

Grand pulled himself up, beaming, his face pink and shiny as if he spent the last hour in a hot bath. Rusty hung off his shoulder, grinning like a lunatic. Together they exuded so much careless happiness that Bells felt her lips fold into a smile despite an effort to remain firm. She produced a dramatic sigh, rolled her eyes and poured her disapproval into one word, "Boys."

"Come on, Bells," said Rusty. "Lighten up! Have a little fun."

"Fun?" she repeated. "We're in the castle of a vampire, you dolts. Have you forgotten?" But the merry crackling of the fire and the relaxed faces of her friends made it hard to believe it was true.

"I don't see any vampires," said Rusty. "Do you?"

"Nope," said Grand.

"You guys are impossible," announced Bells. "It's too hot in here, anyway. I want some fresh air." She rose from the table and stomped to the window, drawing back the drapes. The view arrested her breath. "Wow. How did we get this high?"

"Can I see?" cried Rusty. "Man, this is crazy. Guys, look!"

The view was both spectacular and scary. They were at least a hundred feet off the ground, if not more. Below a carpet of trees stretched to the distant mountains. Lines of rivers glittered in the moonlight. Rare stars speckled the sky, and the moon gazed down at this splendor solemnly like a white face without features.

A sudden chill cloaked the room. Wolves howled, and urgent steps answered them.

The children spun around.

A tall man appeared in the doorway. He was dressed in black, with impeccability and style of someone inordinately wealthy. His face had no wrinkles, yet he seemed ancient. His eyes glinted red and he smiled, revealing sharp, white teeth.

"Good evening, my friends." His voice was smooth and charming, with a hint of courteous indifference. "I welcome you to my castle. You came here freely, and you shall remain my guests for as long as you like. I take it dinner was to your satisfaction?"

His words put them at ease.

"Count Dracula?" asked Bells.

"Yes, I'm Dracula. And you lovely miss would be?"

"Belladonna Monterey," Bells heard herself say, although she wasn't quite sure how. "It's very nice to meet you." She curtsied.

"Is it?" Dracula's lips curled. "Well, I'm delighted you think so."

Peacock felt for the curtain and hid behind it.

"There is no need to be afraid," said Dracula. "Peter Sutton, am I correct?"

"Yes," croaked Peacock, stepping out.

The howling of the wolves erupted to a high-pitched chorus. Dracula smiled wider. "Ah, the music of the night." He shifted his gaze to the children. "You must be tired from your journey. You need to rest. Let me show you to your rooms."

The boys nodded, spellbound.

Bells pinched herself to stay alert. "Thank you for the offer, Count Dracula," she squeaked, "but we don't need to rest, we slept quite well on your friend's page."

Dracula's face was an unreadable mask.

"Your friend Blackey," she clarified. "He sent us here. I'd like to know why."

The Count merely looked at her, cold as stone.

Bells shifted uneasily.

"I like your spirit, Belladonna," said Dracula, striding by the chairs, his fingertips lightly brushing them. "Aren't you scared of me?"

Bells gulped. Grand and Rusty flanked her.

Peacock suddenly lurched to the table, snatched two knives, crossed them and thrust them at the vampire. "I'm sorry I ripped your book, okay? It's because of your sisters! They said, they'll find me and kiss me to death if I won't. There, I apologized, can we go now?"

The Count gazed at him calmly.

Peacock began to shake. "I didn't do it on purpose, okay? What else do you want me to say?"

"Put that down, my friend," said Dracula. "I don't intend to harm you. You are my guest. You have entered of your own free will, and as I said before, you shall stay here for as long as you like."

A strangled cry escaped Peacock. He dropped the knives and bolted for the door. Dracula caught him as if he were a puppet. "I *insist* you stay," he said.

"Please, Count Dracula," said Bells, "please let him go. He didn't mean to rip your book. You heard what he said, it was your sisters who made him do it. He was just scared, that's all."

"Do you always speak on behalf of your friends, Belladonna?" asked Dracula interestedly, ignoring Peacock's pleading and thrashing.

"I—I'm—" Bells faltered.

"Do you think you're smarter than them?" continued Dracula.

"No, I just...I like to analyze things."

"Do you? What a peculiar trait for a *girl*. Please, analyze me. I'd love to hear your assessment." His request was impossible not to obey.

"Well, scientifically speaking, you don't exist," began Bells, bending her fingers. "Number one, *Dracula* is just a book and you're simply acting it out. Number two, you're not a real Dracula character. You're a badling like us. And that means that, number three, you're not even a real vampire, so there is nothing you can do to us. You're bluffing." She fell silent, her heart pounding.

"Do you wish to test me, Belladonna Monterey?" asked Dracula harshly.

"No," squeaked Bells.

"I must say, you're the most stubborn badling I have met in the last century." His eyes glinted. "Come, let me show you to your rooms." Without letting Peacock out of his hold, Dracula seized Bells by the wrist. She flinched but didn't dare to object, terrified by his strength. "Follow me," he threw over his shoulder to Grand and Rusty.

They walked to the end of the passage, down several flights of stairs, then through another passage and down the stairs again until they lost count of the floors. At last they came to another great hall filled with frigid air. It was so cold here Bells could see her breath curling in plumes.

At the end of the hall Dracula stopped and pushed open a door into a spacious guest room.

"Before we proceed, I must ask you an important question," he looked over the children and stopped on Peacock. "Is Belladonna your friend?"

"Yes." Peacock shrunk under his gaze.

"And you'd do *anything* to save your friend, would you?"

"Yes." Peacock shrunk even more.

"Peter Sutton," announced Dracula grandly. "I declare the price for your assault on my book..." He curled his lips. "The price is Belladonna's life."

Bells uttered a mortified gasp.

The boys stared at Dracula, speechless.

"Why does it surprise you?" he inquired. "The prospect of death is the best motivator for lazy badlings like yourselves." He passed a sorrowful sigh. "I must confess, I grew rather bored in my years here. It's only fair to exchange a favor for a favor. If you amuse me and figure out a way to save your friend," he nodded at Bells, "I'll let her go. If not, I'll make you stay in my place." He leaned to them, a putrefying stench on his breath. "Four new badlings, the perfect number for myself and my three charming sisters, wouldn't you agree?"

In one swift move he pushed the boys into the room.

The door swung shut, the bolts slid into place, and all was silent.

They were trapped.

Chapter Seventeen

The Healthy Boy Fight

A well-paced book is like a time bomb. It has a clock. If you won't watch it, it might explode right in your hands. Or else, it might make your heart burst from pounding. At the very least, it will make you bite your nails and wish the minutes wouldn't tick off so quickly.

The boys stared at the door, their hearts—you guessed it—pounding. Victoriously and quite rudely, the door stared back. It had nothing to stare with, and yet it seemed to dare them pry it open.

"He got Bells!" shouted Rusty, shaking the knob that wouldn't budge. He turned around and blurted out the phrase he'd been nurturing since Blackey told them about Dracula's misfortune, "Thanks to you, *moron*." His eyes on Peacock, his fists clenched, he pulled back his arm and with a relish of one having waited for this opportunity since the beginning of time, punched him square in the nose.

Peacock staggered back. "You hit me!"

"And I'll hit you again!" cried Rusty, advancing. For all his height and knobbly build, he towered over his gangly friend who appeared to have instantly shrunk.

Peacock raked his hair in an effort to appear unconcerned. "You want to fight, is that what you want, *monkey?*"

Rusty opened his mouth, searching for a word to retort. When no word came, he hunched, tucked his shoulders, and charged, ramming his head straight into Peacock's stomach.

Peacock's eyes widened from surprise. He swayed and doubled over, gasping.

Elated by this unexpected advantage, Rusty clobbered him left and right.

Grand watched this spectacle with mixed feelings. On one hand, instinct told him to grab them by the hair and pull them apart, like he did with his little brothers. On the other hand, he wanted to shout encouragements and directions to Rusty for a better aim or hook or kick.

He decided to give them another minute.

Rusty pounded on Peacock's crouched back until his arms got shaky. "Man," he wheezed, "this is...hard. It's making me...tired."

Peacock peeked up. "Are you done?"

"I...think so," panted Rusty and clonked him on the head one more time, for closure.

When no more hits came, Peacock said, "Good job, Rusty. Are you proud of yourself?"

"Don't talk to me like nothing happened!" flared up Rusty. "Liar!" And he smacked him in the face, which finally broke the shackles of Peacock's cowardice. He sprung up and pushed Rusty away. "Get off me, *gibbon*."

Grand concluded that he had satisfied his yearning for justice and stepped between them. "Guys, I think that's enough."

"But Grand," pleaded Rusty, "he lied! He lied and he got Bells in trouble!"

"Um." Grand rubbed his nose. "He was scared."

"That's no excuse!"

"Like you never lied before?" snarled Peacock.

Grand sighed. It was high time to employ the maneuver that had never failed him. He grasped Peacock and Rusty by the hair and held out his arms, which, considering Grand's intimidating girth, was hard to ignore and terribly impractical to attack.

It took them another fuming minute.

"Okay," said Grand patiently, looking both of them over. "I'm going to let you go, but if you start fighting again, I won't just stand and watch." He waited for his words to sink in. "And Peacock? I think Rusty is right. I think you should apologize." He released his hold.

Rusty breathed hard, scowling.

Peacock tossed the hair out of his face. "I'm sorry, okay? I already said I'm sorry, didn't I?"

"You said it to Dracula, but not to us," fumed Rusty.

Peacock raised both arms for peace. "Look, I *am* sorry. Seriously. Sorry I was a jerk." And then he added quietly, "I mean it."

"No use for it now," grumbled Rusty.

Peacock blinked. "You want me to say it again?"

"What for? Your sorry is not going to rescue Bells, is it? What a stupid thing to do, to rip a book. Don't you have a brain? And you call me *monkey*."

Peacock gritted his teeth but said nothing.

They stood in silence, contemplating.

"We're doomed," said Grand dejectedly. "Dracula will bite Bells and drink her blood, and by the time we'll figure out how to save her, she'll turn into a vampire and bite us one by one, and we'll turn into vampires too and stay on this page and sleep in coffins during the day and at night we'll go out and hunt—" he felt Rusty's hand on his shoulder. "Sorry."

"No, it's cool, man," said Rusty. "Just not now." He gave him a reassuring grin. "Besides, if Dracula is a badling like us, who says his bite will work? Maybe it won't. Maybe he's bluffing, like Bells said."

"Maybe," agreed Grand. "So what do you think we should do?"

"I have *the* perfect idea," said Rusty, sizing up Peacock. "It's your fault we're here, so *you* get us out."

"And how do you propose I do that?" bristled Peacock.

"I don't know! Figure it out. What are you, *dumb?*"

The word struck Peacock like a slap. He cringed.

"Come on, Rusty," said Grand.

"What?" Rusty clenched his hands. "So *he* can be pissed off at me and call me *monkey*, and I can't? That's not fair. He did it, he needs to solve it!"

Grand rubbed his nose. "Well, we could ask someone for help."

"There isn't anyone to ask," said Peacock grimly.

"We could kill him!" exclaimed Rusty. "We could kill Dracula. We just need to drive a stake through his heart or shoot him with a silver bullet."

"And what if he's a kid like us?" asked Grand. "We don't know if he's the real Dracula or not."

"Right," Rusty deflated.

"Even if he was real, how would we do it? We're locked in, and I don't see any stakes or guns with silver bullets."

"We need to wait," muttered Peacock.

The boys looked at him.

"It's like Grand said," he explained. "If you stay on the same page long enough, it will repeat itself."

"That's right," Grand nodded. "That's what happened in *The Headless Horseman*."

"So if we wait," continued Peacock, "at some point the door will be open. I didn't see Dracula unlock it. Did you?"

Grand shook his head no.

"Wow, Peacock," said Rusty with admiration. "I forgot about that."

Excited to try it, they crouched by the door.

For a while nothing stirred, but just as they were beginning to doubt this brilliant idea, the door shuddered. The latch bolt shifted and slid, the spring released, and the hinges gritted, eager to stretch their bones. The boys looked at each other. Peacock twisted the knob.

The door swung out.

"It worked!" proclaimed Rusty in a thrilled whisper.

"Good job, Peacock," said Grand.

"Thanks." Peacock studied his hands. "It was your idea, though."

Grand shrugged. "It doesn't matter whose idea it was."

"Imagine Dracula's face when he sees that the room is empty," said Rusty to Peacock. They smiled, and thus their peace was sealed. At least until the next squabble.

"Um, guys?" said Grand. "I think we need to leave."

Distant footfalls approached from the hall.

Spooked, the boys ran to the staircase, skipped down to the next floor and stopped, listening.

The footfalls accelerated as well.

"He's after us!" shrieked Rusty.

They took off blindly, racing along dark corridors and great empty halls until they blasted through a postern left ajar. Cold air hit their faces and they halted, panting. They were in a courtyard, a large stone square hemmed by thick walls, stark and foreboding in the light of the moon. Somewhere on the other side the wolves howled, sensing the children's presence. And whoever was pursuing them, broke into a trot.

"Over there!" pointed Rusty.

They dashed through a crumbling arch and found themselves in another square, smaller, full of headstones wedged in the ground like broken, crooked teeth.

"A graveyard," croaked Peacock. He made as if to run.

Grand seized his arm. "No, you're staying."

"What's that?" said Rusty.

The graveyard ended in the familiar dirt wall. And at the bottom of it there was a gap from which a shaft of light shone up, rippling and glinting.

"I think it's coming from another page," said Grand.

They walked up to it. The gap was at least three feet wide. The page below was not very exciting: bright sky, bright sun, and bright sand.

"It's a desert," breathed Peacock. Freezing wind tickled his back, and he spun around, staring into darkness with horror.

"There's someone there," he whispered.

"Where?" asked Rusty.

"Between those tombstones," said Grand. "I think it's the vampire sisters."

Three misty figures rose from the ground and solidified into women in white, their faces pale, their lips scarlet, their eyes shining with hunger. Moonlight gave them an aggressive look, and there was no shadow where they stood.

Peacock screamed, stumbled back, and sunk into the light.

"Peacock, no!"

Grand and Rusty jumped after him.

Chapter Eighteen

The Lunatic Knight

Characters in stories travel in arcs. That doesn't mean they get blasted from cannons, flying—Wheee!—through the sky and dropping in dung. No. That means they go through arcs of growth and arrive at some kind of an enlightening wisdom, which in turn is supposed to change them for the better (or for the worse, depending on the book).

Peacock was coming to a turning point of such an arc.

He sat up, blinking.

Painfully vivid sky stretched overhead. Not a cloud in it, not a bird. Patches of brown grass ran up a plateau where a dozen windmills stood like ancient giants. Their blades rotated lazily, creaking and swishing, as if they were gossiping about the unlucky new badlings that had dropped on their page.

"What is this place?" said Peacock.

"Does it matter?" Rusty dusted himself off. "How are we supposed to save Bells now?"

Grand was studying the landscape. "We've been here before...I think."

Rusty looked at him. "Where, on this page?"

"Um. Maybe it's a different page, or maybe it's a different part of it, but I have a feeling it's the same story..."

He paused. "It's definitely the same terrain—Bells would know. See that hill? I think we were on the other side of it when we met Dapple, the donkey. And this side has the windmills..." His face cleared. "I think we're in *Don Quixote*. I'm sure we are. It looks just like in the book."

"Did you read it?" asked Peacock.

Grand's cheeks reddened. "Sort of."

"Don—what did you call it?"

"Don Quixote. It's the name of a knight. He lived in Spain, in the seventeenth century, I think."

"A knight?" asked Peacock nervously. "A real knight in full armor? With a lance?"

"He only thinks he's a real knight. He's crazy," clarified Grand happily. "He goes on these quests to revive chivalry—his idea of chivalry, anyway—which is attacking everyone he meets. I think if he's a badling like us, he might be even worse, crazy from having to act crazy."

Peacock and Rusty shared a look of utter horror.

Grand failed to notice it. "I'll tell you what happens in the book," he continued. "In the book he thinks he's being romantic and noble, because he wants to win the heart of this lady, I think her name is Dulcinea, so he fights people for her. If he sees us he'll probably attack us."

Peacock gulped. "Sounds like he belongs in a nuthouse."

"Can he help us fight Dracula?" asked Rusty hopefully.

"He has a lance," mused Grand, "but he's weird. I suppose we could try convincing him, but even if he agrees, how will we get back to Dracula?"

"They *must* have their ways for getting around," said Rusty. "They made it to Blackey, right? And to that Prince

Prospero guy. Maybe there's another caterpillar hole somewhere. We could go look for it?"

"Or we could trick him," said Peacock.

"Trick him?"

The boys regarded Peacock with interest.

"You said he wants to win the heart of some lady?"

"Yes," confirmed Grand. "Lady Dulcinea."

"And you said he's crazy."

"That's what the book says."

"Then how about we tell him that Dulcinea is in danger? That Dracula holds her hostage or something?"

Rusty opened his mouth. "Wow, Peacock. That's a great idea. The only problem is—"

"Um, I think that's him right there."

Indeed, it was. Where the blue of the sky met the yellow of the road rose a small cloud of dust. An uneven canter preceded a riding figure: a lanky knight in dented armor upon a mangy horse.

"We better get out of his way before he tramples us to death," observed Grand.

"Why would he do that?" asked Rusty.

"Because he's crazy."

"But not his horse. What if it's a badling like us? I bet it is. I bet it can *talk!*" Rusty didn't get a chance to confirm his theory. Grand snatched his arm and pulled him off the road, into the shadow next to one of the windmills.

Peacock didn't move, facing the rider.

"Peacock!" called Grand in a loud whisper.

"Leave him," grumbled Rusty. "Let him talk to that crazy guy. It was his idea, right?"

"But what if he hurts him?" objected Grand.

"So what? Maybe it'll teach him not to be such a

jerk. Tell me you didn't want to punch him in the face when Blackey said he ripped Dracula's book. He blamed Bells for everything and then tried to run away. That's not cool, man."

Grand considered it.

"Come on, tell me."

"Well, maybe a little."

"See? I knew it!"

"That doesn't mean he's a bad person. He was scared. We all get scared." Grand stepped out of the shadow. "Peacock!"

Peacock didn't reply.

The rider was upon him. He was old, perhaps in his fifties, his face two tired eyes and a mustache. The helmet he wore looked like an overturned bowl, and it gave him a comical appearance. "Behold the giants, Sancho! Look at their thousand arms! They're mocking me, despicable monsters!" He glanced to his right with a look of despair. "Oh, Sancho. Where are you, my faithful squire? Why did you abandon your master?"

His eyes fell on Peacock and he reined his horse to a stop.

"Hello," Peacock waved.

The knight dismounted with a loud groan.

"Who are you?" he cried in a crackling voice, snatched his lance and wearily thrust it forward. Its tip quivered inches away from Peacock's chest.

Peacock flinched, but miraculously remained standing. Encouraged by his own bravery, he started answering when the knight spoke over him, clearly not used to waiting.

"I'm the renowned knight Don Quixote of La

Mancha. What is your name? Answer at once!"

Peacock spread his arms in what he hoped was a gesture of admiration. "Oh, esteemed Don Quixote!" he began, "I've heard so much about you. You're well known for your famous deeds of chivalry and courage!"

Grand and Rusty looked at each other, stunned. It wasn't the Peacock they knew.

"Well known, am I?" Don Quixote straightened. The lance moved about dangerously in his shaking hand.

"Oh yes, you are," said Peacock, gently pushing the lance aside.

The knight didn't seem to notice this sly maneuver. "You say, you've heard of my deeds?" he asked.

"Oh yes, beloved knight." Peacock took a careful step back. "I've heard of your adventures. Allow me to tell you something of which your excellency might not be aware, yet I believe as soon as you hear it you'll rush to her aid, as *she* is in grave danger."

"She?" Don Quixote frowned. "Who is this *she* you mention?"

Peacock drew in breath. "Lady Dulcinea."

The knight's face twisted. "How dare you speak of her, my queen, my beauty, my sun? Who are you and what are you doing on my page? Tell me your name, before I impale you!"

Peacock winced. "No, no, please don't impale me. That sounds painful. My name is Peter Sutton."

"Hmmm," Don Quixote stroked his mustache. "I don't recall a story with a Peter Sutton. Whoever you are, get out of my way. You're distracting me from my quest."

"What's your quest?" asked Peacock. "Maybe I can help?"

"What an insolent young man you are, Peter Sutton. I wager you'll keep pestering me until I tell you. Very well. Perhaps you've come across her, indeed. I'm looking for the new badling girl. Tell me, have you seen her?" He cast a wide look around and grunted.

"The new badling girl?" repeated Peacock.

"Did you happen to see her? Answer at once!" The knight swung the lance so close, Peacock had to duck. "This is an urgent matter! I must find her and present her to my queen."

"What queen?"

"Queen Dulcinea, what other queen is there?"

"You're looking for Bells!" cried Rusty, sprinting out of the shadow. "We're looking for her too! Please, help us save her! Hi, horse," he said to the horse. "What's your name?"

The horse snorted at him angrily.

"Sorry, I thought you were—"

"Get back," hissed Peacock. "You're spoiling my plan."

"I have my own plan." Rusty boldly marched up to the knight. "Hey, Don Qui-something—"

Don Quixote thrust the lance at him, cutting him off. "Do not lie to me! Where is the new badling girl? Where did you see her?"

Rusty's eyes focused on the sharp tip not too far from his nose, "she's with Dracula, in his castle."

"Why, that bloodless hooligan is at it again." The knight whacked the lance on the road. "It's as the queen lamented. Dreadful tidings, dreadful! Tell me your name."

"Mine?" Rusty blinked, relieved that the lance wasn't aimed at him any longer. "Russell Jagoda. But my friends call me Rusty."

"Rusty," said Don Quixote, rolling the word in his mouth. "Like the blood rust on the brave knight's sword. And you?"

Grand timidly stepped out of the shadow. "I'm Grand."

"Grand," repeated the knight, "like a grand duke."

Grand's face brightened.

"I have a nickname too," added Peacock quickly. "It's Peacock."

"Peacock," Don Quixote closed his eyes. "Like an exotic bird of dazzling colors. Azure! Turquoise! Aubergine!"

Peacock gingerly touched his hair. "I always thought it's just blue."

"The name of the badling girl!" demanded Don Quixote.

"Bells," said the boys as one.

"Bells, like the ringing bells of a majestic cathedral," the knight mounted the horse with a grunt. "We mustn't tarry. Lead on, Duke Grand, Dazzling Peacock, and Brave Rusty! Let us rescue Beautiful Bells from the greedy clutches of Dracula!"

"But," began Grand, "how will we get there?"

"Fear not!" cried the knight. "Follow me." And he spurred his horse along the road.

The boys started after him, running full pelt.

Where the last windmill perched like a guarding giant, the road dipped then gently sloped up for another thirty yards. It ended in the ever-present dirt wall. Don Quixote was already there, waiting. Rusty reached him first, then Peacock. Grand came last, labored breaths tearing at his lungs, his face as red as a ripe tomato.

"All here? Up we go!" the knight turned the horse around. It tapped the wall with a hoof, searching for a solid spot, and then it was trotting up, breaking all rules of gravity that have ever existed.

"Holy buckets," said Peacock, his eyes round.

"You can *walk* on it?" asked Rusty.

"Bells...was right...about climbing it. All this time...we could've just..." Too winded to talk, Grand trailed off.

All three of them stared at the wall, none of them daring to try it.

"Hurry!" demanded Don Quixote. "After me!"

Rusty crouched, tucked in his head and jumped. A most curious sensation flung him backward. He didn't fall, only swayed a little, his feet flat on the wall, his body parallel to the road where Peacock and Grand were gazing up at him with their mouths open.

"Wow, this is so cool! Come on, guys, it's easy!"

The horse snorted impatiently.

"We cannot suffer any more delays!" the knight urged them. "Hurry! Hurry!"

Peacock turned to Grand, offering a hand. "Want some help? Want to do it together?"

Grand flushed, embarrassed. "Um, thanks. I think I can do it on my own."

"Okay." Peacock lifted a leg and gingerly stepped on the wall. When nothing horrible happened, he bounced a few times as if getting ready for a leap, then quickly yanked the other leg from the ground and suddenly he was standing next to Rusty. "That felt weird. You sure you don't want some help?"

Grand fiercely shook his head. It took him another concentrated moment to force himself to waddle over the invisible barrier that separated one gravity from another. He crouched and was about to jump when the dreaded rustling noise issued from the sky.

"Who goes there," said Mad Tome. "Who dares disturb my napping?" The lips appeared, then the face, and then it opened in a wide yawn.

"Aww, crap," exclaimed Rusty, "it's awake. Come on, Grand!"

Together with Peacock they grabbed his hands and pulled. He dropped to their feet, rolled on his back but instead of getting up remained still, his mouth open. Peacock and Rusty followed his gaze. A faint *ahhh* went up from them, and for an instant they forgot themselves, lost in the sight.

Both the steppe with the distant windmills and the sky with the blinding sun were now on their left, perpendicular to the dirt wall. Mad Tome's grimace hung directly above them like an unwelcome apparition. And to their right rose another page, dark, shrouded in the night. Its bottom curled up slightly, and beyond *that* the next page was visible, green and lush. A meadow? A forest? It was too far to tell.

The boys looked straight up and saw the pages connect. They were bound to Mad Tome's spine, hanging from it like curtains.

"It's like we're under a book," said Peacock.

"Like if you opened it and put it down like a tent!" added Rusty.

"Um, if that's how it works, then we can just walk out of here," said Grand thoughtfully. "I mean, if we walk long enough, at some point the pages will end, and we'll find the cover and go under it and maybe get back out at our duck pond."

They stared at each other, speechless.

"Are those my new badlings I see?" screeched Mad Tome.

The boys ducked.

"Don't be afraid!" cried Don Quixote. "It can't touch us here. It's not part of the book. But we must hurry." And he urged his horse ahead.

"Where do you think you're going, you dimwitted blimps?" shouted Mad Tome. Fierce wind erupted from its mouth.

"It'll blow us off!" screamed Peacock.

Don Quixote turned around. "It will not, Dazzling Peacock. Do not despair!" Oblivious to sand flying in his face, he hefted the lance and proceeded to carelessly wave it about. "Try me, you abominable beast! Come out and face me in an honest battle!"

"I'll get you later, you piece of tin junk," hissed Mad Tome, its claws snatching at the air in frustration. It couldn't reach them: its arms failed to extend past the page.

The knight brandished his lance with such vigor that he almost toppled out of the saddle.

Mad Tome cackled. "You can't even hold your measly stick, you old buffoon. How do you intend to fight me?"

"Do not vex me with your mockery!" said the knight with indignation. "Spare your breath. You're nothing but a pile of rotting pages. I know my end is near. I'm not afraid of death. And I'll take you with me, you wicked lying rubble. Prepare to meet your swift demise as the penalty for your foul deeds."

"I like this guy," said Rusty appreciatively.

"Agreed," echoed Peacock.

Grand shook his head. "I don't trust him. He said he's looking for Bells on the queen's orders, but Dulcinea is not really a queen, and why would she need Bells? To claim her?"

"He's probably talking nonsense," ventured Rusty. "He's crazy, right? You said so yourself."

Don Quixote waved to them. "After me!"

"I know where you're headed," rustled Mad Tome. "I'll wait for you to arrive, and then we'll have us a pleasant talk about your punishment." It laughed hysterically, although with a hint of bitter disappointment, then yawned and promptly fell asleep, snoring, exhausted by the confrontation.

"It always does this, every time," commented the knight. "One only has to wait. It's what has saved us many times, its propensity for napping and its madness." He patted the horse and cantered off.

The boys jogged after him, across the brown waste to the next page, black under the moonlight.

"Do you think he's a real character?" asked Rusty.

Peacock raised his brows. "You're asking me? I know as much as you do. Ask him."

"Grand, what do you think?"

But Grand couldn't talk, concentrating on moving, sweat running down his face in rivers.

"We have arrived!" shouted Don Quixote. He reined his horse and galloped up the page, instantly swallowed by darkness. The boys followed suit. The ground keeled over and in the next moment they stumbled onto the courtyard in front of Castle Dracula.

Chill cut through their clothes. Wolves howled hungrily not too far away. And from one of the windows, so high up, it almost touched the sky, a figure in a flapping cape was crawling down. It stopped, grew wings and took off to the moon, a bloodthirsty bat on a hunt for new victims.

Chapter Nineteen

The Inside-Out Rescue

What reader wouldn't enjoy a book about valiant knights rescuing wretched maidens from formidable castles? Even badlings read books like that. Not this book, though, or rather, not this *page*. On this page, irritated at not being saved fast enough, the maiden scolds the tardy knights and brings them back on task.

The boys watched Dracula shrink to a dot.

"He left!" exclaimed Rusty. "We can get Bells now!"

Peacock paled. "Did you see the size of those wings?"

"I think he went on a hunt," said Grand gloomily. "It's what he does every night. He hunts innocent people, catches them unaware, drinks their blood, and returns in the morning to sleep in his casket in the dungeon, in the dark and the mold and the death around him."

Peacock's jaw dropped. "You read *Dracula*?"

Grand reddened. "Um...I watched the movie."

"And you didn't get scared?"

"Well, maybe a little," confessed Grand. "There's nothing to be scared about, though. Dracula is very lonely because nobody wants to be friends with him. They all think he's scary and dead. And he's just sad and thirsty and wants company, so he goes out there to make friends the only way he knows how."

When Peacock didn't respond to this, Grand added,

"My mom says living people are scarier than dead ones. She works with dead people every day, she must know. She says when she touches a face of a dead—"

"Guys, come on!" cried Rusty anxiously. "We need to get Bells! What if he bit her? What if we're too late? If we are, it's your fault." He glared at Peacock.

Peacock lifted his arms, either to protect himself from a beating or to start a beating, he wasn't sure himself, when a strangled gasp made him spin around.

Don Quixote did something bizarre. He took off his helmet and bent to the knee, one hand on his heart, another outstretched to three figures that stepped out of the gloom.

Peacock quailed. "The vampire sisters."

The sisters hissed, advancing. Their eyes gleamed, and their lips peeled back, showing long sharp incisors.

"Oh, beautiful maidens!" intoned Don Quixote. "How fair is your skin! How precious your faces! Your lips are rubies that put sunset to shame! Oh, let me feast on your beauty with my ancient eyes. I'm your humble servant, the revered knight Don Quixote of La Mancha."

"Whoa. They're pretty," said Rusty, spellbound.

"Um. I don't think he's a badling," said Grand, nodding at the knight. "I think he's a real character, and I think he thinks they're real too." His comment went unheard.

Peacock and Rusty had fallen victim to the vampire sisters' charm. They stared at them, awaiting instructions. The sisters—one blond, the other two dark-haired— consulted in sibilant whispers.

"Take that one," said the blonde to the taller of the two, pointing a finger at Grand. "Look how plump and juicy he is, just the way you like them."

Every little hair on Grand's neck stood up. He wanted to run but couldn't move a muscle.

"I shall," agreed the tall one with a sneer. "Come, badling." She beckoned to Grand. His legs unlocked, and he obediently waddled up.

"I'll take the little one. He seems so full of life," said the short sister and gestured at Rusty.

He walked to her slowly, stumbling and swaying.

Peacock whimpered. The blonde regarded him hypnotically. He took a step, and another, and another, wanting nothing more but to come close.

"At last," she murmured, lifting his chin. "How splendid it is to meet you face to face. Peacock, is it? I knew you'd do our bidding. You poor badling, did you think ripping our book would kill us?" She gave a burst of laughter. "You were *wrong*. We live in too many minds. It'll take more than that to banish us from existence." She curled her lip and bit into his neck, gurgling in the ecstasy of feeding.

Her sisters snarled, ready to follow the example.

"Grand!" screamed Bells' voice from above. "Rusty! Peacock! What took you so long?" Her head poked out from the third story window. "Wake up, you idiots!"

Peacock blinked. "Bells?"

"Sssss!" hissed the blonde. "Don't listen to her."

"Shut up, you abomination of a woman!" cried Bells. "Guys, push them away! Do it, before they bite you!"

They honestly tried.

Peacock raised his hands a few inches and dropped them.

Grand slumped into the tall sister's arms, not quite knocking her off her feet, but almost, *almost*. Rusty tugged at the folds of the skirt in front of him without looking: it was the first thing he felt under his fingers.

Don Quixote didn't move, stiff as a statue.

And the horse was nowhere to be seen.

"Do I always have to do everything myself?" Bells' furious tone had a sobering effect on everyone, including the vampires. "Where did you go?" she demanded. "And who's this?"

"That's Don Quixote," piped up Rusty. "He's a knight, he came to help us rescue you. He—" The short sister put a hand over his mouth to shush him.

"He certainly looks like he's busy doing exactly that," observed Bells. "Where did you find him? And whose brilliant idea was it?"

"Mine," croaked Peacock.

"You blockhead!" she shouted. "You'll get us all killed! You should've stayed where you were and waited for me. Hey, dead girl, get away from him!" Bells reached behind her. "You! I'm talking to you! Look at me, you dumb rattle-brained bloodsucker!"

She aimed and hurled down a heavy candlestick. It hit the tall sister square in the face, making her let go of Grand.

"Huh?" he spoke from his slumber. "Bells? Are you okay?"

"I'm fine, but you're not! Watch out!"

The vampire lunged back at him.

With a roar of unimaginable strength, Peacock shoved the blonde away and threw himself in front of Grand. "Don't touch him, you ugly carcass! Don't you *dare* bite him, or...or..." He struggled to come up with a horrific enough consequence, when the vampire spoke.

"You're right, badling. Who wants to feed on a fat kid? His blood must be stale from sitting around too much. You, on the other hand, promise to taste *delicious*." She reached for Peacock's neck.

"I'll show you *fat*," muttered Grand and brought his whole weight on the creature, knocking her off balance.

She windmilled her arms and sat back staring up in surprise.

"If you weren't a girl," he explained, "I'd give you a good punch. But you're a girl, so I can't hit you. My mom says boys shouldn't hit girls. I think it's not fair because Bells beats us up all the time. I guess she can do it since she's a friend." He shrugged. "We understand. Do you need help getting up?" He offered her a hand.

The vampire blinked. "This is the nicest thing anyone has said to me since I got here." She put her hand into Grand's and rose back to her feet.

"You're badlings like us, aren't you? You only pretend to be vampires," said Grand with conviction.

She regarded him strangely. "Are we doing a good job?"

"I think you're doing a *great* job." Grand nodded at Peacock struggling in the blonde's hold. "This prop blood you're using looks very real."

"You think this is fake?" The blonde uttered a short laugh and glued her lips back to Peacock's throat. He stopped moving, hanging like a ragdoll.

"Peacock, no!" screamed Bells. "Guys, help him!"

"It's okay, Bells!" answered Grand. "It's not real. She's only pretending."

"No, she's not! She's killing him!" Bells groped for something to throw. "Hey, knight! Don Dummy Dolt or

180

whatever! You're the most pathetic knight I've ever seen! What good is your sword if you can't use it?"

Don Quixote stirred and looked down at his sword that uselessly sat in its scabbard. "Oh, what trickery has befallen me! What mishap!" he cried miserably. "Dracula, you old crook! You fooled me again!"

He unsheathed the sword and swooped on the blonde. She staggered, writhing and snarling.

"You disobeyed the Queen's orders! She will hear of it, mark my words, or I'm not the reverent knight Don Quixote of La Mancha!" He aimed the sword at her chest.

"Put it away, put it away!" she hissed.

Her dark-haired sisters flanked her.

"Please," begged the tall one.

"She didn't bite him," implored the short one. "She was only pretending, like this lovely badling has explained." She looked at Grand with most innocence she could muster.

"There is blood on your mouth, you filthy liar!" screamed Bells. "You bit him! You bit Peacock!" A rain of various objects began pelting the sisters' heads: two silk pillows, a balled up blanket, a ceramic vase, three bronze statuettes, a paperweight in the shape of a bat, and, finally, a heavy book that struck the blonde in the face.

"Why do you hate me so!" she cried. "I'm only doing my job. Do you think I enjoy this? Oh, how wrong you are! It breaks my dead heart to see horror on your mute terrified faces before I sink my teeth into your soft pulsing necks."

"Liar!" yelled Bells, stepping away from the window and looking around the room. She had successfully chucked out everything she could lift and carry and was now contemplating whether or not she should try dismantling the four-postern bed.

Meanwhile, yet another drama developed in the courtyard.

Grand and Rusty slowly gained their senses. Don Quixote tended to them with all the care of a nurse. And Peacock was lying unconscious behind one of the arches, having been stealthily dragged there by the vampire sisters.

"I've done it," admitted the blonde.

The tall sister gasped. "You bit him in earnest?"

"Oh, I simply couldn't resist. What was I to do?"

"But..." the short sister faltered. "Dracula said to wait until he's back."

"He's not real," retorted the blonde. "Haven't you noticed? He deceived us!"

"But he said we can feed on them when he's back," protested the tall sister, "and then all of us will be free to go home, back to our book."

"Listen to me." The blonde lowered her voice. "I don't think he knows himself what will happen. He's merely guessing. And these children," she motioned, "they think we're children like them. They don't realize we've only been here for two days. We have them in our hands, right now. I say let's feast on them, before it's too late."

Alas, too late it was.

A gust of cold wind swept over the courtyard. A glittery sleigh pulled by three horses emerged from the sky and with a thud and a creak landed by the front door.

A regal man in a velvet cloak jumped out. "There they are!"

"I see them, prince," said the woman in white perched high on the coachman's seat. "I'm not blind."

"My queen! My queen!" exclaimed Don Quixote.

He kneeled, kissed the ground and lay still.

"The Snow Queen," whispered Rusty. "What's she doing here?"

"She's after Bells," answered Grand.

Prince Prospero bent to the knee. "Forgive me, my queen."

She didn't reply and, ignoring his outstretched hand and the knight's worshipping figure, stepped down on her own.

"How dare you come to this page unbidden?" hissed the blonde. "Leave at once! Count Dracula—"

"Count Dracula has been captured," snapped the queen. "He's chained to a wall in the dungeon of Prince Prospero's abbey."

"I vow this is true," said the prince with a hint of pride, "I've seen to it myself."

The blonde balked. "What for?" she asked. "What has he done to you other than given you long years of faithful service?"

"Do not pretend you do not know," said the queen. "You're well aware of Dracula's affairs. He schemed against us, and *you* helped him. You, who do not know what it's like to waste away, stuck in this idiotic book, you helped him lure new badlings—not one, but four!—onto *his* page for his own purpose: to spill the blood of one of them to claim as his and give the rest to you. He had no right to act behind our backs." Her eyes glimmered. "But now that you're here, you'll quickly learn what you've been missing. And don't harbor any hopes. You're staying in Mad Tome while *I* am getting out." She walked up to the knight and kicked him with her shoe. "Did you find the new badling girl, you useless piece of junk?"

"I'm here," called Bells from above.

Grand and Rusty passed a terrified sigh.

"There you are," cooed the queen. "I thought I'd never find you."

"Dracula told me all about you," continued Bells. "He's actually a very nice boy and he was very happy that I didn't think him a creep, like everybody else does. He said you're the cruelest and the meanest badling he's ever met, and that you secretly set Mad Tome on other badlings so it would *kill* them."

Prince Prospero gasped.

"Do not assault my queen!" cried Don Quixote, brandishing his sword.

"Oh yes, I will," retorted Bells. "She's not a queen and she deserves it."

"Command me!" the knight fell to the Snow Queen's feet. "Your word is my law. How would you like me to punish this wicked malicious badling? Stab her? Quarter her? Behead her?"

"Rise, knight," said the queen imposingly. "Leave the girl to me. There is other work for you to do. I want you to watch the vampire sisters, to make sure they don't follow us. Can you do this for your queen?" She dazzled him with a blinding smile. "For your *Dulcinea*?"

Grand opened his mouth.

"Anything," intoned Don Quixote in complete servitude. "Anything for you, my lady. My life is in your hands."

"Where's Peacock?" demanded Bells suddenly.

"I'm here," Peacock stepped out of the shadows. He looked unnaturally pale, and when he smiled, two razor-sharp fangs gleamed brightly in the moonlight. He strolled to his friends with a new gait, assured and stately.

"Um, Peacock?" said Grand. "I think you turned into a vampire."

"What are you talking about?" objected Peacock. "I haven't turned into anyone. I'm still me." He sniffed the air around Grand. "You smell nice. I never noticed before for some reason. Very sweet, like...doughnuts."

Grand made a small squeaky noise.

"That's enough talking," interjected the queen. "We must leave before Mad Tome wakes up. Get in." She motioned to the sleigh.

Peacock tossed his hair naughtily. "I'm not going anywhere, I'm staying here."

"Get in the sleigh," ordered the queen.

"Why can't he stay?" asked the blonde. "He's no use to you. I already claimed him."

"*Claimed* me?" Peacock goggled at her. "Are you saying—" his words were cut short.

The Snow Queen had breathed in his face and he slumped, frosted all over. Prince Prospero caught him and dragged him in the sleigh. The queen flicked her gaze to Grand and Rusty. They hastily climbed in, seating themselves on the second of the two icy benches.

"My queen!" cried Don Quixote.

"Stay. I command you to watch the sisters."

"Yes, my queen." The knight unsheathed his sword.

The sisters huddled under the arch, hissing.

Grand tapped Rusty's knee, nodding at Peacock. His hair turned from blue to blond in the matter of seconds and his frosted features began acquiring a rather feminine look.

The Snow Queen climbed on the coachman's seat,

struck the horses, and they swept up to the third story window, hovering close enough for Bells to hop in. She didn't resist: she had no choice. The moment she was seated next to Grand, the sleigh shot to the dirt wall with incredible speed.

The world careened.

The ground became the wall, the wall the ground.

Bells was too stunned to speak.

The queen sprayed snow from her sleeves, covering bare soil with a blanket of white. The horses touched upon it and galloped forth, leaving Dracula's page behind them.

Chapter Twenty

The Sleigh Chase

Most books have villains, evil destructive characters that do evil destructive things. To conquer them someone has to face them. That's one scary prospect. Luckily, most books also have heroes who shoulder this noble chore. But what if the villain is the book itself? And what if this book doesn't have any heroes to face it except four desperate children?

Huddled on the hard seats, they peered up at the passing pages of Mad Tome. On the front bench, Peacock shifted closer to Prince Prospero, still dazed from the Snow Queen's spell. On the back bench Bells and Rusty sandwiched Grand, and for a good reason: his body radiated enough heat to keep both of them warm.

"We're idiots, absolute and total idiots," whispered Bells to Grand, her cheeks flushing. "All this time we could've just *walked* back."

"We didn't know," objected Grand. "How could we know?"

"We could've figured it out," said Bells resolutely. "We could've tried and tested every possibility, including gravity reversal. Some scientist I am." She crossed her arms. "Now we're stuck here and it's my fault. I'll know better in the future."

"Don't be so hard on yourself."

"It's Peacock's fault, not yours," piped up Rusty.

"What's that?" Peacock turned his head.

Bells' eyes widened. She stomped on Grand's foot who in turn pinched Rusty who choked on whatever it was he wanted to say. The source of their distress was unsettling.

Peacock looked like an identical copy of the blond vampire sister. Even his voice was not his own anymore. He didn't seem to be aware of the change, regarding his friends with his signature mockery. "Why are you staring at me like this? Is something wrong?"

"Nothing, nothing," said Bells quickly. "I was just talking about...how much I was worried about you."

"Seriously? And you guys were listening to that?"

Grand and Rusty vigorously nodded.

"I can't believe it," he turned away. "Girls and their worries." Prince Prospero glanced back and whispered something to Peacock. They laughed.

It appeared to Bells that they were making fun of her and of all things girly. A curious sensation spread through her chest, an anticipation of sweet, long-awaited vengeance. "I'll see what you have to say once you realize you're a *girl*," she said inaudibly.

"Did you say something?" asked Grand.

"He replaced her," whispered Bells. "She bit him, and he replaced her."

"I see that."

"Did you hear what the Snow Queen said? About the vampire sisters helping Dracula lure us to his page so he could spill our blood and claim us? So if she spills my blood, I'll replace her?" Bells glanced at the queen's sparkling mantle, at her pale bluish hands snapping the reins and shuddered at the thought.

"I think so," hazarded Grand. "The Headless Horseman wanted to behead me, so I think—"

"Hey, not fair," blurted Rusty, "I can't hear what you guys are talking about."

Bells pushed her head behind Grand's back. "Peacock has changed into the vampire sister because she spilled his blood."

"Whoa. Is that why? I thought it was because the Snow Queen breathed on him."

"No, it has nothing to do with that, that's just her own power. At least that's what the book says. Anyway..." Bells pulled out from behind Grand's back and leaned over his knees, fervidly talking to both boys.

"This is it, guys. That's how they turn new badlings into themselves. Remember Boulotte, Bluebeard's wife? She was upset she didn't bring her scissors. And then the puppy in Wonderland—"

"That's right," interjected Rusty. "It wanted to bite me. And it told me I'd replace it if it did. I forgot!"

"Shhh," Bells cast a nervous look at Peacock and Prince Prospero, but they were engaged in a conversation and didn't pay them any heed. The Snow Queen shouted at the horses, the horses whinnied, and the wind swished by the sides of the sleigh, twirling up an occasional snowflake.

Relieved, Bells continued. "And then the knight, Don whatever his name—"

"Quixote," supplied Grand.

"Don *Quixote*," repeated Bells, "he put his sword to the blonde's chest, remember? Why was she so afraid? Vampires don't die from being cut by a sword. It all makes sense. She was afraid he'd cut her and she'd turn into him, a crazy old man! I'm sure she didn't want *that* to happen. We're lucky the badlings have been holding back. I think it's because they agreed to vote on who gets to claim us. That's what they wanted to do at that masquerade. Only it went all wrong, so now anyone of them can do it, if they wanted to."

"Crap," breathed Rusty.

That single word expressed their collective feelings on the matter so accurately, they fell silent.

"So Mad Tome must've gotten one of *Dracula's* pages and killed the real Dracula," said Bells at last. "And that boy, the badling who replaced him, must've somehow sent a message to his sisters back in the book, pleading for them to find a new badling. Unfortunately for Peacock, that must've happened when he was reading it. So they told him to rip it. They knew that if he did, Mad Tome would get him. That's how it all started."

"It didn't help that I couldn't read past the first page of *The Headless Horseman*," muttered Grand.

"I should've finished reading *The Snow Queen* to Sofia," said Bells.

"I'll read *Alice in Wonderland* when this is over," promised Rusty, "and that book about the little black hen, Blackey."

They went quiet again.

"These kids, the badlings, they just want to get home," said Bells sadly. "Remember what Dapple said? He said if we destroy Mad Tome, we can return. I think he meant that all of us can return. I wonder if they tried it before and failed. Maybe that's why they're so mean to us." Her eyes were shining when she finished.

"I think there's more," whispered Grand. "I think—

"

Without letting go of the reins, the queen spun on her seat and silenced him with an icy glare. "That's enough idle talk. If I hear any more of this," her eyes fell on Bells, "I'll claim you right here and now. Am I clear?"

"Yes," squeaked Bells, willing her teeth not to chatter.

The queen turned back to her horses.

"She heard us," whispered Bells.

Grand didn't reply, frozen under Peacock's hungry stare.

"Want to sit next to me?" Peacock patted the bench. "We have more space here than you guys over there."

"It's best to leave the girl where she is," said the prince.

"No, I meant Grand." Peacock pouted. "He smells better."

"What?" asked Bells, offended. "Are you implying I stink?" She suppressed an urge to sniff herself, just to be sure.

"You can't claim a badling, not yet," said the prince conversationally. His face suddenly drained color. "Oh, horror. Whatever evil has possessed my tongue. I didn't mean to misspeak, my queen! I beg your forgiveness! Oh, how can I—"

"Hush!" she shouted, her eyes wide with fury. "Save your breath. I don't need your measly apologies."

Prince Prospero shrunk into the seat.

"It matters no longer," professed the queen. "Our time is near. They might as well know what awaits them." She looked at Bells. "Come, sit with me and not with those silly boys." Her breath reached over like an arm, chilling

Bells to the core. Her eyes became two icy lakes polished to perfection. Bells wanted to skate on them, to splinter them into shards and assemble them into mosaics. The vision became so real she stretched out her hand to touch them and felt it cramp.

The Snow Queen gripped it, yanked her up and over the heads of Peacock and Prince Prospero, and deposited her on the coachman's seat.

"Are you warm enough?" she asked.

Bells stiffened: it felt like she was sitting next to a fridge.

"I'll tell you a secret," said the Snow Queen slyly, "I don't like boys. They're filthy and obstinate and have no appreciation for beauty. Many of them have come, and many of them I could've claimed, but I didn't. I've been waiting for a *girl*. *She* whom I could offer gems of wintry splendor, *she* whose heart would still from the play of northern lights, *she* who'd relish dwelling in my icy palace after I'd departed, but not before we'd talk about girly things for hours on end." An arrogant child flashed through the queen's silky expression, the one she once was and had almost forgotten. "I haven't talked to anyone about girly things for years."

Despite her numbness, Bells shuddered. "Girly things?" she asked, working to move her tongue. "I don't like talking about girly things. I'm a scientist."

The queen's eyes flashed with disappointment. "I'll *make* you like it," she snarled, reached up to her crown and broke off a crystal shard.

There it is, my death, thought Bells with strange calm, watching the queen raise her arm to deliver the fatal blow. *I need to dodge it.* She tried moving. Her body wouldn't oblige. *I need to do something!* The image of startled Boulotte passed through her mind, and Bells decided to do an outrageously girly thing, something she purposefully avoided to do in the past but that warranted to be the only effective solution to her current problem. She summoned whatever strength she had left, opened her mouth and screamed.

She screamed like a girl.

At first she thought it produced the desired effect.

The horses reared, snorting.

The queen's arm jerked, and the shard flew out of her fingers. She lost the grip on the reins. The animals, sensing their freedom, raced forward, breaking into a mad gallop as if chased by the wolves.

Bells got knocked back into the seat and saw the real reason for the outbreak of this pandemonium.

The face of yawning Mad Tome filled the air.

"It's waking up!" cried Prince Prospero.

"I've noticed!" The queen stood tall, slashing at the reins, a fearsome and powerful deity not to be trifled with.

They were nearing a familiar looking page. The sleigh accelerated, snow spuming from under its runners, and then it jumped over the bend in space. At once the page in front of them became the ground, and the ground they rode on became the dirt wall.

The sleigh bounced, nearly throwing Bells off the seat. She clutched it, peering at the unfolding landscape: bare hills, dark woods, and an abbey girded by a stone wall, two naked trees standing sentinel by its gate.

"The Red Death page," she said to herself.

The sleigh came to a screeching stop.

"We have arrived." The Snow Queen offered her

hand to Prince Prospero who helped her descend. "What are you waiting for? Get out."

Grand and Rusty awkwardly hopped off.

Peacock stepped down in small measured steps, his face twisted with shock as he finally noticed that he wore a long woman's gown and that long hair spilled over his shoulders. He mutely stared at his friends who mutely stared back, unsure how to comfort him or what to say.

Bells climbed out last, still slow from numbness.

The Snow Queen regarded her with distaste. "We shall hold a council on who gets to claim you." She gestured to the open doors already crowded with expectant faces, eager to slash or scratch or bite, to escape their predicament and to leave new badlings in their place.

Chapter Twenty-One

The Wrong Council

How do you divide four things among eight things? You cut each thing in half. How about four things among a hundred things? It depends on the thing, of course. If it's four doughnuts, you break them into a hundred tiny pieces (good luck with that). But what if the things to be divided are four people?

The children reluctantly entered the abbey. The crowd parted to let them through, every eye staring, every mouth whispering, every limb tense, wanting to grab yet holding back in the presence of the Snow Queen. She strutted smoothly with her head high, leading the assembly to the black suite. Here she halted, spun on her heels, and addressed them in a formal tone.

"We, the badlings of Mad Tome, intend to hold a council for the purpose of determining your future placement."

Bells stole an uneasy glance at Grand. He shrugged, nodding at Rusty who was gawking at Peacock.

Peacock had somewhat acquainted himself with the idea of his change and was determined to appear as if it didn't bother him in the slightest. "No need to decide anything about me," he said smugly, "I'm going back to Dracula's page, *hunting*." He wet his lips.

"You don't get to go anywhere until we vote," stated

the queen. "It's our vote that will determine your future."

There was a murmur of agreement.

"Do you absolutely have to vote?" asked Bells, alarmed. "Wouldn't it be better to let us choose the characters we get to replace? I mean, scientifically speaking, if you let us do that, the success rate—"

"That's enough!" shouted the queen and waved a hand.

It acted a signal.

A throng of burbling, jostling bodies unceremoniously shoved the children through the door and pushed them into four black chairs that were set up in the middle of the equally black room with glowing red windows. People and creatures alike bedecked every sitting surface: sofas, ottomans, settees, divans, windowsills, dressers, wardrobes, commodes. When no more spots were left, fights broke out. Some tried sitting on each other's shoulders, others settled on the floor. At last, they quieted, all eyes on the children.

Bells recognized a few of them, like the caterpillar and Alice and the Red Death and, according to Grand's description, the scary looking Headless Horseman; but most were unfamiliar, their faces hostile and grim, their voices murmuring in subdued displeasure.

"She broke the rules—Did you hear that? One already has been claimed!—Keep it quiet—They know, someone told them—But who would?—Does it matter?— They're ours—I want that one—You don't get to pick!— Get your hands off me—You stepped on my foot—" and so on, like a packed classroom before the start of a lesson.

"They're treating us like prisoners," said Bells.

"Looks like it," agreed Grand.

Rusty made no comment. He kept staring at Peacock who finally snapped his jaws right in his face and made him jump.

"Whoa, dude, cut it out!"

Peacock sneered, revealing a pair of fangs. "What happened, Rusty? What's wrong? Don't you want to beat me up? Go ahead, I'm not stopping you."

Rusty edged away.

"Are you scared?"

"Nope."

"Come on then, *do it*."

"I would've," said Rusty fiercely, "but I don't raise my hands at *girls*."

Peacock drew back as if punched.

Rusty sniggered.

"Stop it." Bells stomped on his foot, but her face lit up with a smile of immense satisfaction.

The murmur in the room abruptly ceased. All eyes shifted from the children to the sofa directly across them. The Snow Queen looked down on the badlings who occupied it, waiting for them to scramble out of the way. That done, she lowered herself in the middle, to her right Prince Prospero, to her left the ghost of Bluebeard, the ghost of Blackey perched on his shoulder, the ghosts of dead wives shimmering behind.

"I ask everyone to be quiet," began the queen.

There was no need: the silence was absolute.

"We have gathered here—"

"I've suffered the most damage!" twanged a voice.

"Who dares to interrupt me?"

No one replied.

"Show yourself!"

Prodded by his neighbors, the Headless Horseman rose, holding out his head. It grimaced, moving its lips and tongue in an exaggerated fashion. "I've been traumatized. The consequences are dire. I cannot perform my story without being terrified of a new badling stalking me across the page. It is my right to demand compensation! I claim the fat one." He pointed at Grand. "He terrorized me by following me around. He deserves to suffer in my place."

Grand couldn't believe what he was hearing. "I terrorized you?"

"That's entirely unfair," said the caterpillar languidly, taking the hookah out of his mouth and breathing out a ring of smoke. "If anyone can claim him, that'd be me. I've been first in line for years, according to our last assembly. Bluebeard, you decreed it. Have you no record—"

"Bluebeard is a ghost," interrupted the queen. "Whatever he decreed is no longer valid."

"Besides," continued the caterpillar, in an unhurried manner, "he managed to escape my pupa. It is a blow to my self-esteem. I've been working hard to morph into a genuine caterpillar, and I must tell you, it's not easy. You get to walk across your pages, but not me. These pitiful stumps you call *legs* provide me little locomotion aside from crawling and creeping and on a rare occasion—"

"Silence!" screamed the queen. "Anyone else who speaks out of order will be dismissed, therefore forfeiting their right to claim a new badling. Need I repeat it?" She glared at them, fearsome in her fury.

There was a surge of whispers and a few angry glances, but no one openly challenged her. Not yet.

"Our time is short," intoned the queen. "We must

proceed to vote."

Applause erupted. Someone stomped. Someone whistled.

She raised her hand for calm. "But before we do, may I present to you a gift, a gift we've been waiting for, for years." She paused, letting her words sink in, then continued in a tone of one disclosing an important secret. "A way for all of us to go home, every...single...badling."

The room grew still.

Stunned faces watched her with breathless anticipation.

"The badling by the name of Grand, stand up and tell us what you had in mind," commanded the queen. "Tell us about your method."

Everyone's attention shifted to Grand. He blinked. "Method?"

"Your method to destroy Mad Tome," snapped the queen. "We want to hear it."

"It's not a method, it's just an idea. But...how do you know about it? I haven't told anyone except my friends..."

The ghost of the little black hen quickly flew up and hid behind the sofa.

"I have my ways," said the queen. "Go on. Don't keep us waiting."

"I bet it was Blackey," muttered Bells. "I bet he spied on us, little snitch."

Grand shifted his weight from foot to foot. "Um," he began, "I thought if we could somehow get the ducks at the pond to find Mad Tome and rip it—" His expression brightened with a sudden idea. "Or we could just walk along the dirt wall and get out by the pond and then we'd be able to destroy it for sure."

Bells stared at him.

Grand turned pink. "I mean, it'd be better if *we* did it because ducks are not really interested in books, they're more interested in worms, or doughnuts." He sighed.

"Wait a minute!" someone shouted. "What do you mean, go back to the pond? You want us to let you go? Just like that?"

This was picked up by another cry. "Look at the vampire! Look! That's supposed to be a boy! One of Dracula's sisters claimed him without our vote!"

A roar of outrage erupted from all sides.

"He said back to the pond!—They're planning an escape!—She bit him, I heard it from Don Quixote, he saw it with his *very* eyes—Seize them! Seize them at once!— Have we waited for nothing? Who says we need to vote?— Grab them while you can! Get the fat one!—No, that one, the girl, get the girl—" They leapt from their seats.

"Sit down!" screamed the queen.

No one paid her any attention. They hustled and elbowed and pushed, hemming the children in a rapidly shrinking circle. Faces snarled at them. Wings spread. Tails twitched. Teeth clicked.

"Quiet!" thundered the Snow Queen and unleashed a wind of such force it froze everyone solid.

In the sudden silence someone banged on the glass. One of the windows shattered, and in poked the beak of Hinbad.

"You forgot about us, huh?" he said, regarding the scene with one curious orange eye.

The window next to him imploded. "Congratulations," said Haroun, trying to squeeze in his whole head. "Mad Tome is waking, in case you didn't know."

The third window broke. It was Hossain. "Dude. You people are too loud." He stared at the frost-covered badlings, then at the Snow Queen. "Awesome trick! That's a cool way to make them shut up."

The queen heaved, worn out by her effort.

"Anyway," continued Hinbad. "Did you vote yet?" He passed his eyes over the figures until he spotted Bells. "I claim that one. She's clever."

"You?" Haroun screeched in shock. "No way! *I'm* getting her."

Hossain pecked him. "Didn't you say Mad Tome is waking? We better get out of here before it gets really angry."

As if to confirm the accuracy of his prediction, the ground shuddered, shaking the whole abbey, which had a thawing effect on all within. There was a pause, an intake of air, and then a crunch and a crackle of splintering ice and stretching limbs and flexing joints, and in the next minute the mayhem erupted anew.

"So, like, we can give you a lift," screeched Haroun.

"But not to everyone at once!" clarified Hossain. "First come, first served. That cool?"

They were met with a squall of terror. Sofas were overturned, ottomans were tipped, settees, divans, commodes were pushed aside to make way for the frenzied mob. Some badlings dashed for the doors, others for the windows, yet others went for the children, reaching at them with anything that was sharp: talons, teeth, daggers, claws, and even a hairpin in Alice's trembling hand.

Before any of them inflicted damage, a low rumble

rolled through the sky, an amplified sound of yawning and stretching, and then from below a rattle of chains, a slam of a door, and an ominous beating of wings.

The light dimmed. Darkness oozed into the room, and with it, freed from the dungeon prison by the faithful ghost of Blackey, Dracula flew in and alighted next to the children, sweeping his competitors off their feet.

"You're mine," he told them, "*mine*. I claim you all." His bat-like face twisted in a snarl of triumph.

"You don't need to claim us. We can destroy Mad Tome together!" cried Bells. "You said you're tired of being here. Don't you want to get home?"

"Let that not concern you, Belladonna Monterey." Dracula's eyes flashed red. "You'll learn to love your new life, just like I learned to love it before you." He bared his fangs.

"Bells!" screamed Rusty. "Behind you!"

She ducked.

Dracula's jaws closed on nothing. He reached for Bells just as the Snow Queen smote him with a powerful blow. She grabbed Bells by the arm. "You're *mine!* I found you first! You landed on *my* page!"

But Dracula was not to be outdone. He grasped the queen from behind and lifted her clear off the floor. A surprised expression spread over her pallid features. She released her hold on Bells, and next she was hurtling out of the room through one of the broken windows.

Dracula watched her fly, enjoying a moment of gratification.

It was this moment that saved our friends. They looked at one another, took big gulps of air, and bolted for the doors, running full pelt until they were out of the abbey.

Fierce wind slapped their faces. Dirt rained on their heads. The hills swarmed with panicked figures, and the sky was roiling and flashing yellow.

"Who dares to wake me?" thundered Mad Tome, its lips dark clouds, its eyes streaks of lightning.

"What do we do now?" squealed Bells.

"Where is Dracula?" wailed Peacock. "I want to go with him! Why did you drag me away?"

Grand wheezed, speaking in bursts. "This is it...we will die...this crazy book...will rip us...to pieces..."

"Over there!" Rusty pointed. "The Roc chicks! They're taking people on!"

At the end of the page lay Haroun, Hussein, and Hinbad, their wings flat on the ground, serving as ramps. The badlings climbed on top of them like a tide of insects. The first to get fully loaded, Haroun took off, flying up then parallel to the dirt wall.

Mad Tome stretched its claws with an unmistakable intent to crush the bird and everyone it carried. "You think you can escape me, you wretched badlings? Think again!" The tips of its claws snapped, missing them by the inches. Haroun screeched and swooped down, zigzagging, until at last he reached the bottom of the next page. He dove under it and was gone, successfully escaping the danger.

Mad Tome roared, caught the edge of the page and ripped it, howling in pain.

"It's mad," muttered Grand.

"It's destroying *itself*," echoed Bells.

Peacock didn't share their sentiments, nor was he watching the commotion. He studied his friends with a peculiar air, as if he wanted to bite them and was deciding on who would taste better. And just as he set his eyes on Grand, Rusty interrupted him.

"Come on, guys," he shouted. "We can still make it!"

Bewildered, they sprinted forth and reached Hinbad just in time, joining a huddle of badlings already seated on his back. Hinbad screeched, flapped his wings, and soared up.

Then several unpleasant things happened in a rapid succession.

Upset at the badlings for defying its orders and hurting from a wound it brought upon itself, Mad Tome began fluttering pages, generating a windstorm and sending Hinbad into a plummeting spin.

As if that wasn't enough, Dracula came out of nowhere, snatched Peacock, and vanished out of sight.

Next, from the mass of the badlings desperately clinging to Hinbad's back, the Headless Horseman emerged and caught Grand in a headlock. "Hinbad! Let me off! It's my page!"

Hinbad screeched agreement and instead of passing under the prairie veered over it and quickly slowed down. The horseman jumped, taking Grand with him.

While Bells and Rusty stared at this, unable to help, the remaining badlings started giggling.

"We got you! We got you! We tricked the Snow Queen! We got two new badlings, the boy and the girl!" They ripped off their masks, and Bells saw with horror that what she perceived as hair was fur, and who she thought were either kids or short people were not human at all.

"Monkeys," she gasped. "Where did *they* come from?"

Chapter Twenty-One

Rusty grinned. "Hey, monkeys! How are you doing?"

The monkeys didn't appear to be in the mood to return his greeting. They curled their lips, showing sharp yellow teeth.

"Stop! I command you to stop! You're carrying my badling!" came a shout from behind. It was the Snow Queen flying in her sleigh. She was about to overtake them.

Startled, Hinbad rocked off balance and instead of skimming under the page ahead of them flew directly at it. Bells and Rusty glimpsed lots of green, and in the next second they were smashing into a carpet of leaves, flowers, and lianas.

Chapter Twenty-Two

One Monkey's Mischief

When reading a book, beware of paper cuts. Once you shed blood at the hands of a character, you become it. As you've seen, Peacock has suffered this fate already, successfully turning into one of the vampire sisters. Grand was yet to face his decapitation. As for Bells and Rusty...well.

Pursued by the speediest steeds in Mad Tome—the three horses of the Snow Queen—Hinbad was not to be outmatched.

"You try and catch me, you crazy icicle!" he screeched. "I didn't learn to fly for nothing! I can *totally* outfly you, watch me!"

Unfortunately, because Hinbad was young and giant and overconfident, he focused more on asserting himself than on where he was going. The monkeys screamed directions, trying to prevent the crash, and failed.

Rushing full speed ahead, Hinbad saw the rising page a tad too late. He careened, desperately flapping his wings, and then realized that this maneuver happened only in his head. In reality he propelled forward headlong, tore through the tent of the jungle, and slid into the rich soil the way a knife slides into butter. His whole body quivered from the impact. The monkeys rained off his back, scattering into trees. And Bells and Rusty somersaulted into a cluster of flowers that stunk like decomposing corpses.

There was a silence that follows big explosions, then it erupted with noises.

Bells sat up, dizzy. She brushed off leaves and twigs and gawked around.

The jungle seethed with life. Insects buzzed. Birds shrieked. Everything pulsed and dripped and wobbled. There were no visible paths leading anywhere. Tree branches curled like outstretched fingers aiming to snag her hair. Flowers emitted a nauseating odor. And when she moved, the ground squelched, reluctant to let her go.

"Are you okay?" she asked Rusty, her nimble fingers redoing the ponytail.

"I'm fine," he said, his head down. "You?"

"I think so." She patted herself, failing to notice a peculiar tone to his voice. "Nothing is broken. And we're alive, which is a good thing. But these flowers stink, which is a bad thing." She waited for him to comment or at least to snigger.

He did neither.

"What's wrong, Rusty?"

He looked up, a hand on his cheek.

"What happened to your face?"

"Nothing."

Bells frowned. "Let me see."

"It's nothing, really." Rusty backed away, but Bells was faster. She peeled off his fingers and gasped. A shallow gush ran from his eye to his chin in a jagged scarlet line.

"It's cool, man. You don't need to worry. I cut myself when we fell. On a...on a stick! Right there." He vaguely pointed beyond the flowers and gave her a weak smile.

Bells' eyes widened. "They scratched you."

"Who?"

"The monkeys!"

"No, they didn't."

"You're such a bad liar. It doesn't look like a cut, it looks like a scratch and it looks bad, Rusty. You're bleeding. You're—" she stopped herself, turning cold.

"What?"

Their eyes met.

"What's happening?"

"Listen," she said quickly, "just...stay calm, okay? Stay calm."

"Why?" Rusty cried. "What's the matter?"

Bells stated as evenly as she could, "You're changing into a monkey."

"No." Rusty clasped his face. Soft fur sprouted under his fingers. "No!" he shrieked and jumped to his feet.

"Don't freak out, please. We'll find a way to fix this!" But as she said it, Bells wasn't so sure. She couldn't take her eyes away from Rusty's back where a tail unfolded in a loop. His face darkened to black leather, as did his hands, the rest was overtaken by grey fur.

"It's that monkey," he said, "the one that sat next to me, it scratched me when we started falling!"

A terrible thought struck Bells. She quickly looked over her arms, her legs, then felt her face. "Did it scratch me too? Rusty, tell me, do you see any cuts?"

But Rusty succumbed to panic.

"This is awful!" he shrieked. "Pinch me, I'm dreaming! I want to wake up! Grandma! Grandma, get me out of here!" And he took off.

"Rusty, wait!" Bells dashed after him.

It was useless. Carried forth by his new monkey's

agility, Rusty expertly hopped from tree to tree and soon disappeared.

Bells ran a bit more then stopped, blocked by an impassable tangle of vegetation. "That's just great," she muttered. "Why did you have to run, Rusty? How am I going to get through *this*?"

She peered at the liana that hung down like a green twisting snake, pondering if she should climb it, when a loud noise made her jump and wheel around.

Something smashed into the jungle, something heavy. Then something snorted, and something crunched.

It was the crunch of *snow*.

A gust of wind chilled the humid air. Bells' skin erupted in goosebumps.

"The Snow Queen," she whispered.

"Bells, look!" came a call from above. "I can climb trees like a monkey!" Rusty didn't resemble himself anymore, save for his tattered clothes. He wrapped his tail around a liana and whizzed down.

"Careful!" cried Bells. "You'll fall like that."

"No, I won't. This is fun!" He scratched his head. "Want to try? I can teach you. It's easy."

"Listen to me," said Bells desperately. "We can't climb trees right now."

Rusty's face wrinkled. "Why not?"

"Because we need to find Grand! And Peacock! And—" she broke off. "Don't you remember?"

"Remember what?" Rusty caught something in his fur and studied it, then quickly put it in his mouth.

"Rusty! Eww! You're not a monkey, you're a *boy*! We're in Mad Tome. A monkey has scratched you and you replaced it, don't you understand? And the Snow Queen just got here. She's after me. We need to find Grand and Peacock and get back to the duck pond."

Rusty blinked. "The duck pond?"

"Do you want to stay a monkey forever?" asked Bells.

"Totally! Look what I can do!" He scaled the nearest trunk and swung down from a liana, only to climb back up for another go, an amused expression on his leathery face.

Bells clutched her forehead. "You don't change, Rusty, monkey or not." Her words rang out uncomfortably loud. The jungle was silent. "Rusty?" She had a feeling of eyes on her, many pairs of eyes looking down from the canopy of leaves.

"Rusty!"

The branches shook and groaned. Scores of furry arms reached for Rusty at once and grabbed him, stopping his mouth. He struggled, mutely staring at Bells. Dozens of wrinkly faces exactly like his started giggling. It was the monkeys.

One of them picked off a large nut and threw it at Bells. She cowered. More nuts pelted the ground like huge hailstones.

"Get her! Get her!" they screamed, hooting and ululating.

"Rusty!" called Bells. "Don't give in! Fight them! You have to—Ow!" A nut struck her elbow, hitting a nerve.

"There you are, badling *girl*." The Snow Queen stepped out from behind the tree. Her mouth twisted in the smugness of a predator that has at last cornered its prey. Steam rose from her, and every plant she touched immediately frosted over.

The monkeys issued a squeal of terror, dropped the

rest of the nuts and fled, Rusty trapped in their midst. The sounds of them tearing through the jungle quickly faded.

Bells stood quiet, massaging her elbow and searching for a way to escape. Behind her was an impenetrable thicket of vegetation. To her left and to her right rose trees that only monkeys could climb, the gaps between them tangled up with lianas. The only exit from this nightmare was up ahead and it was blocked by the queen.

"Poor badling," she cooed sweetly, advancing. "You look so tired, so dirty, so bruised."

Bells drew back and stepped on something slimy. It protested by releasing an odor of rotting flesh. It was a cluster of flowers, the same kind she and Rusty encountered upon their rather unpleasant landing in the jungle.

She dashed around it.

"What's your hurry?" cajoled the queen. "Come. I'll clean your face. I'll give you my cloak. It will shield you from this insufferable heat." Her exhale froze the flowers into an icicle bouquet. The good outcome of this was, they stopped stinking. The bad outcome was, they crumbled under the queen's shoe, the last barrier between her and Bells.

I'm doomed, thought Bells. *This is it, I'm doomed.*

She imagined herself as the Snow Queen, sitting on an icy throne, arranging and rearranging crystals into sparkling mosaics.

This is horrible. I'll die from boredom!

The queen was beside her.

"Wait!" cried Bells. "You're just a girl like me. Don't do this. You want to get home, right? I can help you. Let me go and I'll walk up the dirt wall and get out at the pond and tear Mad Tome in half. I promise. And then you can go *home*! See your mom..." Bells faltered. For some reason it was the wrong thing to say.

The Snow Queen hissed, steam clouding her face. "Home? I don't want to go home. I'm better off here." And with a greedy glint in her eyes, she doffed her icy crown and took a swipe at Bells, missing her by an inch. Bells staggered. Her foot snagged on a root and she fell. The queen smiled, the crown poised in her hand like a knife. "Say goodbye to life as you know it, Belladonna." And she slashed her.

Bells focused on the sharp tip, waiting for the pain. But it didn't come. The crown swiftly moved away without touching her. The Snow Queen hiccupped. A puzzled expression spread over her features. She rose and hung in the air, swinging left and right.

"Humph uh uphm uhm mumph?" screeched a familiar voice.

Bells squinted. "Hinbad?"

The Roc chick towered over the clearing, the Snow Queen swaying in his beak. He spit her out and watched her tumble with one amused orange eye. "I said, is she giving you trouble? We were supposed to vote and stuff, like who gets what new badling and—hey, icicle lady, you're not going anywhere."

The queen was stealthily crawling behind a growth of ferns. Hinbad snapped her by the cloak, shook her like a poisonous snake, and flung her into the emerald distance.

They listened.

There was a cry, a snap, a thump, and blissful silence.

"That's better," concluded Hinbad, prancing to Bells. The ground shook under his weight. "That felt so good. I wanted to do it for such a long time."

"Thank you, Hinbad," squeaked Bells.

He fastened an eye on her. "You're welcome. I like you. You'll make a great Roc chick."

"I will?"

"Don't you want to fly?" He looked up. "There she goes."

The Snow Queen's sleigh burst out of the jungle and hastily swished out of sight.

"I have a feeling she'll be back," said Bells.

"Do you want to fly, then?" Hinbad lowered his head level with hers.

She gulped. "Do I...have to decide right now?"

"What's there to decide?" asked Hinbad, puzzled. "Flying is the best thing in the world. Haroun and Hossain will be so jealous that I claimed you." He made a grating noise that resembled a chuckle.

"Can I find my friends first?" implored Bells. "I'd like to say goodbye to them," she measured her words carefully, "like you'd want to say goodbye to your brothers if you were to leave them forever."

Haroun blinked. "Why would I want to say goodbye to them? They'd never say goodbye to *me*." He screeched in agitation.

"Sorry, that's not what I meant," stammered Bells. "I just want to see them one more time to...to tell them that I'm going to be a Roc chick and that I'll be flying so they'll be jealous of me because they can't fly and I can!" She forced a smile.

"Sure!" Hinbad nodded happily. "I'll claim you right away so you can fly up to them and show off. Wouldn't that make them choke with envy?" He lowered his voice. "So, like, I'm not supposed to do this, Haroun and Hossain told me to wait for them, but they're not here to stop me, are they? It'll be a great surprise for them, wouldn't it?"

"Well..." Bells twisted her ponytail, "if I replace you now, my friends won't recognize me. They'll think I'm you and run away from me screaming."

"Huh," said Hinbad, jabbing his beak at something squirming in the grass, tossing it up and gulping it so fast, Bells failed to see what it was, but she thought it looked like a fat anaconda perfectly capable of swallowing an eleven-year-old girl whole, and her stomach rolled over itself.

Hinbad belched. "You're clever," he continued, nonplussed. "I didn't think about that."

"You can always claim me later," said Bells hopefully. "Could you maybe take me to them? You're so powerful, so big, your flight is so smooth and speedy. I bet you fly faster than your brothers." She watched the effect of her words take hold.

"I *totally* am." Hinbad unfolded his wings, uprooting a couple trees in the process. "I am *the fastest*. Mother told me I'd never fly as well as Hossain, but I'm better than him. I'm better than both of them."

"You are," Bells lauded. "You're graceful and swift. May I once more experience the pleasure of traveling with such a capable flyer?"

"You may!" screeched Hinbad. "Get on. I'll take you to the Monkey City."

"The Monkey City?" repeated Bells. "That sounds familiar. What book is that from?"

"*The Jungle Book!*"

"I should've guessed," she looked around. "Now it

makes sense."

"Did you read it?" asked Hinbad.

Bells blushed. "No, but I watched the movie."

"You should read it. It's a great book. Getting on?"

"Er." Bells glanced up. "You sure it's safe to go? I mean, isn't Mad Tome looking for us?"

"Nah, it's napping," said Hinbad with confidence. "It tired itself out with that tantrum. It always does."

"How do you know?"

"Can't you hear it?"

Bells listened.

Sure enough, underneath the din of the jungle ran a hum, a rustling snore that could be mistaken for the murmur of leaves.

"So that's how you can tell—"

"We have to go, though," interrupted Hinbad. "Before my brothers find me." Evidently he was more terrified of his brothers' wrath than that of Mad Tome. He flattened a wing. Bells climbed on his back and they took off, soaring above the sea of trees that shifted and rippled like green water, with splashes of color erupting here and there in the shapes of startled tropical birds.

Chapter Twenty-Three

The Queen's Betrayal

It's unfair that it's easier to destroy a book than it is to write it. Imagine how long it would take you to meticulously craft every sentence, every paragraph, every chapter, then print it all out and bind it into a book. Now imagine how fast you can shred that book and toss the scraps out the window. If only it were that easy with Mad Tome.

"Hinbad!" called Bells over the wind. "If we rip Mad Tome, will that change my friends back?"

"Huh?" he screeched. "I can't hear you!"

"It's okay!" cried Bells. "It's nothing. Just talking to myself." She banged her head on his back. "I hate this. Scientifically speaking, nothing makes any sense. Non-scientifically speaking, nothing makes any sense either. My brain will explode." She took a deep breath and lapsed into intensive thinking.

Okay, let's examine our options. If we destroy Mad Tome, will it make Rusty less of a monkey and Peacock less of a vampire? In other words, will it turn them back into themselves? I believe there are two possible outcomes.

Outcome one: our theory about Mad Tome being a typical villain whose powers disappear once it's dead is right. That means when it's gone, every single badling, including Rusty and Peacock, will return home the way they were before.

Outcome two: our theory about Mad Tome being a

typical villain is wrong, in which case if we destroy it Rusty and Peacock will turn into ghosts, as will all the other badlings. This means that we can't damage it in any way. Not that we can—it's too big—unless we walk out of here to the duck pond, or the ducks for some reason decide to rip it, like Grand said. Oh, I wish he were here! I hope that headless idiot hasn't done anything horrible to him.

She shuddered at the thought.

At least I know where he is, and I know where Peacock is, and I'm about to see Rusty.

Bells sighed.

Okay, back to the facts. Or, one fact, really. Assuming that most of the badlings—not counting the real characters or the Snow Queen—want us to destroy Mad Tome, what is the validity of outcome two? It's null. Why? Because according to outcome two, that would destroy them as well. However, because they want us to destroy it, it points to the validity of outcome one. Which means that we must destroy Mad Tome, because once we do, everything will return back to how it was before.

Satisfied, she closed her eyes and leaned into the wind.

Hinbad started slowing down.

The jungle had come to an end. In front of them lay the ruins of an ancient Indian city. Fragments of crumbling walls jutted out like broken teeth. Every surface, every outcrop and shelf teemed with monkeys. They saw the descending bird and hooted. The Roc chick touched the ground. The shock of landing jolted Bells, and she slid off his back a bit faster than intended. A jostle of furry bodies crept to her with an obvious intent.

"Hello, monkeys!" she tried. "Have you seen my

friend Rusty?"

They grunted, tightening their rows.

"You took him here. I saw it. Rusty, can you hear me?"

More grunting, angrier this time.

"Okay, that didn't work." Bells groped in her mind for the right thing to say, realizing that *that's* what she should've thought about, not the obliteration of Mad Tome. It looked like she might be obliterated herself. Then an idea struck her.

"Listen, you're not monkeys, you're children," she said hoarsely. "I know you want to get home, at least I think most of you do." She passed her eyes over them.

They halted, their leathery faces puzzled.

"If you shed my blood, then only one of you gets to escape—which is not even a real escape because you'll have to stay in Mad Tome. But if you help me find my friends and let us go back to the pond, we'll get rid of Mad Tome and then *all* of you can escape. You can all go home!"

The monkeys scratched their heads, apparently thinking.

"You're not who you think you are," added Bells.

This was greeted with confused looks.

Bells let out an exasperated sigh and looked up at Hinbad for help. "Do you remember who you were before you got here?"

"Huh?" he blinked his orange eyes.

"What's your real name?"

Hinbad's talons clawed at the ground. "I don't remember," he screeched, scaring the monkeys off. They scattered into the ruins, immediately poking out their heads and creeping back.

A globe of water rolled out of Hinbad's eye and splashed on the stones.

Bells flinched, startled.

"All I ever wanted was to fly," said Hinbad miserably. "That's the only thing I remember." He spread his wings, scattering the monkeys again.

"I'm...I'm sorry." Bells patted his leg.

"Please, don't tell my brothers I told you. They'll kill me. We're not supposed to tell new badlings who we really are."

"They're not your real brothers, are they?"

Hinbad opened his beak to answer.

"Shut up! Shut up! Shut up!" screamed the monkeys and swarmed him in a moving groping blanket.

"Get off me, fuzzy bugs!" He shook like a wet dog.

"Stop! You're ruining your only chance!" cried Bells, retreating. "Remember! You're not—"

A monkey leapt at her. "I got her! I got her!"

Bells dodged it and bumped into another one. "No, you didn't! *I* did!" Two more monkeys pushed through and made a grab for her. She fell, rolling into a ball. They raised their hands to scratch her just as Hinbad smote them.

"You're not getting her, she's *mine*," he screeched. "She said I could claim her. You said I could." He regarded Bells hopefully.

"Yes," she panted, quickly touching her face, her arms, and her legs. There wasn't a single cut. "Let's look for Rusty." She encircled Hinbad's leg, clinging to it like to a tree.

He obediently nodded, passed the crumbling walls and stepped onto a plaza overgrown with creepers. At the end of it sat the remnants of a once magnificent palace. The few pillars that didn't collapse jutted out like bony fingers. The floor plates were cracked, torn apart by roots. And in the shimmering haze beyond stretched a tangle of streets lined with ramshackle abandoned houses.

"A king used to live here," screeched Hinbad. "He kept his elephants here. Mother liked to hunt them."

"Don't you feel sorry for them?" asked Bells. "Poor elephants."

"You wait," Hinbad cheered. "When you become a Roc chick, you'll like them. They taste like snakes, only a bit more chewy and with five ends."

Bells gulped. "Er, okay. Rusty!" she called.

"Rusty!" picked up Hinbad. "Hey, fur balls, go find him for us, will you?"

The monkeys stole up to them in a grumbling mob. "We are strong and tricky and smart!" they shouted, the air around them crackling with threat.

"I'll squash you like bugs!" warned Hinbad.

The monkeys eased off, but only for a moment. "We are wicked and free and bright!"

"Rusty!" called Bells. "Rusty, where are you?"

"We're the best people in all the jungle!" screamed the monkeys.

Bells drew in a lungful of air. "Rusty!" she yelled.

"Here!" came a feeble cry from one of the houses. "I'm here, Bells! I'm okay! I'd get out but they won't let me!" Rusty's head appeared in a window. Two monkeys smacked him, pushing him down.

"You dumb pinheads!" shouted Bells. "Let him go!"

"She called us dumb! She called us dumb!" Scores of them rushed at Hinbad. He shook like a wet dog, and they fled tails high, squeaking.

A gust of wind blew from above.

Hinbad looked up. "Haroun? Hossain?"

The Roc chicks flapped their massive wings, staring down amusedly at the strange congregation.

"Dude, you cheated," said Haroun smugly, alighting next to his brother. The force of his descent sent the monkeys rolling.

"Yeah," echoed Hossain. "You were supposed to wait for us."

Hinbad didn't get a chance to reply.

A freezing squall hit the plaza. Enveloped in a glittering cloud, the Snow Queen's sleigh arced through the sky and landed with a terrific thump. Summer died, strangled by winter. The strip of jungle around the Monkey City, so green a moment ago, was now white. The queen rose, surveyed her handiwork and, satisfied, swiftly stepped down.

"I call to your attention!" she proclaimed.

The monkeys quieted.

"I came here to complete our task that was so rudely interrupted. Three out of the four new badlings have been claimed without our collective vote."

There were grunts of protest.

The queen nodded. "I'm as upset as you are, rest assured. That's why I'm here. You know you can rely on me to do my duty. I decree that the last new badling must be claimed correctly, according to our agreed upon procedure. I'm going to propose the most deserving candidate, and we will vote." She gave Bells an icy stare. "The candidate to claim the badling girl is—"

"I've something important to say," announced Bells loudly, her blood boiling. She let go of Hinbad's leg and braced herself: all heads turned in her direction. "I think everyone here deserves to know that the Snow Queen tried cutting me with her crown to claim me *without* your vote."

A murmur passed through the plaza.

The queen narrowed her eyes. "This is an outrageous lie."

"No, it's not!" screeched Hinbad. "I saw you corner her in the jungle. I saved her. *I* get to claim her, not you!" He looked over the assembly. "Why are we listening to this crazy icicle anyway? I'm throwing her out."

Hossain blocked his way. "Chill, brother."

Hinbad gawked. "You're with her?"

"Dude, come on," said Haroun, "you broke the rules."

The monkeys knuckled closer to the Roc chicks, chattering excitedly, and a couple of them shrieked. "He broke the rules! He broke the rules! Did you hear that? He broke the—"

"Silence!" commanded the queen. "You'll do as I say, you bunch of selfish brutes. Bring her over."

Before Bells could understand what was happening, a throng of furry arms gripped her and dragged her to the Snow Queen.

"It was so naïve of you to think you could escape your punishment," she began. "None of us have *ever* escaped it, and neither will you. There's nothing special about you, Belladonna Monterey, to warrant an exemption."

Shouts of support erupted from the crowd.

"This will teach you how to read books to the end."

"Teach her! Teach her!" chanted the monkeys.

The queen drew herself up, standing impossibly tall.

"It was *my* book you kicked aside, *my* story you didn't finish reading, *my* page you landed on. It is *I* who deserves to claim you. I and no other. Vote!"

A pandemonium ensued. Half of the monkeys cried, "The Snow Queen! The Snow Queen! Vote for the Snow Queen!" Another half cried, "Make her a monkey! Make her a monkey!"

"She said *I* could claim her," screeched Hinbad.

"Dude, she doesn't get to decide!" objected Haroun.

The air between them crackled with spite, and the pandemonium around them escalated to the raging bedlam.

Fights broke out. Bits of fur flew up in grey clumps. Fists collided, faces snarled. The Roc chicks pecked at each other. The horses struggled against the harness, kicking and neighing. The clamor rose to a deafening roar, and the monkeys who held Bells let go, swept up by the frenzy. The Snow Queen seized her in an iron grip, a victorious gleam in her eyes.

"Any last words?" she asked.

Bells shook. She was mad, mad at the Snow Queen, at the monkeys, at the Roc chicks, at all the badlings, at her friends, mad at the whole world. She had nowhere to retreat, nowhere to run. She couldn't just grab her bike and take off like she always did, and she suddenly thought of her mother. *Come back this instant!* were her last words.

Bells looked at the queen. "Was it your mom?"

The queen stiffened. "What?"

"Was she mean to you? Your mother? Is that why you don't want to go home?"

There was a flicker of fear in the queen's eyes. It quickly faded. "What's this nonsense you're saying?" she spat.

"It was your mother, wasn't it," pressed Bells. "She was calling you names. She didn't approve of you, didn't approve of whom you wanted to be, so you decided to run away to teach her a lesson."

The queen recoiled, hands over her eyes. She appeared to have started melting. Her cloak glistened with droplets of water, and the crown slipped off her head, dissolving as it went. She looked so pitiful that Bells regretted her words.

"I'm sorry," she squeaked, "I didn't mean to—"

The Snow Queen shuddered as if recalling a memory. "You're a cruel, cruel child," she said coldly, "you don't deserve my beautiful palace. I changed my mind. I don't want you." And with these words she snatched the closest monkey and cut its cheek with her long sharp nails.

There was a second of vacuous silence. Then the monkey cried a terrible scream of pain, a scream of a child, a child who has been betrayed, and all at once the badlings stopped their quarrels, staring at the queen, stunned at her unspeakable treachery.

Hinbad recovered first. His orange eyes blazed red. "How could you?" he screeched. "How could you claim one of our own?"

"I'm not going back, I'm *not!*" shrieked the queen, hopping into her sleigh. Hinbad was upon her, tearing at her cloak. White flakes fluttered up and met those falling from the sky. Only it wasn't snow.

Bells caught one of them. "Paper." Now she could hear it. The crackling noises mingled with raspy wails of doom. "Mad Tome," she said, "it's Mad Tome. Something is shredding it to pieces."

Chapter Twenty-Four

The Unrivaled Curiosity of Ducks

When your friends are in peril, and you yourself are in peril, and even the villain you have to conquer is in peril, what do you do? You show peril that you mean business.

Bells set her teeth.

I need to get out of here, she thought. *I need to end this ridiculous charade that I have started in the first place. I'll need to go alone, because looking for Rusty in this mess is useless, and looking for Grand and Peacock is out of the question.*

She surveyed the plaza for a way to the dirt wall.

It failed to present itself. Instead, an ear-splitting crack assaulted her ears. Pieces of pages rained down, some as big as birds. The Monkey City swarmed with badlings, characters, and ghosts. They were falling from above, no, they were *pouring*, blotting out the light and shaking the sky with their cries.

"Hinbad!" called Bells. He stopped pecking at the queen, his attention diverted by the mayhem. "I need you to fly me to the duck pond. Can you do that?" She marched up to him and knocked on his leg.

"Huh? Fly *where?*" He hopped to the side, just in time to dodge a windmill that crashed with a tremendous rumble.

A spray of dust hit Bells in the face. She coughed,

groping around. "We need to go *now*! Please!"

"Help! Help!" screamed the monkeys, clinging to Hinbad. He shook them off. "Haroun! Hossain! Where are you?" His screech drowned in the mournful wail of ghosts. "It's killing us...stop it...stop it..." Their cloudy shapes drifted to and fro, desperate, helpless. The Snow Queen's horses panicked and broke off from the sleigh. The queen herself was nowhere to be seen. And above it all Mad Tome raved and raged and writhed, its cries of woe a terrible solo against the background of anguished screaming.

"Ohhh, they hurt me so," it moaned. "Ohhh, why do they hurt me..." It hacked and slashed blindly, grabbing at anything and everything that moved. One of its claws got stuck in a tangle of lianas. It jerked, and the page tilted sharply, tossing everyone into a jumble.

Bells felt her feet detach from the ground when a reckless idea struck her. It was the best she could come up with, considering the unfortunate circumstances. She leapt for the claw, and as it freed itself, she snatched it.

Mad Tome peered at her with bleary tear-stained eyes. "Alice, is that you?"

Bells dug her nails into the hard leathery surface, afraid to say anything and give herself out. Her heart hammered. Her ears rang. She swooned, almost falling off.

I won't faint, I won't faint. I won't faint!

"Alice, it's as you said," wailed Mad Tome. "They have betrayed me. After everything I've done for them, after I've risked my life to hunt for new badlings—as *they* asked me to, mind you—they turned against me. They have brought a terrible menace on me, Alice. You and Don Quixote are all I have left. Find him. Have him skewer them on his lance!"

Bells didn't dare to breathe.

"They torment me, Alice. Ohhh, they torment me so! Alice?" Mad Tome waited. "Why aren't you saying anything? Alice? Alice!"

Bells coughed to clear her throat, hoping she sounded Alicey enough. "I'm here, Mad Tome, I'm here. I came to...to see how you're doing. Are you doing okay?" It was obvious that it wasn't doing okay in the slightest, but Bells' scrambled mind failed to come up with anything better.

"You must help me chase them off!" cried Mad Tome.

"Chase whom off?"

"The ducks!"

Stunned, Bells nearly released her hold. "The *ducks?*"

"They're ripping me, Alice! They're ripping me apart!" There was pain in Mad Tome's voice, an age-old misery, as if it was no longer a malevolent villain but simply a book, a big tome of unread pages, sad and disillusioned and dying.

Bells buzzed with too many feelings at once: surprise, relief, astonishment, dread, and, strangely, giddiness, giddiness at the absurdity of it all.

"The ducks are ripping you apart?" she repeated. "The ducks at the duck pond?"

"Well, where else?"

"Are you kidding?" Bells giggled. "I can't believe it!"

"You're not Alice," rustled Mad Tome, squinting. "Who are you? Answer me, before I slash you to bits and chuck you into oblivion!"

Its face hung so close Bells could reach out and touch it. It was crumpled and torn like a discarded piece of paper: two rips for the eyes, two holes for the nose, and a huge gash for one toothless mouth, a puffy tongue lolling out of it like a strip of damp cardboard. It seemed to hold itself together by the threads, stubbornly refusing to disintegrate.

"New badling," it sneered in recognition. "You came to me yourself, how convenient. Let me show you what happens to naughty children like you, you careless foolish *girl.*"

The insult left Bells winded. She sucked in air and let it out in a hiss. "Come on, ducks. Come on. Show this pile of stupid pages—"

"What's that you're saying?"

Forgetting danger, Bells pulled herself up, propped hands on her hips, and proclaimed, "I'm saying, you're just a pile of *stupid pages.*"

"Stupid pages, am I?" said Mad Tome, amused by this display of audacity.

"No, I'm sorry. I got it wrong." Bells flipped her ponytail and stood even taller. Her worries left her. Her fears retreated under the pressure of hurt, hurt from the old stinging wound. Never in her life did she feel so offended by being dismissed as a *foolish girl*, and she was going to prove Mad Tome wrong. There was an odd clarity in her mind: she knew exactly what to say next, and nothing was going to stop her.

"You're a nasty cancerous wart on the face of literature," she delivered sharply. "You're not even a book, you're a helter-skelter mindlessly put together heap of misplaced pages that is shamelessly boasting and bragging about its grandiose importance of making children read more books by kidnapping those of us who for some reason abandoned one book or another and forcing us to suffer through bits of stories, when in fact it accomplishes nothing."

Mad Tome stared.

"I'm sorry to inform you, but what you're doing has a negative effect. Instead of compelling us to read those books, you scared us out of our minds, and we'll now avoid them like a plague." She paused. "Well, maybe not all of them. I kind of liked the Red Death story, actually."

"I'll punish you for this," hissed Mad Tome. "I'll pick the worst, the scariest, the most horrific page of all, and I'll put you there for an eternity, to make you wish you were dead. Only there will be no death for you, I'll see to that *personally*."

"Oh, really?" Bells crossed her arms. "And what page would that be?"

"A page from a horror book."

"A classic then," nodded Bells. "My favorite."

"It'll be filled with torture!" bellowed Mad Tome. "With blood! With anguish you daren't imagine! Aren't you scared?"

"Scared of whom? *You?* Pfft," Bells scoffed. "You're just a book, a tome of random pages torn out of other books. You don't even have your own story, only bits and pieces of others. That's why you're mad. You wish you were a real book, but you aren't."

"What do you know about who I am?" asked Mad Tome bitterly. "How dare you presume?"

"Look, I'm sorry if I hurt your feelings, but you kind of hurt mine," said Bells. "I admit, I don't really know who you are or how you came to existence, but does it matter? You're dying. Why won't you let us out?"

Mad Tome slumped. The bottoms of its frayed eyeholes sagged, getting wet. "I used to be a real book," it said softly, "a long, long time ago."

"You did? Which one?" asked Bells.

"*Aesop s Fables*. Children read me so often, my pages started falling out, and then one day I found myself an empty cover. I was surprised at how it made me feel. I thought I'd be angry, but I wasn't. I was happy of my misfortune; it told me that children loved me. So I set out to look for my pages, to collect them and rebind myself anew. Unfortunately, I didn't find them. They were lost, gone forever." Mad Tome paused, reminiscing.

"That's terrible," muttered Bells. "I'm sorry I said you're not a real book."

It didn't hear her, gripped by the presence of memories. "But I found other pages," it said grimly, "pages that children left unread, that fell out from sorrow and were dying. I started gathering them, first a handful, then more and more. It was hard to stop, hard to feel empty again. And there were so many, *so many*! How could I not do it? The sheer amount of them baffled me, then angered me, then enraged me. I swore I'd find every child who did this and deliver a punishment, a punishment they deserved." Mad Tome smiled cruelly. "I decided to make them read until they were sick, until they begged for forgiveness, and I called them *badlings*, for the atrocious, horrible things they did to books." It leered at Bells.

The words were out of her mouth before she could stop them. "But you weren't satisfied with that, were you? It wasn't enough. You wanted to hurt them more. So you made them replace the real characters, but that wasn't enough either. You started killing them, turning them into ghosts, and snatching more pages and more badlings, until you became so bloated, you nearly burst and that's when you went mad. It's *you* who deserves to die, not us. Let us go!"

Mad Tome cackled. "Just like that? Let you go?"

"Yes! Because if you won't..." Bells frantically groped for an appropriate threat.

"Because if I won't?" nudged Mad Tome.

"The ducks will kill you anyway!"

A peal of hysterical laughter racked the book, and Bells lost her footing, falling to hands and knees.

"The ducks!" shrieked Mad Tome. "The ducks have found worms and waddled off. No one will stop me from ending you, you negligent brat. You're all the same. You grab a book, flip through it and toss it, like it's an ugly toy. You upset its characters. When another child picks it up, they can't perform. They make mistakes and stumble, and guess what happens. The child sets the book aside and becomes a badling." Rage twisted Mad Tome's mouth. "Be gone, all of you. Be gone!" It raised its claw to obliterate Bells.

Alas, it was wrong about the ducks. They didn't waddle off, they were merely contemplating.

Mad Tome's face suddenly twitched, then cracked, and then, with a final tug, tore in half.

The ducks tilted their heads, disappointed. The thick leathery thing that lay at their feet sure smelled like doughnuts but for some reason didn't have any doughnuts in it.

They had pulled it out of dirt not too long ago, lured by the sweet smell of crumbs that Grand left behind. At first they pecked at the paper until it turned to mush, then they went for the binding. Ducks are not particularly intelligent, but they're stubborn, and this wiggling brown thing kept their interest, promising edible delight. What if it was a huge flattened worm?

Two ducks clamped their beaks on the opposite ends of the thing and gave it a hearty shove. When it attempted to crawl away, they dragged it to the pond and dunked it into water. If ducks ever feel proud of themselves, this was the moment. They puffed out their chests.

The thing squirmed, making itself look highly appetizing. All it took was another pull. Mad Tome's ancient casing, already soggy from sitting in the dirt and now completely soaked, couldn't withstand the abuse. It gave and fell apart.

The ducks blinked at it, confused.

At first nothing happened, then the water started rippling. Where the scraps of Mad Tome floated, children emerged. First a couple, then a dozen, then the entire surface of the pond bubbled like boiling stew, birthing forth coughing, dripping badlings.

The ducks quacked in alarm and rushed to the shore where they huddled into a frightened flock on yellow maple leaves, next to a pile of four bikes carelessly tossed one on top of another.

Chapter Twenty-Five

On the Importance of Doughnuts

The smallest kindnesses (or follies) can bring about the biggest fortunes (or disasters). If Grand didn't feed doughnuts to the ducks, they wouldn't have followed the trail of crumbs, found and destroyed Mad Tome, accidentally releasing the badlings. And if Bells didn't stop reading *The Snow Queen* to Sofia, or if Peacock didn't rip *Dracula*, none of this would've happened.

Only it did.

And it wasn't over yet.

Bells sat stock-still in the shallow end of the pond. She was submerged to her waist, although she hardly registered this fact and the fact that the water was cold and the air was crisp—the air of a September morning. To her left was a tall skinny boy and to her right a petite girl, both staring ahead with vacant expressions.

Behind the boy sat Grand. "Um. Is this our duck pond?" He stirred up the water, gazing at the leaflets of duckweed floating in circles.

"Holy buckets," croaked Peacock a few children away. "I'm *back*." He absently raked his hair and stopped, frozen, then pulled a few strands down, looking at them cross-eyed. "My hair, it's my hair, my blue hair." He felt his teeth. "I'm not *her* anymore."

"Guys! Guys! We made it! We're *out*!" Rusty

energetically sloshed over. His voice jolted Bells from her stupor.

"Rusty!" she cried, standing up. "You're not a monkey anymore!"

"I know! I kind of miss it, though."

"Can this be true? Did the ducks really do it?" She rubbed her eyes, to make sure the pond stayed in place. It did. It wasn't in a hurry to vanish.

"Look at all the badlings." Rusty swept his eyes over the kids. "Hey, guys. Cheer up. Mad Tome is gone!"

They didn't react, silent and still. The sight of them was unnerving, even spooky. At least a hundred of them sat along the shore, their faces blank, their reflections quivering in the pockets of dark water. Where it was deeper, more of them bobbed up and down, only their heads showing, their bodies submerged.

Rusty shivered, then immediately found a new reason to be giddy. "Grand! Peacock!" He waved at them. "Man, I thought I'd never see your face again."

Elated at this bit of news, Bells quickly glanced at Peacock to make sure he was back to himself. Assured that he was, she demonstratively turned away, still miffed at him for implying that she stinks and for wanting to leave them at the last second.

She wrung out her ponytail and plodded over to Grand. "Hey, it worked. Just like you said it would. The ducks did it. I can't believe it. Can you believe it?"

"I guess." He stood. Rivers of water cascaded off his shoulders. He wiped his face and nodded at the motionless children. "I don't like this."

"Yeah, something is wrong," agreed Bells. "They're acting really weird." She looked back at the petite girl who sat still, ominously silent. "Let's get out of here. The water is freezing."

They clambered onto the shore. A piece of something dark lay half-buried in the dirt. Bells stooped to pick it up. It was a scrap of leather, flimsy and wet, patches of mushy cardboard stuck to it. She turned it over. What remained of ornate letters, shallow depressions once filled with golden paint but now empty, spelled two words.

"*Aesop's Fables*," she read. "It didn't lie to me after all."

"What's that? What did you find?" Rusty ran up to her.

Peacock trudged behind him. "Did you find another book?"

"No," said Bells, "I found what's left of Mad Tome." She gave it to Grand.

He traced the letters with his finger. "Um...I thought it didn't have a name."

"It did. It was an actual book. It told me just before it died," explained Bells. "It said children read it so many times, it had lost all of its pages so it started looking for them but couldn't find them. Instead it found pages from other books, the ones that the badlings didn't finish reading."

"It *told* you?" said Peacock.

Bells didn't answer.

"Man, that's insane. We were *inside* this thing." Rusty scratched his head. "I still have urges to climb things, you know?" He seized up the maple.

Bells rolled her eyes. "You always had those urges, Rusty."

"I sure don't miss being a vampire," said Peacock to

Bells, his tone demanding a reply. She was about to say something, when Grand tapped on her shoulder.

Beside them emerged the petite girl, that same girl who sat next to Bells. She had pale blue eyes and two braids the color of linen. She couldn't have been older than ten, maybe pushing eleven. Her small frame was clad in an old-fashioned frock adorned with ribbons that dripped dirty water. Her lips had a bluish tinge, but she didn't shiver.

"Hello," said Grand uncertainly.

"You," she pressed a contemptuous finger to his chest. "It was your idea." She shifted her eyes to Bells. "I *told* you I didn't want to come back. Are you deaf, or dumb, or both?" She glared at her.

The children in the pond began stirring. One by one they slid out, hemming Bells and the boys in a gloomy resolute circle. Their steps produced rhythmic squelching, and their faces exuded spite.

"Did you hear what I said?" demanded the girl.

Stunned by this rudeness, Bells blinked at her mutely.

"What a dummy. Stupid like these stupid ducks." The girl picked up a rock and threw it at the maple, causing the birds to scatter.

Bells watched her with horror, recognizing herself in the girl, and finally recognizing the girl. "Snow Queen?"

"Thank goodness, you're not as dumb as I thought," declared the girl. "And I have a name, if you please."

"Of course you have a name," said Bells with mock politeness, thinking that if this little thing insulted her any more, she'd deal with her as she dealt with Sofia. "Can you tell us what it is?"

"My name is Mary," said the girl and raised her chin.

"Mary, Mary, quite contrary," recited Bells automatically.

Mary's eyes widened. "Stop it! I forbid you to tease me!"

Compelled to redeem himself, Peacock spoke up. "Listen, guys, what do you want from us? We saved you from Mad Tome, we brought you back, what else do you need? Nobody is holding you here. Go home!" His plea fell flat against silence.

Mary crossed her arms. "Did you hear him? He's sending us *home*."

The children sidled up to her. Most of them were strangers but a few looked oddly familiar, like the dollish girl with the wavy hair, or the tall boy with a long bloodless face, or the kid who stroked his chin as if it had a beard. One girl sobbed soundlessly, five more consoled her. A puny boy dressed in a suit touched his head as if unable to believe it was there. And way back someone tried to take off, flapping arms up and down like wings.

"They're all nuts," concluded Peacock, turning to Bells. "You know, cuckoo, crazy, mental?"

She sighed. "You're such a moron."

"Hey, I missed you too," he said flamboyantly, and then added, "I was worried about you."

"You? *Worried* about me?" Bells' eyebrows went up. "Did I hear you right?"

"Seriously, I'm not kidding. I have this new appreciation for girls."

Bells cocked her head to one side. "Oh, do you?"

"Yeah, it's like..." he searched for the right word. "It's like you feel all this stuff, all this worry about *everything*, and it drives you bananas. You want to talk about it, talk and talk and talk, just to get rid of it, you know?"

Bells smirked, amused. "Go on."

"Enough of this rubbish!" interrupted Mary. "Or I'll have Henry decapitate you all!" She pulled the puny boy out by the sleeve. "Tell them, Henry. Tell them you'll do it."

Henry bubbled something incoherent.

Frustrated, she pushed him back. "If you can't perform your duty when your queen asks you, Louis will do it. He's infinitely more capable than you. Louis!" She raked her eyes over the crowd, singling out the kid who stroked his chin. "Louis, do you have your ax on you?"

"Sorry," mumbled Louis.

"You left it behind?"

"What did you expect?" said the tall boy sharply. "You thought we'd crawl on our knees and do your every bidding? *Traitor*."

Mary gasped, her chin trembling. She flung herself to the ground and started sobbing. It was a well-calculated show. A group of girls rushed to her, throwing reproachful looks at the boy. He scoffed and stalked away. There was a surge of murmurs.

"I will decapitate them, my queen!" came a hoarse cry.

Mary sat up, dramatically wiping her eyes that were completely dry. "Gabriel? Do it, Gabriel! Avenge your queen!"

A wispy kid stalked out on knobbly legs, waving around what looked like an antique toy sword.

"So Don Quixote wasn't a real character either," said Bells softly and looked at Grand.

He raised his hands for peace. "Um, Gabriel? I don't think we need to do this. I already went through a decapitation, and it wasn't nice at all. The Headless Horseman sliced off my head and tied it with a twine to my hands. It felt very awkward to hold it. It vibrated like there were thoughts moving about."

Gabriel halted. "Did they, really?"

Grand nodded.

Bells went white as chalk. Her eyes were glued to Grand, or, rather, to his head.

"Very funny, Grand. You scared her," said Peacock.

"I didn't mean to. Honestly. Bells, it's okay. Don't worry. I'm fine now. It wasn't all that awful, I promise."

"Wow, man!" exclaimed Rusty. "You felt your thoughts *move*? What was it like?"

"Well, you kind of sense them buzz and flow, like..," Grand hesitated.

"Like an electric current?" offered Bells.

"Um, something like that. And when you think too much, it heats up."

"What, the *head*?" cried Rusty.

"Yeah, so when it does, you have to stop thinking, because if you don't—"

"—you think your brain will melt to sludge," finished Bells, inspired, "and you imagine it leaking out of your ears and falling to the floor with a hideous plop." She broke off, blushing.

Grand stared. "That's exactly it. How did you..."

"I just never tell you," admitted Bells, casting her eyes down. "I think about this stuff, but I don't tell you about it, because, well, I'm not supposed to think about awful bloody things like that, as a *girl*."

"Who says?" said Rusty. "It's the coolest stuff ever! Bells, you're the best *girl* I know."

Bells looked up at him. "Really?"

"Um, I think that whoever says what girls are supposed to do or not supposed to do are a bunch of slowwitted dolts, and they can all eat dirt from the duck pond," stated Grand.

"Slowwitted dolts," repeated Bells, "I like that."

"Can you tell us more?" asked Rusty. "What happens to the brain after it plops to the floor? Does it crawl away?"

"You want me to?" asked Bells breathlessly.

The boys nodded, as did Gabriel and a group of girls that assembled nearby, listening with vivid interest.

"Enough of this disgusting nonsense!" cried Mary, elbowing her way through to Bells. "Better tell us the truth about what you did. Yes, Mad Tome is gone, but why are we here? Why aren't we home like we're supposed to be?"

Bells opened her mouth, dumbstruck. "What?"

Mary spun around to face the badlings. "You see? She's playing stupid. They all are. But don't fear. I'll tell you. It's because they did it on purpose."

Her tirade produced an uneasy muttering.

"I say, they knew exactly what they were doing, and they deserve to be punished for planning and executing this atrocious crime." Mary haughtily looked at Bells and the boys. "We shall consult about your punishment. Follow me," she called to the children, "let's go where they can't hear us."

Disconcerted by this new revelation, the mob trailed after her to the opposite end of the pond.

Bells watched them depart with a bewildered

240

expression. "Did you hear that? She just accused us! She accused us of planning all this beforehand with the intent to hurt them. What a snake. I think she still believes she's the Snow Queen and can do whatever she wants. What should we do about her?"

"Why do we need to do anything?" asked Peacock. "We can just leave."

"But—" began Bells. A sneeze interrupted her.

"Exactly my point," said Peacock smugly. "You'll get sick if you stay here any longer. You're soaked! We all are."

"Peacock is right," agreed Grand. He was the only one who didn't shiver, standing still and unperturbed like a mountain.

"So you say we abandon them?" demanded Bells. "Just like that?"

"I dunno." Rusty wiped his dripping nose. "We could call the police?"

"And tell them that a bunch of kids fell out of a book?" Bells snorted. "They won't believe that for a second."

"Right," agreed Rusty.

"Don't they know their way home?" wondered Peacock.

"Seriously?" said Bells. "Did you see Mary's dress?"

"Yes," he said, taken aback by her tone. "What's a dress have to do with—"

"Boys," said Bells with feeling. "You don't notice things until they're pointed out to you, do you? Did that dress look like something girls wear now? Like something I would wear?"

"*You?* But you never wear dresses."

"Okay, fine, not me, some other girl."

"How would I know?" protested Peacock. "It looked like a normal dress to me."

"It's old, you doofus. Very old. It looked like a dress from the last century."

"Does anyone have any food?" asked Grand. A fat shameless duck nipped at his pants, clearly demanding a doughnut.

"I'm leaving," said Peacock and ambled over to the bikes.

"Wait!" called Bells. "We're not done talking yet."

He was about to deliver a biting remark but was distracted by a new occurrence.

A fight broke up among the children at the other end of the pond. There was shouting and pushing and crying. Led by the tall boy, about half of them were leaving, headed for the trail that cut through the park. Another half scattered into trees, randomly running in all directions. A handful that was left struggled against Mary and Gabriel. Mary shouted commands, her sharp little face white with fury.

"Looks like they're disputing over something," observed Bells. "I wonder what it is."

"Who cares?" Peacock saddled his bike. "Let's go. I never wanted to get home so bad in my life."

Bells stared at him.

"What? We're not responsible for them, we're not their parents."

"Don't you *worry* about them?"

Peacock started to retort then stopped, his eyes shining. "I'm a *boy*, remember? An insensitive irresponsible unfeeling boy."

"And a jerk," snapped Bells.

Chapter Twenty-Five

"And a jerk," agreed Peacock.

"Dolt. Idiot. Blockhead. Doofus! But mostly a jerk." Bells sucked in air, and added, "I'm glad you're not a girl anymore. You don't deserve it."

A corner of Peacock's mouth crept up and he said, "I'm so glad I'm not a girl anymore, you have no idea. It was awful. It wasn't just my head, my very bones were flooded with *worry*."

"Peacock!" shouted Bells, looking for something to throw at him.

He ducked, miming terror. "Don't beat me, don't beat me!"

"Hey, that's my job," Rusty sniggered.

Absorbed in this hilarious banter, neither of them noticed a change that overcame Grand. He fixedly watched the remaining children, now quiet. A nagging coldness spread over his gut.

"So you're not mad at me?" asked Peacock.

"No, I'm not mad at you," Bells assured him. "If not for you and those vampire sisters, we wouldn't have done this. It was crazy and scary and a little bit sad, but it was also amazing. Don't you agree?" She suppressed a sneeze.

"Maybe there's another book buried somewhere," said Rusty. "Want to look?"

"Rusty." Bells clasped her forehead. "I think we've had enough for the day."

"I'd do it again," said Grand slowly, his eyes on the children, "if we had time to prepare, pack sleeping bags, snacks, doughnuts..." he trailed off.

"What is it?" said Bells and froze.

The day was warm for September, the sun was high, yet an unpleasant chill crept over the grass. The water in the pond throbbed, furrowing in ripples. The ducks fled with agitated cries. And a few maple leaves seesawed to the ground like bits of ancient yellowed parchment.

The remaining children shambled toward them, only they weren't children, not anymore. Time took hold of them, time they had spent in Mad Tome. Bent and shaky, they looked like living breathing corpses. A layer of fog paved their way, swirling in tongues.

"Um," said Grand. "Is this when we run?"

But they couldn't, shocked into paralysis.

The corpses limped closer.

Fortunately, the journey proved too much for their brittle bones. One by one they crumbled to dust, coming up in puffs of pulverized matter. Unfortunately, not all of them were content with such fate. The old hag in the lead, her skin paper-thin, her frame skeletal, stubbornly kept moving. It seemed she drew energy from her eyes, two bulged pale-blue globules that shone with vicious hatred.

Chapter Twenty-Six

Girls, Books, and Diamonds

To you the last page of a book heralds the end of the story. Not to the characters. The moment you're done reading it and slam it shut (or, preferably, gently close it), they gather to congratulate themselves on the job well done. "One less badling in the world," they cry, "one less badling!" They hope whoever reads the story next won't have to taste a badling's misfortune.

"But," you think, "Mad Tome is gone!"

This Mad Tome is gone, that's true. And yet, who knows how many more of them are out there, lurking in hidden places, waiting for you to find them? They might have varying appearances and different names, but rest assured their purpose is the same: to teach bad children who abandon books a lesson.

But back to the pond.

"Disgusted, are you? Scared? Did not expect me to look like this, did you?" wheezed Mary through her toothless mouth. "This is what will happen to you, *badlings*. One day you'll forget what you've been through and leave a book unread." Exhausted by her speech, she bent over, hacking and coughing.

The children watched her struggle for breath, too petrified to move.

At last she raised her head, no more than a skull

wrapped in vellum. Her mouth opened and closed, producing no sound. Her eyes shone with jealousy and spite.

"What happened to you?" asked Bells.

"Don't provoke her," warned Rusty. "She'll be gone soon, like the rest of them."

Peacock covered his mouth. "This is sick, I'm going to be sick." The bike tumbled out of his hold.

"I could really use a doughnut right now," muttered Grand. "A fresh sugar-glazed doughnut and a long dreamless nap."

With an inhuman effort, Mary took a step. There was a snap like that of breaking twigs: the bones in her legs splintered. That didn't deter her. She took another step, and another, balancing on stumps, held together by will alone.

"Badlings!" she rasped. "How pleasant it is to see you in flesh and blood, when I'm no more than a bag of bones. This happened at your hands. You're responsible for my torment." Her eyes flashed. "You think you have escaped my fate? You're mistaken. Mad Tome will come for you, like it came for me. I did not wish it to end like this. I wished to live on, in books, *forever*. You have robbed me of immortality!" She curled her bony hand into a fist and shook it. "I curse you! I curse you to never—"

But her curse was cut short by a duck, that same insolent duck who pulled out Mad Tome and who always begged Grand for doughnuts. It waddled over to Mary and pecked her, which was enough to turn Mary to dust. Her skull caved in, her body collapsed, and she went up in a gritty cloud.

Startled, the duck took off.

"Whoa, man," said Rusty, "that was crazy. See? I told you she'd be gone."

"They're *all* gone," said Bells. "That's horrible. I didn't expect that to happen. I thought they'd go home, but they simply died. They all died!"

"Then we don't need to do anything about them," concluded Rusty. "Problem solved!"

Bells glared at him. "How can you be so insensitive? Maybe we shouldn't have destroyed Mad Tome, maybe we should've stayed."

"And be the puppets at the mercy of stories?" Peacock snorted. "No, thanks."

"Um, it wasn't us who destroyed it, though," ventured Grand. "It was the ducks. And we don't know if all the badlings died, some of them left. Maybe they're still alive."

There was a reflective pause.

Rusty scratched his head. "These ducks are weird, man. Why would they tear up a book? They're not dogs, they're ducks!" He looked at his friends, suddenly animated. "So get this. Grandma got me these nice sneakers for my birthday, right? Guess what. I forgot to put them away and the dogs ate them. Like, they chewed off the leather! All of it!" He grinned, waiting for a positive response, but the mood was too somber to dissolve.

"It must've been the doughnuts," pondered Grand. "Maybe they smelled it."

"I'm cold," grumbled Peacock. "Can we go now?"

Bells looked at him and through him, still reflecting. "I think after this I'll either read every book I come across or not read any of them at all," she frowned. "Although I suppose I'll have to read books when I study science. Can you imagine if—"

Distant voices floated from the trail.

The children glanced at the mounds of dust, the spots where the badlings expired. It could be construed that those were piles of ash leftover from multiple fires, and if the voices belonged to adults, the outcome of such an encounter would be bad, very bad indeed.

"Crap." Rusty hurried to his bike. "We better get out of here."

"Most excellent idea," mocked Peacock. "Not that I suggested it for a while now."

The voices turned to the pond, joined by a pair of footfalls.

In a flash the children mounted their bikes and sped off, furiously pedaling in the opposite direction.

Bells quickly gained the lead. Teeth clenched, ponytail whipping, she pumped her legs with an admirable cadence. Ignoring the path, she raced across the lawn and swerved onto the main asphalt road. It was mostly deserted in this corner of the park, cool and shadowy under giant maples.

"Hey, Bells! Wait up!"

The boys were lagging.

Feeling rather jubilant at having outraced them, Bells slammed on the breaks a bit too hard. The back tire locked. The bike skidded and bucked from under her. She fell headlong, scraping her hands and knees bloody.

The boys squealed to a stop.

"Are you all right?" asked Grand.

Bells sat up. Her head throbbed, her cuts stung, and yet, incredibly, she was smiling. "Never been better. Feeling alive and whole, you know?" She sniffed her bloody palm and licked it.

"Hey!" protested Rusty. "That's gross!"

"No, it's not. It's just blood. What's so gross about it? Besides, it makes me feel like I'm *me*. Like I'm real and not some character in a book." She licked it again.

"Tastes kind of salty, doesn't it?" Peacock stretched out a hand to help her.

So did Grand.

Bells hesitated, but only for a moment. She gripped Grand's forearm and hoisted herself up. His already red face colored crimson.

"Thank you, *George*," she said politely.

"Um. You're welcome, *Belladonna*." He gasped, mortified.

Rusty sniggered.

Peacock busied himself with lifting his bike.

"It's okay. I'm starting to like it, actually," said Bells, remembering how Blackey pronounced her full name, with reverence and style. "Belladonna Monterey. It doesn't sound so bad, does it?"

"*I* like it," said Grand timidly. "It's very queenly. It fits you."

"Really?"

"I think so."

Bells stretched tall, back straight, chin high. Her dark eyes flashed with something new, something regal. She gazed at the gap between the trees ahead, the place where the park ended and the street began.

"Did you know that *Monterey* in Spanish means 'King's mountain'? And *Belladonna* in Italian means 'beautiful lady.' It's actually a name of a poisonous plant that's also called the 'deadly nightshade.' Its leaves and berries are highly toxic. If you eat them, you'll hallucinate. And if you eat too many, you'll die. They used to make poison out of it in the middle ages. A drop could kill a horse." Bells came up with this horrid fact on the fly. She had no idea how strong the poison really was, but she thought it sounded quite impressive, and she surveyed the boys, waiting for an awed reaction.

None followed. The boys obviously didn't understand the significance of her statement.

"You never told us," said Rusty.

"Well, I'm telling you *now*," she said irritably and picked up her bike. "Let's go."

"But I thought," began Grand, "I thought you didn't want to go home. I mean..." he held on to his bike to stop his hands from shaking, "you can hang out at my house for a while, if you want. There's a big funeral tomorrow, so mom is at work, and Max and Theo are with my auntie for the rest of the weekend—" he stopped abruptly. The idea of spending an afternoon alone with Bells struck him speechless.

"We could hang out together," blurted Peacock.

"I can't," sighed Rusty. "I promised Grandma to help her walk the dogs. Can I stop by later?"

"Yeah, can I come later too?" asked Bells. "I want to show my mom something first. Would that be okay?" She felt her pocket, a terrific sense of pride filling her chest.

"Sure," agreed Grand, pushing at the pedal to roll it up. "I have doughnuts," he added hopefully.

Bells suppressed a giggle. "Doughnuts? Doughnuts sound good. I like doughnuts, especially the old-fashioned ones. They're denser and more buttery, so when you bite them—"

Chapter Twenty-Six

"Will you stop talking about food?" snapped Peacock. "I'm feeling queasy."

"Hey, chill," warned Rusty. "Or I'll shove an open book in your face, make you start reading it, and then run off. I'll make sure it's about vampires, too."

Peacock paled. "That's not funny."

Rusty patted him on the shoulder. "Hey. Relax, man, I didn't mean it. All cool."

"Sorry," muttered Peacock. "I was just really scared."

"We understand," said Bells. "We were all scared. Don't worry about it."

"Yeah? Okay," Peacock smiled. "I guess I'll see you guys later." And with that he was off.

They watched him tear along the road until he vanished from sight. Something about his departure made them quiet. A light breeze rustled through the maples. A leaf detached. It twirled and fluttered like a yellow bird, coming to rest at Rusty's feet.

He started. "Right. I'm going too. Grandma must be getting worried." He gave Grand and Bells a parting nod, straddled his bike and left, his head bobbing, his knees comically sticking out.

Bells turned to Grand. "I want to go alone, if you don't mind. I just...I need to be alone for a while before, you know..."

He sighed. "It's fine. I get it."

"Wish me luck."

He awkwardly patted her on the shoulder. "Good luck."

"Thank you. Here we go." Bells kicked off and started pedaling, concentrating on gaining speed.

Not more than ten minutes later she dropped her bike by the garage door. Her mother's car was parked in the driveway, which meant that both she and Sofia were home unless they went somewhere on foot which was highly unlikely.

Bells mounted the steps to her house. *I wonder how much time has passed,* she thought. *Is it the same day? Looks like it. So it's still Saturday. That means I was only gone for a couple hours or something like that. Then why are they here? They should be at Sofia's singing lesson.*

Bells reached for the doorknob and stopped. Her hand was bloody and smudged with dirt, dark lines of grime under each fingernail. Her clothes were still damp, caked with bits of mud and leaflets of duckweed. She sniffed herself.

Great. I stink like a dog.

'Don't you dare come back here unless you're clean!' rang in her head.

Bells contemplated, then patted her pocket and decisively opened the door.

The house was quiet.

She tiptoed from floorboard to floorboard, avoiding those that creaked then stopped by the kitchen, suddenly hungry.

I'll just grab a quick snack then I'll go to my room and think about what to do next. She slowly crept in, freezing at every step, but no one was there to reprimand her. Once in the kitchen, she let out a long exhale and reached for the cupboard.

Someone stifled a sob.

Bells jumped, wheeling around, fully expecting to see Mary's rotting corpse that managed to rise from the ashes, follow her here, and was about to complete the curse.

But it wasn't Mary.

It was her mother, the famous opera singer Catarina Monterey. She didn't look herself, however. At first Bells didn't recognize her. She sat slumped in the chair, a wadded napkin in her hands, her eyes red, her face puffy.

"Mom?" said Bells.

"Belladonna." Catarina's voice caught at the end. "Bells," she corrected herself.

"Were you *crying*?" Shocked, Bells didn't know what else to say. Her mother never cried, not even when her father left them. A squirming feeling of guilt wormed itself into Bells' stomach, and she had an urge to confess to her every crime—especially the crime of returning home filthy—and ask for forgiveness. She even thought she might take a shower and wear a dress, just to make her mother happy. But Catarina's next words demolished this ephemeral wish.

"Your choir practice—"

The feeling of guilt was quickly replaced with defiance. "I'm not going," declared Bells. "Not now, not ever. And you can't *make* me."

Catarina only shook her head.

Heart pounding, Bells shoved a hand into her pocket and slammed the gems on the kitchen table, smudging the pristinely white tablecloth with flecks of dirt. The diamonds, each the size of a quail's egg, glittered dully. It gave Bells an immense satisfaction to watch her mother's eyes widen.

"What's this?" she asked.

"It's what you wanted," said Bells, bursting to explain and barely holding back, waiting for her mother's reaction.

Catarina picked up the biggest gem and turned it in her hands. "It can't be..."

"Yes, it can. It's payment," said Bells levelly, as though it was not a big deal. "I'm paying you to never *ever* make me go to any of those ridiculous singing classes. I don't want to sing, I want to do science, and this is my payment for you to leave me alone. I suppose it'll cover rent and bills and even college."

Catarina stared open-mouthed.

Bells continued, determined to deliver a crushing answer to every one of her mother's doubts. "You told me not to crawl back here, asking for money. Well, I didn't. I came *with* money. And you wondered how I was going to make a living. I think I just made it. There. Is this enough?"

"Where did you get them?" asked Catarina.

"I dug them up," said Bells proudly, "while I was doing scientific explorations. How is this for a *poor scientist?*"

"But where?"

Bells thought to say, *on top of a mountain in the nest of a giant bird,* then decided against it. It sounded too crazy, and her mother surely wouldn't believe her. "I didn't steal them, don't worry. I just...found them. There's lots more. In fact, there is a whole valley of them—" Bells bit her tongue.

"Valley?" Catarina dabbed the napkin at her eyes and stood, towering over her daughter. "Belladonna Monterey," she began.

Bells sighed. "Here we go."

"You'll have to explain this. Precious gems like these don't just lie around in some valley."

"Yes, they do," disagreed Bells, feeling that she was going to lose this match. There was no stopping her mother now.

"Where exactly did you find them?" demanded Catarina. "I must explain to you how this works. They don't belong to you, Belladonna. It doesn't matter that you have found them. They belong to the owner of the property. Do you understand?"

Exasperated, Bells snatched the diamonds and stormed out of the kitchen.

"Belladonna! Come back this instant!"

She answered with a slam of the door.

Finally, she thought, *I'm alone. Okay, what do I need to do? First, I need to pack my things. Then I need—* Her thoughts were cut short by an unexpected presence.

"What are *you* doing here?"

On the floor, leaning on Bells' bed, sat Sofia, an open book in her lap. She looked up, her face tearstained. With horror Bells saw that she had wrapped herself in *her* blanket and rested both feet on *her* pillow.

Whatever feelings of longing for her little sister she nourished had expired in an instant.

"Get out of my room," commanded Bells. "I want to be alone."

"I'm grounded," said Sofia tragically and wiped her face with the hem of her dress.

"You're disgusting," said Bells.

"And you're dirty," retorted Sofia. "Mom will scold you for this." She pointed to Bells' bloodied knees.

Bells opened the door. "*Now.*"

Sofia pouted. "I don't want to be alone in my room. Please?" She looked so miserable, so crestfallen, that Bells softened. "Okay, you can stay for a little bit. But don't ask me questions and don't get in my way." She marched to her dresser then suddenly stopped. "Wait. Why aren't you at your singing lesson?"

"I told you, I'm grounded."

"Why? What did you do?"

Sofia played with her skirt before answering. "I didn't want to go until you came back."

"Oh." Bells deflated. "You didn't?"

"Nope," Sofia sniffled. "Mom got so mad. She said I was to sit inside all day and read this stupid book, but I don't want to read it. *You* always read to me. Why do I have to read it?" She pushed it away.

"Wait! Don't do that." Bells' stomach lurched. She reached for the book and turned it over. A familiar face regarded her with an icy stare, a sinister smile frozen on it in mockery.

"*The Snow Queen*," whispered Bells. "Let me finish reading this to you. Is this the page you stopped on?"

"I don't want to," whined Sofia. "It's a dumb story anyway."

"No, it's not. How do you know?"

"What's going on here?" Catarina stood in the door, hands on her hips, ready to dispense a dose of parenting to her arguing daughters.

"Belladonna is being mean to me," complained Sofia.

Bells stared. "No, I'm not. How am I being mean? I offered to read you a book."

"And I said, I don't want you to." Sofia kicked it out of her hands, sending it flying.

"Don't do this!" cried Bells.

"It's *my* book. I'll do what I want!" shrieked Sofia, jumping up. Bells went after her but was seized by Catarina.

"Let go!" she tried wiggling out of her mother's hold.

"You need to stop teasing your sister," admonished Catarina. "What kind of an example are you setting for her? Think about that."

Sofia showed Bells the tongue, smugly opened the book and grabbed a page as if to tear it.

Bells went cold.

"Sofia!" Catarina released her grip and stalked to Sofia who stubbornly pressed her lips together and proceeded ripping out page after page, throwing them at Bells' feet. They softly landed on the carpet, multiple faces of the Snow Queen glaring at her from every angle.

"NO!!!" screamed Bells and slid to the floor, hands on her face in horror.

Naturally, you're wondering what happened next. Of course, it was as expected. Only I can't tell you about it, because that's a different story and it belongs in a different book.

This story is over.

Congratulations, you made it to the end!

You're not a badling after all. Isn't it a great feeling? Now, be a good sport, close this book, and go read another. But remember to finish it—you know what will happen if you don't.

Mentioned Books

(don't open them if you don't plan to read them)

The Snow Queen by Hans Christian Andersen

Don Quixote by Miguel de Cervantes Saavedra

Alice's Adventures in Wonderland by Lewis Carroll

"The Masque of the Red Death." *Complete Stories and Poems of Edgar Allan Poe* by Edgar Allan Poe

"Bluebeard." *The Complete Fairy Tales* by Charles Perrault

The Headless Horseman by Mayne Reid

"The Story of Sindbad the Sailor." *The Arabian Nights Entertainments* by Anonymous

The Surprising Adventures of Baron Munchausen by Rudolf Erich Raspe

The Little Black Hen, or the Underground People: A Fairy Story for Children by Antony Pogorelsky

"Hansel and Gretel." *Grimm's Fairy Tales* by Jacob Grimm and Wilhelm Grimm

The Secret Garden by Frances Hodgson Burnett

"Nose, The Dwarf." *The Little Glass Man and Other Stories* by Wilhelm Hauff

Dracula by Bram Stoker

The Jungle Book by Rudyard Kipling

Aesop's Fables by Aesop

ABOUT THE AUTHOR

Ksenia was born in Moscow, Russia, and came to US in 1998 not knowing English, having studied architecture and not dreaming that one day she'd be writing. The Badlings is her fourth novel. Her other books are Irkadura, Rosehead and Siren Suicides trilogy (which is really one book in three parts). She lives in Seattle with her boyfriend and their combined three kids in a house that they like to call The Loony Bin.

ABOUT THE BOOK

The Badlings was edited by Sarah Liu, who is never ever a badling. Final formatting was completed by Stuart Whitmore of Crenel Publishing. Text is in Adobe Garamond Pro. Final digital assembly of the print edition was completed using Microsoft Word and Adobe Acrobat. The electronic edition was mastered in ePUB format using Sigil.

68164191R00162

Made in the USA
Lexington, KY
04 October 2017